A COLD HEART

DOUG SINCLAIR

Storm

This is a work of fiction. Names, characters, businesses, places, events and incidents are either the products of the author's imagination or used in a fictitious manner. Any resemblance to actual persons, living or dead, or actual events is purely coincidental.

Copyright © Doug Sinclair, 2025

The moral right of the author has been asserted.

All rights reserved. No part of this book may be reproduced or used in any manner without the prior written permission of the copyright owner. This prohibition includes, but is not limited to, any reproduction or use for the purpose of training artificial intelligence technologies or systems.

To request permissions, contact the publisher at rights@stormpublishing.co

Ebook ISBN: 978-1-83700-032-6
Paperback ISBN: 978-1-83700-033-3

Cover design: Blacksheep
Cover images: Depositphotos

Published by Storm Publishing.
For further information, visit:
www.stormpublishing.co

ALSO BY DOUG SINCLAIR

DS Malkie McCulloch Series

Blood Runs Deep

Last to Die

A Deadly Flame

For Maaike, who continues to support me in this ridiculous obsession of mine. Love you, schateke.

ONE

Elizabeth lifted her coffee cup, but it made it nowhere near her lips; her fingers told her it was cold and far beyond drinking. She checked her watch for what had to be the tenth time in an hour, then realised what a waste of time that was. There would never be a right time to do what she needed to.

Needed to do? Yes. What choice did she have? She had no other option. No alternative but to turn her back on thirty-plus years of doing all she could to be a decent and – what was the phrase? – upstanding citizen. No way out of a trap of everyone's making but her own.

She rejected her own thoughts; she hadn't allowed herself a pity party in twenty years. Not since...

No. Not going there. She always felt filthy after dropping her guard and letting her mind go back to that time.

But this was no pity party. She'd been there, often enough. At the bottom of the hole, where it reached its blackest and most hopeless, and she'd clung on. To what? She realised only now she had no idea what it was that had got her through those days and months and years. How the hell had she made it through five years of that? What stubborn rage of determination had she found to dig her fingers into to stop her from giving up and letting herself drop to the bottom, checking out, even bring on her own end?

She shook herself. Thinking like that would achieve nothing. She had to do this. She would do it. She had it in her, she told herself, but it rang hollow in her own mind.

Sophie need never know what her mum had done. She could enjoy her own imminent fresh start free of the brutality she left behind each night when she came home. She deserved that, didn't she? Everything else fell away. Nothing mattered more.

Unless she found out, of course.

She must never find out.

She went over it again in her head. What she planned to do wouldn't even make it into the local papers or go out on the Livingston community radio station. It would go down as a statistic, nothing more. As long as she didn't get caught.

She was going to get caught. She knew it.

No, she'd thought it through. More than was good for her. After all, it wasn't like she planned to rob the Almondvale branch of RBS, was it?

No, nothing like that.

But it would be enough.

Enough to ruin her life if she got caught. Hers and Sophie's. She'd fallen so far from her previous life, dragged her family down into degrading poverty, but she could make it so much worse if...

And what about Andrew? For better or worse, they'd said. Would she have made that promise if she'd known what would hit them all just when things had started looking so good? Of course she would. She'd meant it with every fibre of her being while things were good, while they grew together and rounded off rough edges to fit together better and better with each passing year. Until Andrew's bombshell, delivered with such glib impatience by an overworked GP.

Even following that appalling news, they had pulled together and managed, and life had been good for them.

Until for Sophie, it really wasn't.

Sophie needed a fresh start, an end to the misery she'd already suffered for more years than any mother should have allowed.

Elizabeth fell back on her habitual decision-making tactic: asking, what's the worst that could happen? Three lives ruined. That's what.

She stood to do it, had no option but to do it, but found herself, coat and scarf donned like a suit of Primark armour, back at the cafe counter ordering another coffee, another excuse to put it off.

She saw the barista do a double take at a traitorous tear that dropped onto her cheek before she could wipe it away. She didn't deserve the boy's sympathy. She didn't recognise herself.

She forced a smile but could get no words out. His face nearly broke her; the look of someone whose kind heart recognised a soul in trouble but wasn't yet old enough to know how to offer comfort.

Back at her table, she wiped her wet cheeks and checked her watch, again. Twenty minutes until closing time. Until thousands of people would pass her by wrapped in their own lives, their own troubles, and crowd the exits in their haste to go anywhere but here.

Should she wait? Until only last-second shoppers waited at tills and security guards had nothing on their minds but a pint and a Saturday-night chippie?

She lowered her head and shook it, tried to dislodge multiple horrible scenarios that crowded her mind, confusing her and competing to build the worst possible scenario of all the ways this could go wrong. She lifted it again to see the barista – Charlie, his name badge had said – watching her with a conflicted look on his face. Probably torn between sympathy and a desperate hope she'd let him get away bang on finishing time.

She lifted her cup again. The coffee tasted bland; would an extra shot have helped her, sharpened her senses, energised her for the task ahead?

Enough.

Circumstance had forced her to do this, an act she'd never before have condoned in anyone else, let alone considered herself.

Barista Charlie deserved a healthy tip, if only for obviously stretched patience, but if she could afford to tip in cafes she wouldn't be in this bind in the first place.

She stood, took her cup to the counter: the least she could do. Charlie took it from her with a smile.

'Are you OK, lady?'

She glanced at him and nearly lost it. He meant it. Whatever the young man had going on in his own life, he found the capacity to care about a stranger. She remembered a time when she was the sort of person who considered other people's unseen struggles. Someone letting a door swing shut in her face might have just had a life-changing diagnosis from a GP, like Andrew had. Someone forgetting to thank her in a shop might be contemplating their own redundancy. In fact, her own work clients often behaved in atrocious ways, and she'd learned to understand why, to allow for the fact that other people's lives could change them as much as she...

'Lady?'

She flustered, gaped at him, could find no words. She held out a tenner in her sweating palm; ten pounds more than she had spent on her own well-being in months.

Charlie pushed her hand back to her. 'No charge, lady. You look like you need some kindness today.'

Tears spilled. She hung her head in shame. Sympathy from a stranger. Would he care so much about her if he knew what she was about to do?

TWO

Malkie listened to his inner idiot, argued with it for a second, then let the idiot win.

'I need to hear you say it, partner.'

Steph's eyes blazed, and Malkie knew he'd fucked up. Again.

She took a long, slow breath in through her nose, then let it out between lips tight with anger. She spread her fingertips as if she could radiate her fury at him through her palms.

'I will not do anything stupid to Dean Lang.' She added 'sir' as a barbed afterthought. She'd always been too damned good at them.

Malkie sighed. 'Fuck's sake, Steph. I worry, you know? And stop calling me "sir". You know I hate it.'

Her eyes smouldered for a few seconds longer before she could get any more out. 'He's a waste of space, and a waste of oxygen, and if I ever touch him again, he'll grass me up to Thompson and I'll have wasted a perfectly good career. So, no, I don't intend to let that little bastard get under my skin and make me ruin my life. OK?' She thought for a second. 'Just let me make the arrest when we finally get to nail the bastard for something.'

Before he could thank her for letting him speak his mind – neither of which actions ever ended well – she spoke over him again, delivered one more hurtful, verbal sting.

'Sir.' Her eyes dared him to push his luck.

Malkie slumped back in his chair. He cast his eyes over his shoulder again; still no one at the desks this side of the filing cabinets that some of his less pleasant CID colleagues saw as the demarcation between 'just uniforms' and the people that actually caught bad guys. Malkie loathed those kinds of colleagues.

He gazed at his fingers interlaced in his lap and allowed himself a heavy, self-indulgent sigh. 'I'm sorry, Steph. I worry. You already gave Barry Boswell a good kicking, bloody hospitalised him, for fuck's sake. I just don't want you – No, I mean I don't want your Da—'

Steph's lip curled in disgust and her eyes blazed.

'Sorry. I don't want the fucker baiting you so badly again you might rock up there with the best of intentions to just put the fear of God up him, but then...'

He couldn't force the next words out. Steph did it for him. 'Kick the living shit out of him?'

Malkie glanced at her. Language, with a capital 'L', from Steph was just one worrying sign he'd observed over the past few weeks that the Steph he knew and loved – most of the time – was struggling.

He shrugged, hoped she'd let him off with that.

She didn't. She leaned forward, her eyes dangerous. Again.

A lump dropped into Malkie's gut. *Fuck's sake. More?*

'You mean like *you* did?'

He gaped at her. She couldn't know. Could she? Would that fucker Lang have risked telling her? And in a heartbeat, he knew; yes, he fucking would. The bloody animal would guess neither he nor Steph could afford to escalate it any further.

Steph still had – as she reminded him, often – a career ahead of her and Malkie had a pension he needed to protect, now more than ever since his dad had moved in with him after his home burned to the ground. He choked back anger. Recent evidence had suggested the candle that caused the fire that killed his mum and made a widower of his dad had not fallen over accidentally. He dreaded reopening the accidental-death finding of the Fire Scene Investigator report, wasn't sure he – or his dad – could handle it right now.

'Malkie. Have the decency to pay attention when I'm pissed off at you.'

He returned to the present. *Steph. Arse-kicking. Again. Deserved. Again.*

'What the hell do you mean? I've—'

'Don't you dare tell me you've not been near him. Don't you bloody dare.'

Malkie slumped again. Damage limitation time.

'He told you.'

'Of course he bloody told me. He said – and I paraphrase here – "If that lard-arse comes near me again, I'll have you both," so whatever you did didn't scare him quite enough. What the hell were you thinking? You're not a fighter.'

He could see no escape other than to level with her, let it all out, take the kicking and hopefully move past it. He sat forward, tried to take one of her hands in his, but she sat back and folded her arms across her chest.

'It was eating me up inside watching you get so upset over what that fucker Boswell did to you. To you and your mum.'

Steph's eyes glistened, but she held back any uncharacteristic tears she might feel welling inside her.

'So, I went up there. Just to have a word. I hoped I could

scare him away with just my warrant card and some dire promises.'

Steph's eyes widened in what Malkie recognised as her disbelieving scorn face.

'But he said things about you. Things I couldn't let him get away with. Honestly, Steph, I don't think I've felt anger like that before in my entire life. I lost it. I almost dangled him off his balcony. I think I told him that if I heard another word from him about you, I'd—'

'You'd what?' She had that gleam in her eye now; she wanted to know just what he'd put the fucker through.

'I said "I will come back here, and you will suffer an unfortunate accident." Something like that.'

She stared at the floor somewhere off to his left, nodded her head, seemed to consider his words.

'"*You will suffer an unfortunate accident.*" Really? You said that?'

He saw the gleam move down to twitch at her lips, and knew the worst was over. 'Ha, ha, bloody ha. I was improvising.'

She laughed so hard she let out the tears she'd suppressed not two minutes ago. She bent forward at the waist and howled, thumped her fist into her thigh as if the hilarity was all too much for her.

Malkie sat. And waited. He deserved this.

When she could breathe again, she dried her eyes on a tissue and moaned as if struggling to hold back another outburst.

'You finished?'

She erupted again, spilled more tears, waved a hand at him, pleading for mercy.

'Stop. Please. Oh God I hurt.' She clutched her stomach and held her hand up to fend off any more pearls of Malkie comedy.

He couldn't bring himself to smile, despite the rush of relief he felt; his punishment was over. This time.

When she'd regained control of herself, she sighed and smiled at him. 'Bless your little polyester socks, Malkie.'

He huffed his displeasure and folded his arms. She placed one hand on his arm and squeezed. 'I don't deserve you.' She waited for him to look at her. 'Sir.' She let go, sat back, held her fingers to her mouth to fend off another fit of laughter.

Malkie's pride took a battering, but nothing it hadn't learned to survive over too many years. He waited, made her look at him again.

'I need to know, Steph. I need to know you won't go anywhere near him.'

She heard the tone in his voice, quiet but insistent, and brought herself back to her senses. She smiled at him, and he recognised the fondness she reserved for very few people and which he could never bear to lose.

'Malkie, I promise I have no intention to go anywhere near my so-called stepfather, Dean Lang, or Barry Boswell, the animal who raped my mother and...'

Her face soured; she'd let her mouth run off to a place neither of them wanted to go.

Malkie stood, cut her off. 'Neither of us wants to hear that, Steph. Means nothing, right?'

She studied him, stood, punched him on the arm, gentle and lingering.

'No, partner. I'm not him, right?'

'Fuck, no. Those irritating personality defects are all your own, young lady.'

'Pot, kettle, Malkie. Pot, kettle.' She stood, glanced at her watch. 'Don't you have a daughter to introduce yourself to?'

He scanned her face for signs she was lashing out, aiming for his current most vulnerable spot. He saw none; she wouldn't.

'Aye. I'm heading there now. Thanks for that.'

She walked away, shouted one habitual last comment over her shoulder, timed to perfection as she passed through the doorway to the Livingston Police Station reception before he could think of anything to hurl back at her.

'She'll adore you. Or hate you. Like Marmite. Good luck.'

Malkie pulled his jacket and coat on and headed for the same door.

Time to open a door to a whole new phase in his life, one that – he found himself able to believe – could mean a new start for him, a chance to get something right that fundamentally deserved to be done right.

As he reached for the button to unlock the security doors, he found himself risking the ire and often obvious disdain that desk sergeant Bernie Stevens always reserved for him.

'G'night, Bernie. Hope the rest of your shift passes uneventfully.' He flashed her a grin he was sure would annoy her.

She surprised him – stunned him, in fact. Instead of her usual barely concealed sneer and disapproving shake of the head, she sat back in her chair and studied him, her face a mask of consideration, no trace of scorn apparent.

He stopped halfway through the door. This wasn't right. Wasn't normal.

'You OK, Bernie? I mean Sergeant Stevens.'

She actually smiled. A small smile, possibly mocking. 'I'm fine, Malkie. I mean Detective Sergeant McCulloch. Have a lovely evening, won't you?'

Malkie headed outside, rattled by Bernie's uncharacteristic civility. As he followed the footpath toward the Almondvale and McArthur Glen shopping centres, he marvelled at how quickly a day can turn around. A social interaction with Bernie Stevens that didn't leave him feeling like shite on her shoe. Wonders would never cease.

He chose to take it as a good omen and found himself

picking up the pace as he headed for his first ever coffee and cake with his twenty-six-year-old daughter.

THREE

As she approached the store, she imagined every eye on her. Sweat broke out on her forehead. She wiped it away then worried someone might have noticed. She saw a security guard walking the floor. His face struck a vague chord in her memory but no name came to mind. He looked like the kind of man interested only in swaggering about and basking in the imagined admiration of every woman lucky enough to witness him in all his uniformed glory. His trousers hung low under a belly so fat she doubted he could run up a stair let alone chase someone. A walkie-talkie hung from a loop on his shirt, tight around his fleshy neck, the buttons at his waist struggling to contain him. She watched from a bench outside, looked for any pattern in his wanderings, found none except frequent detours to the till desk inside the entrance. Two girls seemed to humour him and his apparently hilarious comments, before rolling their eyes behind his back and waving their hands as if to banish some unwelcome odour.

Where had she seen him before? And why did it bother her? Did some memory of him lurk in her troubled mind or did she fear him only because he was the man who would come after her if she got noticed?

She scolded herself for delaying the inevitable. She recalled the scratches she'd seen on her daughter's wrists, scratches she was certain ran further up her arms, under her school-shirt sleeves. When Elizabeth had first spotted them, she'd turned away from the bathroom door before – she hoped – Sophie saw her. They needed to talk about it. Just as soon as Elizabeth could find the right time.

The security guard took up a challenging pose in the shop doorway. Feet apart, arms folded, scanning all who passed for any potential threat to his professional domain. As Elizabeth entered, she was horrified to see a glimmer of recognition cross his face, but his eyes dropped below her neck and lingered there. She caught an acrid whiff of body odour and had to suppress a gag reflex.

Inside, she wandered, picked up a few items she'd have chosen if – she had to laugh – she could ever again afford to spend money in a shop like this.

With three garments over her arm, she made for the designer section. Her stomach spasmed when she found them. Jumpers. Black. Plain V-neck. Carla Castaligna, Milan, the label said, with a black cat's-head logo. £350. The price had her choking back anger. The massive wealth divide between parents of the fortunate few and those like her almost made what she was about to do feel justified. But then, she used to be a mother who would spend this much without thinking. Not anymore. Now, if she got caught, would it make any difference if she stole a £5 Primark jumper or one of these? She reeled at the prices. £350 for a logo.

She nearly turned away again. This was all wrong. She fingered the fabric; it felt softer than anything she'd worn for far too long. But for that price? Good grief, this was stupid. She recalled the phrase in the guidance the school had issued to incoming students.

Plain black trousers or skirts, shoes, blazer optional. Then had come the sentence that had struck her as both good advice and a vile nod to the sad facts of growing up in modern times. Expensive designer clothing was discouraged, primarily – it claimed – because of the risk of damage or loss. Students walking around school in jumpers that cost three times that of an entire off-the-peg uniform was considered insensitive to those parents who couldn't afford designer prices. That didn't stop wealthy parents doing it anyway, which meant people like Elizabeth had to do things like she was about to, so her daughter might not end up a victim of spoiled little rich girls and their eager acolytes. She'd wondered before if parents like theirs were just doing what she was doing: whatever it took to give their kids the best chances in life?

But their choices wouldn't get their kids taken from them. Elizabeth's could.

The unfairness of it choked her. She never asked life to deal her such shitty cards. Her duty to her daughter outweighed any expectation society demanded on her to shut up and put up. If something as stupid as a jumper with a £350 logo could go even some way to keep Sophie from the bottom of another brutal and merciless teenage pecking order, then a jumper with a £350 logo she would have.

One last glance around the store; the security guard was having another crack at the girls at the till, who looked to be running out of urgent, closing-time jobs.

Before she could talk herself out of it, she found Sophie's size and hid it between the coats over her arm and headed for the dressing rooms, all the way fighting a frantic urge to run for the front door and take her chances.

One of the girls called out to her, grinned at her partner,

and darted out from behind the tills. 'I'll be with you in just a second.' The second girl looked daggers at her pal's escape.

Gillian, according to her name badge, rolled her eyes as she approached. 'Thanks for the excuse.' She nodded towards the security guard at the front desk. 'Stinky's on form today.' She barely glanced at the coats on Elizabeth's arm. 'Three, is it?'

Elizabeth gaped at her. Was it going to be that easy? She nodded at Gillian, who frowned back.

'Are you OK, lady?'

Elizabeth felt about to throw up, had to remind herself that this girl, probably no more than six or seven years older than Sophie, wouldn't lose a penny, that shops like this accepted a certain level of undetected theft as an unavoidable fact of everyday retail.

'Lady?' Gillian's concern now evident and seeming genuine.

'I'm fine, thanks. Just one of those days, you know?' She clutched the coats and her hidden shame to her side but forced herself to relax. She wondered if Gillian's mum would do the same for her daughter. She seemed like a nice girl, probably deserved a mum like that.

A mum like her? A criminal?

Gillian placed a hand on her arm. 'You still have five minutes, miss. And any of those will look brilliant on you, by the way. You've got the figure for them, know what I mean?'

Elizabeth forced a smile and entered a cubicle. She sat, had to choke down sobs of shame. This wasn't her. She made herself acknowledge the words: shoplifting, theft, crime. Bad enough if it was just a cheap bargain-store jumper. This was a Carla Castaligna. Would that make a difference to her punishment if she got caught? Would it cross a line from a fine or community service to actual prison time? A moan escaped her lips. She clamped a hand over her mouth and rocked backward and forward on her seat. She risked a glance around the side of the cubicle curtain, saw Gillian back at the till, laughing with her colleague, the security guard out of sight somewhere.

She heaved in a breath, held it, released it, slow and shaking. She removed her own coat and blouse, then cut into the fabric where the security disc was attached – thankfully only an inch from the waistband hem so she could stitch it up later – and hid the tag and the hanger behind the seat. The jumper was designed for emaciated models and girls like Sophie who could eat her bodyweight in calories without gaining a pound, but with her own clothing back on and her scarf tightened to hide every hint of what she wore beneath, Elizabeth felt like a blimp on legs.

She walked – as calmly as her weak legs would let her – towards the front door.

Gillian turned to her and smiled. A patronising and pitying smile that Elizabeth couldn't bring herself to resent.

'None of them any good, no?'

Elizabeth kept walking but forced herself to shake her head and smile back.

She made it out of the shop to the mall hallway.

No sign of the stinking security guard.

She was going to make it.

He appeared from her left and looked her up and down with his special professional security guard scrutiny.

She froze. Her guts turned over. She felt her face drain of blood.

Stinky stepped towards her, his face switching to eager predator mode.

She swallowed. Tears brimmed. Stinky's face showed his realisation: he knew. He might have no idea exactly what he knew, but he knew.

She bolted. Her job kept her active, if a bit achy in the lower back, so she hoped she could make the doors to the street outside before Stinky even got up to whatever speed he was capable of. She'd read somewhere that security guards were told by their employers never to chase shoplifters out of their own shop, but that the same employers would hammer any guard who didn't.

She reached the exit out onto Almondvale Boulevard, barged the door open with her shoulder, and glanced back. Stinky was still coming.

She moaned, fear rattling through her, and hurtled out into bitter February cold. Heedless of traffic, she started onto a road crossing, narrowly missed a passing van, and stumbled back onto the pavement.

Stinky reached the door and leaned on the frame. He heaved in great gasping breaths and sweat dripped from him. 'Fuckin' stop.'

Elizabeth glanced up the road. She saw a long line of cars starting to move through green lights at a junction. If she timed it right she might make it.

She watched him, then the approaching cars. Would he follow her across busy traffic? If he got hurt... No, she'd made her choices and his were his own. If he hurt himself because of her, she'd deal with that guilt later. When she thought the timing was as good as it would get, she launched herself across the road. Over her shoulder, she saw Stinky push himself off the doorway and barrel after her. She sprinted to the other side and turned, expected to see Stinky stopped by the now-passing traffic.

He stumbled. Fell forward. Pitched into the road. A VW hatchback bore down on Stinky as he struggled to lift his bulk from the road.

The hatchback's brakes screeched.

People yelled. Others fumbled with mobile phones.

Stinky bounced off the hatchback's bumper, rolled once, then slammed against a roadside barrier.

Elizabeth tasted acid. She'd caused this.

She staggered backward. And again. Shook her head as her mind spun. One voice in her told her she'd had no choice, that Sophie wouldn't survive another six years of bullying.

She took off, bumped into a scruff in scuffed shoes and a grubby coat. He stared at her. She stared back. Something in his eyes told her he was trouble.

She bolted again. Fear lent speed to her legs, and she ran faster than she thought she was able, hauled in lungfuls of icy air as her feet pounded at the pavement.

He'd looked dead. Stinky had looked dead. She'd chosen to put them both in harm's way. She'd made it across the road intact. But he...

Worse, she felt surer than ever that she knew him from somewhere. Whoever he was, she knew him to be bad news, the worst kind.

What had she done?

FOUR

Malkie barely had time to recognise the sound of the collision before a small woman dressed for a typical freezing Scottish February barged into him. Her terrified look suggested she'd witnessed the incident. Or was she involved? He couldn't see details yet because the railings either side of a crossing had been draped with giant vinyl banners advertising cheap meals and karaoke at a nearby chain pub.

The woman closed her coat lapels over her chest, over a T-shirt, a woollen jumper and a body warmer; no wonder she was sweating and red-faced. She bolted. Malkie reached for her but heard a commotion from the road and saw a crowd of eager spectators gathering. He headed for the road, his priority always to treat anyone injured.

He watched the woman run for a second, her legs pumping away under her heavy woollen coat, her arms flailing at her sides as if clutching at air to pull herself along as fast as possible. Three layers plus a winter coat. Even in February...

In the road, he found a blue Volkswagen stopped on the crossing. A large man in a security guard's uniform lay on his back, blood seeping from a head wound and one leg bent at an ugly angle. His mind flashed back to a young man in a much worse state, back in November. He had survived against everyone's expectations, but a whole lot of shite had kicked off from that incident.

Malkie pulled his phone from his pocket and quick-dialled Steph.

'RTC, Steph. Almondvale Boulevard, north-west entrance into the Almondvale Shopping Centre. One casualty, not aware of condition yet.'

'OK. I'll get some Uniforms out there. Five mins.'

The Livingston police station occupied a full half of the Civic Centre alongside the courts and social services and the Procurator Fiscal's department. A short footpath led across the lawns across the River Almond to the two town-centre shopping paradises, the footpath Malkie had taken on his way to meet the daughter who – until only weeks ago – he'd thought had been miscarried, then had discovered had survived. Parts of his mind he would never be proud of suggested that an RTC would provide a perfect excuse to call her and cancel.

While he pushed through a crowding gaggle of mobile phone videographers, he saw the victim move, but barely. The man muttered something through blood bubbles on his lips. Malkie leant closer, leaned his ear to the man's mouth.

'Get off my back. Fuckin' hurts.' He raised one arm as if to sit up but fell back again, his face spasming in agony.

'I'm not, mate. No one's touching you.'

Sounds like a spinal injury. Poor bastard.

He placed a hand on the man's chest, more to reassure him than to hold him down.

'I've called it in, mate. Ambulance will only take minutes to get here from St John's.'

The driver of the Volkswagen – who looked barely old

enough to have started shaving – appeared next to them, hands on his hips, his eyes raging but his posture defensive.

'Idiot ran out in front of me. I had no chance. And I was doing bang on thirty, officer.'

Malkie filed the driver's whining under *Methinks the boy racer doth protest too much*. He memorised the lad's number plate although his chances of driving off were zero given the cars stuck behind him and the nosy crowd ahead. 'I need you to stay here until we can interview you, OK?'

The lad stared, appalled, at the man in the road.

'Mate? Are you listening? What's your name?'

He shook himself. 'Adrian. Aye. I'll wait. Wisnae my fault so nae problem there, officer.'

'Adrian what?' He held back on a sigh of frustration.

'Adrian Burns. I was only doing thirty.'

Malkie nodded at him and indicated he should step back.

Steph and two Uniforms arrived minutes later. She crouched beside Malkie.

'Ambulance en route. What happened?'

'Not much I can say at the moment. Woman on foot charged into me on the north side of the road, looked terrified, she bolted. I didn't see the impact so obviously I needed to check for casualties as a priority.'

She glanced at him. 'Aye, I wasn't checking on you, mate. Just getting up to speed.'

Malkie sighed; he knew his tension came from repeatedly avoiding the young lady – his daughter, he reminded himself – waiting to meet her dad for the first time at the age of twenty-six, somewhere inside the same shopping centre the victim had come from.

Steph took his arm, pulled him up and away from the victim. 'Responders are here.' He saw a Uniform pushing spectators back while the other bent to assess the injured man. 'This isn't one for us. A response vehicle and another couple of Uniforms are en route. But you'd better call your daughter.'

He shook himself from staring at the injured man, from memories stabbing behind his eyes, of a young man, battered and bloody and reaching for him.

'Malkie.'

He returned to the moment.

Steph, her hands on his arms, concern on her face. 'This isn't like Robin Wilkie, mate. This is nothing like that. Let the Uniforms handle this for now. But call Jennifer, aye? She'll understand.'

He dragged his thoughts back to the present. 'Aye. Jennifer...'

Steph headed for the fresh-faced boy racer, Adrian, standing in front of his car, now studying the damage to his vehicle.

Malkie dialled his ex, Sandra Morton; the only woman he'd ever slept with, the woman who he'd once thought had ruined him for all other women, forever. The day she admitted that their daughter – he still stumbled over that word – had survived and grown to adulthood, she had also sworn that she had estranged herself, and their child, from her vicious and violent brothers. One of them had stabbed the teenage Malkie for dumping their beloved sister. He'd nearly left the hospital in a box.

'Malkie?'

Sandra. Her voice grated on him like fingernails on a blackboard; he still struggled not to attach a world of regret and bitterness to any thought of her.

'Malkie. Are you there?'

'I'm here. I'm outside the shopping centre, but I just witnessed an RTC, and I can't leave. Can you apologise to Jennifer for me, and reschedule, please?'

He heard muffled words, then a new voice came on. His

daughter. The first time he'd heard her speak. He both loved and feared the rush of emotion her voice triggered in him.

'Malkie? It's Jennifer. Hi. It's, er, lovely to finally meet you. Well, you know what I mean.' She sounded as nervous as he felt at the prospect of meeting her.

'Hi, Jennifer.' He found himself loving the sound of the word for what it now meant to him. He reminded himself he knew nothing about her, or how far from the Morton family tree Sandra had managed to get her to grow up.

'I'm so sorry. I—'

'It's fine. Mum explained. Go be a policeman, Malkie. We can reschedule.'

Tears threatened to escape him. His daughter.

'Thanks, Jennifer. I really am sorry, but my job... You know?'

'What kind of a copper would you be if you walked away from someone who needs your help, right? Please, don't worry about it. Mum and I will finish our coffees and talk about you.'

He laughed. She laughed back. Then, a long, pregnant silence.

'Well, bye for now, then.' She gave him another few seconds which he failed to fill with anything, then she disconnected.

He gazed back towards the Civic Centre. His place of work. The base from which he and others did what they could. She'd sounded almost proud of him.

He roused himself. The response vehicle and two more Uniforms had arrived and taped off a section of the road from behind the boy racer's Volkswagen to the other side of the victim. Spectators pressed against the tape; phones held high to capture as much of the event as they could over the shoulders of the response officers. Two-tone sirens signalled the arrival of an ambulance, and the audience pulled back – with scowls and bad grace but no loss of fascination – to let it through.

Steph returned to his side. 'How did it go?'

'Fine. We'll reschedule.'

'Not what I meant, and you know it, old man.'

He looked at her, felt affection from her that he knew she'd never waste on another soul.

'It was fine. She sounds... grown up, like, you know? Civilised?'

'Did you expect her to have taken over the family businesses and turned into Cruella De Morton or something?'

'Ha ha. Comedian. No. But it felt... OK.'

'OK?' Her eyebrows arched. Another talking-to incoming? 'I mean it felt... Good. Aye, it felt good. She didn't sound like a mouth-breather, sounded quite polite. Maybe Sandra meant what she said about splitting from her rotten family.'

'She has.'

'Eh?'

'I checked because I knew you'd be too stubborn to give her a chance. Sandra is now a staff nurse at St John's, been in nursing since she left school at sixteen. Jennifer works in Advocacy. That's where good people help other good but troubled people to not fall through the cracks and end up in more trouble.'

'I know what Advocacy is, smart-arse.'

She grinned. 'In fact...'

Her look promised trouble, like she was enjoying this. 'She regularly signs in to the Civic Centre for meetings with Social Services on the floor above ours.'

Malkie gaped at her. 'You mean I might have passed her and not known who she was?'

'Very possible, Sherlock.'

'Well, fuck me.' He returned his gaze to the accident, to the distraction of the job.

'No thanks, and please stop offering.'

They waited. Malkie would have to log a statement; he

hoped he wouldn't be recorded officially as the first responder, but he'd been the first copper on the scene.

The ambulance crew took less than five minutes to stabilise the man and load him for transport to St John's. The audience drifted away, some already calling people, he presumed to relate the exciting end to their afternoon and to spread their photos on social media.

We really are the pinnacle of evolution, aren't we?

As the Uniforms busied themselves with crowd-dispersal and an initial search of the road for evidence, Malkie and Steph wandered back towards the Civic Centre. As they passed the entrance to its main building Malkie couldn't help wondering if he really might have passed by his own daughter and not realised. He could ask her to let him know the next time she had an appointment with Social Services, but then she might think he'd been checking up on her, and the last thing he wanted was her to think he was abusing police resources to check her out.

He turned to Steph as they walked. 'Hang on. How did you get all that info on Jennifer without a case reference to justify PNC database searches?'

She smiled and shook her head. 'Really, old man?'

He felt small and slow-witted. Steph often had that effect on him.

'We get as much info from social media, these days, as we get from that damned computer. Social media, mate.

'She has accounts on Facebook and Bluesky, and she's dabbled in Instagram. Oh, and she's on LinkedIn. That's like Facebook for professionals. Means she's a professional person with a career in mind.'

'Really? She's a professional person? A career girl?'

Steph tutted. 'A career person, you dinosaur.'

'Aye. OK. Fair point.'

She punched his arm. 'You'll get the hang of it, mate.'

'Of what?' They'd reached the doors to the station reception.

'Modern life. Parenting. Maybe even adulting if you study hard.'

Part of him resented the – admittedly spot-on – assessment of his educational requirements, while another part of him recognised a whole new thing to terrify him.

Parenting. Fuck's sake...

FIVE

Back at his desk in the station – or rather, the desk Malkie kept messy enough to ensure none of his hot-desking colleagues would consider inhabiting – Malkie stared at the email on his screen that he'd not yet found the courage to send.

This one email threatened to sabotage eight hard months he'd spent dragging himself to a place where his dad could rely on him. When his mum had died in a fire that gutted his childhood home and left his dad homeless, he'd fallen apart. His dad had lain in St John's recovering from burns and breaks and heartache while Malkie had hidden himself away from everything. He'd been put on medical leave, which was supposed to give him space to process, to deal with the fallout from such an awful tragedy, but it had only given him too much room to fill and nothing to fill it with. So, he'd wallowed. He'd found himself – not quite wishing – but wondering what if both his parents had died that night. Together. Nobody deserved to lose a partner of fifty years. Then he'd loathed himself for even considering his dad's death could be any kind of benefit to anyone.

He sighed, read the email again. He could have boiled it

down to eleven brutal words: 'New evidence suggests my mother's death may not have been accidental', but he knew Susan Thompson – his boss and old flame – would need more to justify taking the suspicion seriously. As always, Police Scotland's J Division struggled every day to cover increasing levels of drug use and domestic abuse, arson attacks and racial discrimination, drunken brawls and muggings and burglaries and a terrifying spike in fatal stabbings worsening across the whole of Scotland. He needed to hit a vague and unquantifiable threshold of reasonable suspicion to allow Thompson to assign resources to reopening a case the Fire Investigation Unit had already signed off on as accidental, seven months ago.

He moved the mouse pointer to the 'Send' button but couldn't press it. His dad had left the decision to Malkie, claimed he couldn't assess the new evidence as well as Malkie could with his professional expertise. Malkie suspected the old man simply couldn't bear to make the decision for his son, couldn't condone turning both their lives upside down all over again. Both wanted to see the fucker who murdered his mum rot in Addiewell for however many years 'Life' meant these days, but at what emotional cost to them both if that didn't happen?

He heard a door slam somewhere and allowed that to distract him. He locked his PC screen and stood to investigate. He knew he was avoiding his responsibilities, hoping that five minutes away from the damned email might lend him some perspective.

As he passed the ladies' toilet, he heard an impact from inside, then – he could swear – moaning. No, not moaning. Growling? Pissed-off groaning? He glanced around the huge open-plan office, saw only heads down over reports and PC screens at the far end where the Uniforms sat. He knocked on the door then eased it open a few inches.

'Hello? You OK in there?'

Silence.

'Hello?'

Nothing.

He considered walking in but knew how badly him walking into the ladies' loos could end. It could be one of his colleagues but equally it could be one of the ladies from the other side of the building, the admin and HR lot, who often had to traipse around to the actual *polis* side of the office because building management still hadn't repaired one of only two cubicles in their toilet.

He gave it five seconds more but heard nothing, so he wandered back to his desk. As he sat back down and nudged his mouse to get the log in prompt to appear, the door opened.

Pamela Ballantyne stepped out, dabbed at her eyes with a tissue, smoothed her jacket and her trousers, breathed in then released it as if expelling some heavy burden. When she turned back to the CID desks, she spotted Malkie, and her face darkened.

She sat at a desk far from Malkie, as usual. She nodded at him, her composure returned and every inch the professional.

'DS McCulloch.'

Malkie nodded back. 'DS Ballantyne.'

Malkie waited for more. Hoped for more. He and Ballantyne – or Pammy, as she was known to anyone not within her earshot – had never clicked with each other. While Malkie had aligned himself – unofficially, of course – with his old pal and old flame who had overtaken him up the greasy pole, DI Susan Thompson, Ballantyne had hitched her wagon to DI Gavin McLeish, who then turned into a walking car crash of a senior officer who had repeatedly demonstrated the perverse prevalence in all corporate environments of what he'd heard called The Peter Principle. McLeish had fucked up twice that anyone knew of. First, he'd got Malkie a handful of manky syringes in the wrist by barging into a teen boy band party against all known protocols and putting Malkie in the untenable position of choosing between stopping the needles from ending up in McLeish's neck or risking taking the hit himself. McLeish had thanked Malkie only once and with about as bad grace as anyone could. Malkie's preference to play down the incident for the sake of a quiet life had allowed McLeish and his corporate-babble-spewing gob to talk himself into a DI position that Malkie had gladly vacated months previously. McLeish had then outdone even himself by trying to run a covert informer on the inside of an ugly and violent local crime family and been played like an out-of-tune fiddle. As per The Peter Principle, McLeish had weasel-worded his way out of trouble again, and even – somehow – managed to turn a monumental fuck up into a 'valuable lesson learned' and wangled himself a trial period in a Major Investigation Team. Malkie hadn't – yet – had to suffer the ignominy of McLeish swooping into Livi J Division and lording it over him, but it could only be a matter of time.

Pammy Ballantyne had realised, too late, that she'd fastened her career aspirations to a man who turned out to have a short memory for loyalty, as the worst kinds of pole-climber often did.

'You OK, Pam?'

Her eyes snapped up, full of danger, daring him to add the forbidden second syllable.

'I'm fine, Malkie. Mind your own business, please.'

'Sorry, Pam. Just worried. Heard you kicking the fuck out of something in the ladies' loo, you know?'

She glared at him, but he also saw her cover the knuckles of her right hand with her left hand then turn away from him, to her PC. He noticed a redness around the rim of her eyelids. Could the cold and ever-hostile Pammy Ballantyne have been crying?

Not kicked. Punched? What's got you all riled up, Pammy? Not like you to let a mere mortal like me see a chink in your armour.

As fascinating as Ballantyne's obviously troubled mind was to him, he tore himself away from watching her heave a heavy sigh, lean on her desk and lower her head. He returned to the email he needed to make a decision on.

Send or delete? Rake everything up again but maybe get an answer to the question that now troubled both him and his dad and would never let itself be forgotten? Or bury it. Let it fester and rot and add further to the irrational anger he felt at himself for – For what? Not being there? For giving her the birthday candle that he now knew took no part in her death?

Having answered his own question, he clicked 'Send'. Then he breathed. 'What the hell am I doing?'

Ballantyne turned. Malkie expected to see her revel in his apparent admission of having committed another in a long line of fuck ups, but he saw her do a double take as she looked at him.

The look of defensive sarcasm and superiority he expected from her evaporated. She seemed to reappraise him, reconsider. He realised his troubles must be writ plain on his face, so painful had his decision been, and he could only assume that even Ballantyne could recognise a soul in trouble.

Her eyes tightened as if processing something, then she turned away again. No disappointed shake of her head. No curl of her lip. Nothing. As much as the thought of Ballantyne exhibiting any kind of sensitivity astounded him, Malkie couldn't shake the disturbing feeling that he'd just witnessed – he struggled to articulate it even in his own mind – a softer side to DS Pammy Ballantyne.

He shook his head, had a stern word with himself, then opened a case file on the security guard's RTC to record his statement as de facto first responder.

He itched to recall his email to Thompson, dreaded the ramifications if she agreed with his concerns.

The candle that had started the fire that killed his mum had never been the one he'd bought for her birthday and left burning on her bedside table. The fire had started on the windowsill, where every other candle he'd ever bought her had sat, unlit and gathering dust, for years. Next to the window. The open window.

Did some fucker murder my mum?

SIX

Elizabeth walked home. She'd taken a bus to the shopping centre to avoid her car registration being photographed entering and leaving the parking area, then she'd been too worried to let herself be caught on any bus CCTV.

She sat in her armchair, the one Andrew could no longer use because he lacked the strength in his arms to stand from the cushioned depths of living-room furniture. The jumper sat on the coffee table. Black wool. Three hundred and fifty bloody pounds. For a jumper. How had the world become so stupid?

She'd have spent that kind of money on clothes, once. These days, she'd needed to visit a food bank for the first time in her life in order to save money for the basics when Sophie started at big school: black trousers, socks and trainers, white blouse. Recently it had seemed like Sophie was getting better. Until Friday. She had come through the front door and ran straight up to her bedroom, and neither Elizabeth nor Andrew saw her again until morning. She couldn't bear to think it had started again.

Could one stupidly expensive jumper change things? Had life become that screwed up?

She feared to touch the thing, as if further handling of it might pollute her, remind her she was about to dress her only child in stolen goods. If she'd been allowed to leave unnoticed with the thing, she knew it would have barely registered anywhere but the store's inventory checks. One of her clients, Emily, had a grandson who – she claimed – only stole from shops to sell on at much cheaper prices to friends and family who couldn't afford supermarket basics prices. Elizabeth never had the heart to tell Emily that she'd heard the lad was also known for nicking TVs and laptops from sleeping households that would struggle to replace them.

Did that make her less of a criminal? Less of a potential embarrassment to herself and to her daughter? Why had that stupid idiot chased her so much further than he was supposed to? What was £350 to a store that charged more for one jumper than most people she knew spent on feeding their kids every month? Why hadn't he stopped at the exits, where he was supposed to? Why did he have to go and turn her already-shameful act into – into what? Had he lived? She had to hope he'd survived.

She grabbed her phone and opened a browser. On the *West Lothian Courier* front page, she found a brief report of the incident in a sidebar. She stopped reading at 'critical but stable and taken to St John's hospital' and sighed in relief. When she read on, she saw nothing to suggest anyone had yet identified the reason why he'd run out into the road, beyond a few helpful witnesses who mentioned 'some woman he was chasing'. No description. At least none reported. Might she survive this?

She shook herself, slammed her fist down onto the arm of the chair. She harboured not a scrap of regret about what she'd done. Sophie had suffered too much already at the hands of toxic little shits in her classes. Elizabeth's top priority had to be her daughter's mental health, even taking priority over taking care of Andrew, and her own pride.

When Sophie started at her new school, she had bemoaned the loss of her few supportive friends, but she had understood Elizabeth's wish for her to escape a past no twelve-year-old should ever have to suffer.

She'd worked so hard to escape that life. Had it been fifteen years ago that she'd left? She suspected she'd never stop carrying the damage he'd caused her. Andrew had been patient, had given her all the time and all the space she'd needed, and for that she'd love him forever. Sophie had been like a final sealing-off of all that Elizabeth had endured before taking her life back, living proof of having left behind what she'd once thought would kill her.

She stood, suddenly furious with herself.

No. Damn it, no. She'd survived that vile bastard. She could survive this. She would not allow fallout from her actions to cause Sophie any further shame, any further punishment. She'd die before letting it hurt her daughter. She'd never felt more certain of anything in her entire life.

She laid her head back, just for a few minutes. She had an hour before she had to leave for her first client of the evening. Thirty minutes before she needed to cook. Sophie had happily adjusted dinner times to bang on five o'clock so that Elizabeth could cook and eat with her and still make her first appointment each evening.

She did seven mornings and seven evenings a week, with housework and catching up on her sleep every afternoon. Andrew did what he could except on his therapy afternoons like today. Since his diagnosis, they'd had to have too many conversations that ordinary, good people should never need to have, too many words shouted from the end of a tether. They always, somehow, managed to talk each other back to a place where they could move forward, together.

She reminded herself how the doctors had told them Andrew was lucky, if that was the word for it; his kind of MS was the kind that might respond to treatment, and might – they had to hope – be held at bay long enough for him to see Sophie grow to adulthood.

She felt a headache brewing, so she reached for the box of painkillers that sat on the coffee table. With two pills chased down by a glass of water from the kitchen, she closed her eyes again. Twenty minutes she had now; it would have to be enough.

Her phone rang, and she almost sobbed. The day she could shut the world out completely would be the day she could maybe start to fight back.

'Hello?'

'Liz?' A nicotine-ravaged voice barked down the phone at her.

'Hello, Isa. What do you want?'

A moment of silence. 'Hello to you too, Liz. What's got you so rude? You're usually so polite and posh.'

'What do you want, Isa? I'm busy.'

'Nae need to snap. Nicola's phoned in sick. Again. Saw her on Facebook last night, drinking shots with her pals in Cinderella's, so the wee skiver is at it again. I'm going to report her again.'

Elizabeth heaved a heavy sigh. 'Isa, if you get rid of her, it'll take another three months to replace her, and I can't take on any more shifts. God knows, I'd love to, but I can't. Andrew and Sophie—'

'We'll get another European one, if we can still get them; they work like machines for peanuts and they don't talk back, neither.'

'Fine, but don't get rid of Nicola until you replace her. I'm not kidding. There's no way I can take on any more shifts just now.'

'A'right, I'll pick up your slack. I've always been able to handle more shifts than you could.' Elizabeth didn't miss the unfounded accusation in Isa's now-disapproving voice.

'Oh... Sod off, Isa. I do what I can.'

'Good. You need to do Mrs Gowan at half five. She's on Nicola's list and no one else can cover.'

Elizabeth shot out of her chair. 'No. I can't. I need to cook for Sophie and Andrew, and I've had a... horrible afternoon. I'm... struggling, just now.'

'Why? What's happened?' Elizabeth didn't need to see Isa's face to know her question came more from salacious nosiness than anything like concern.

Elizabeth dredged her mind for anything she hoped might persuade even Isa to show a rare scrap of compassion. She came up blank, except for...

'I saw a man run over today.' Before she could stop herself, she forgot a lesson learned nearly too late during the fight against her own historic abuse: she embellished. 'I nearly got hit too. It was horrible, very upsetting.'

'That security guard guy at the Almondvale? Did you see him? Did he die?'

Isa took a breath, but wasn't finished yet. 'How come you nearly got hit? Is that why you're humpty? You're never humpty so you must have had something to do with it, right?'

'I'm not humpty and I'm not hurt. I'm just tired.'

'If you're not hurt, you can do Mrs Gowan's five thirty. There's no one else. Your regular six o'clock, Mr Stevenson, is right round the corner from her.'

'No, I—'

Isa disconnected the call.

She cried, then. Quietly, so Sophie wouldn't hear her; she had too much battering her already, but she was going to have to do it, couldn't afford to lose her job, not after Andrew had to stop working. She glanced at the clock again. Ten minutes, and she'd need to spend five of them apologising to Sophie for having to make her own dinner.

No. Not happening. She could throw a crisp bake and some

chips into each of the bins in the knackered old air fryer she'd got from eBay, one for Sophie and one for Andrew for when the Livi Mobility taxi dropped him home. She rattled round the kitchen like a dervish, laid out plates and cutlery and ketchup, then put her coat back on, still lying where she'd dropped it on the sofa, and headed upstairs to let her daughter down again.

SEVEN

Thompson intercepted Malkie as he tried to sneak out the back of the station, past the custody suite and the charging bar. He nearly made it through the first pair of doors which would have covered his escape but her voice from one of the conference rooms stopped him in his tracks.

'Malkie. Interview room, please. Just a few minutes, I promise.'

Better to take it now, get it over with?

He turned, saw her walk slowly towards him, concern written across her face. Malkie had often reminded her that they were no longer the mates – nearly much more – they'd been during training at Tulliallan, but she seemed incapable of settling into a traditional DI/DS relationship with him, still stubbornly refused to let their shared past go. If he was honest with himself, he remained no less fond of her than the day she'd broken the news to him that she'd passed her DI exams and would soon be his boss. She'd squirmed under his gaze for long, long seconds until admitting he'd allowed himself to get booted back to DS precisely because he would never be the kind of copper who could sit behind a desk all day. The day he'd got himself demoted was one of the best of his career, even if openly celebrating the fact would have gone down with management like a lead balloon.

They sat at the table in the interview room. Thompson took her time phrasing her first comment. Malkie wondered if the knuckle-draggers he'd so often had to interrogate in rooms like this felt the way he did now: like a cold lump of something had dropped into his guts.

'First thing: are you OK?'

He thought about this. From anyone else but her or Steph – or maybe his favourite DC Louisa Gooch – he'd have dismissed the question as a glib throwaway social box to be ticked. But from Thompson, he knew better.

'Susan, I'm fucked if I know, if I'm honest.' He rubbed his hands over his eyes and down to his jaw, as if he could wipe away the fog that descended on his mind as he'd considered the most truthful way to answer her question.

'If I don't ask for a reappraisal of the case, I might never stop worrying some fucker got away with murdering my mum. If I do and I catch the bastard, I might—' He held his hands up as he saw a warning flash across her face. 'If *we* find the bastard I would have to deal with the fact that at worst he'll spend his remaining days getting his bed and board provided free in a comfy cell with cable TV and a PlayStation.'

Thompson sighed. 'I wish I could make the decision for you, Malkie. I really do.'

'I know. You're not bad for management, Susan.'

'Watch it.'

They sat in companionable silence for a while, Malkie wondering what the hell was the right thing to decide. The path that would do the least damage to him and to his dad. He felt paralysed by the enormity of the decision. He believed he could handle the worst that reopening the investigation might do to him, but his dad... Could the old man survive finding out the worst if it panned out that way? Might Malkie spend the rest of his days fearing he'd chosen wrongly? His dad would never admit it if Malkie's decision caused him more hurt, more pain, but Malkie would know. Would that drive a wedge between them? An elephant in the room that would follow them for the rest of both of their lives?

He leaned forward, rested his elbows on his knees, stared at the floor.

Susan didn't push him, gave him time.

What would be the biggest offence against justice? To find the bastard who killed his mum and pray he went down for it? Or let it go for the sake of an easy life, knowing the bastard would never pay, never have to face the damage he'd done?

And so, it hit him. If his mother had been murdered, even if her death had never been the intention of the person who set the fire, the kind of animal that could risk doing something like that would never feel a shred of guilt. Worse, would Malkie ever know if he walked past that person, ignorant of the bastard's smugness at having got away, literally, with murder?

'I want the investigation reviewed, Susan. Please.'

Thompson leaned forward, rested her forearms on the table. 'OK, Malkie. I'll look over the case notes again, and the fire investigation report.'

She paused, waited for him to sit up and look at her.

'You realise you can't be anywhere near this, right? I mean don't even go asking that Fire Investigator guy for updates.'

'Callum Gourlay.'

'Aye. Him. You and he were getting pretty chummy while you investigated that bonded warehouse fire. You can't be in contact with him if the Fiscal sanctions a formal case review. You know that, right?'

Malkie already knew he couldn't make any promises on that front, but he'd make sure nothing he did came back to bite

Thompson on the backside. But she needed something from him.

'Let me call him once. Now. Let him know there's a chance his findings might be reviewed. Then I'll leave well alone. Can you let me just do that? Before any new findings surface?'

She stared at him, and he knew she'd be weighing up her concern for him against her professional responsibilities.

'One call. Before you leave here tonight. Then no more until whatever conclusion this all comes to. OK?'

'Fine. Thanks.'

'It's not just you that'll hurt if this goes bad, Malkie. You know that, right?'

'I do, Susan. I really do.'

After a further few seconds of appraisal, she nodded then stood. She opened the door but stopped before walking through it. 'Take care, please. This could hurt you. And your dad.'

He felt a pall of dread settle over him, a foreboding that rattled his resolve.

As Thompson turned to leave, Malkie asked a question he dreaded hearing the answer to.

'Who will you put on it?'

'It's going to have to be Pam Ballantyne, mate. I want to keep it local until we get some idea if it's going to grow arms and legs and maybe embarrass the division.'

Malkie thought on this, realised he felt less unhappy about it than he might have expected.

'Are you going to be OK with that, Malkie? Pam Ballantyne?'

'I think I am, Susan. She's nothing if not thorough.'

Thompson chuckled. 'That's one way of describing her, aye.' She wandered off to her own desk, shaking her head and chuckling to herself.

Malkie closed the door behind her and pulled his mobile from his pocket. He found Callum Gourlay's number in the phone book and hit the call button. The ten seconds before the call was answered seemed to drag on forever.

'Callum Gourlay, Scottish Fire and Rescue Service, Fire Investigation Unit, can I help you?'

Malkie grinned. 'Do you read that off a card in case you forget any of it?'

'Hah! Cheeky sod. How the devil are you Detective Sergeant McCulloch?'

'I'm good, Callum, but cut that DS shite right away, please.'

'Fair enough. What can I do for you?'

Malkie feared his delay in answering would set Gourlay's nerves off already, and he wasn't wrong.

'Malkie? You're going to dig, aren't you?' Gourlay's voice suggested just how bad an idea he thought that would be. 'Are you sure about this, mate?'

'No, I'm really not, Callum, but it's happening. One of my colleagues will be assigned to review the investigation. Informally, for now. I won't be allowed within a mile of it, for obvious reasons.'

A long silence on the line told Malkie that Gourlay had looked down the line to where this could go.

'Am I going to be investigated too? My report, I mean?'

Malkie couldn't give him the assurance he needed. 'I don't know, mate. I wouldn't think so. Your report said quite clearly that the root of the fire was on the windowsill, not on her bedside table. Which means it wasn't my birthday present to her that started it. It had to be one of the candles she'd collected over the years and never lit. But you couldn't know that. I imagine your job is much like mine: gather all the available evidence without forming an opinion too early?'

'Aye, that's what we do. Avoid forming any conclusions until we know we have all the available facts.'

'Then, I think you'll be fine. You reported your findings

accurately. If anyone messed up it was me, not reading the report thoroughly enough to notice exactly where you said the fire started. I just saw "candle in her bedroom" and jumped at the worst conclusion.'

'You must have been in a rotten place, mate. No one can blame you for being distracted at the time.'

'Thanks, Callum, but I should have gone back to it, reread it when some time had passed.'

'Do you know how many people even ask to see the FIU report into house fires that killed their loved ones? Hardly any. They ask us for our opinion and accept what we tell them. They rarely read every word of the report; it's just too painful for most.'

'I appreciate what you're saying, but I'm a police officer. I should have read the whole thing. In detail. Made sure I was fully informed.'

'Ach, stop that shite, man. You didn't set the fire. It wasn't even the candle you lit that started it. Whatever else comes out of this, you need to hang on to that: it was not you.'

Malkie felt his throat constrict as a lump of grief threatened to set him off. Gourlay waited.

'I need to go, Callum. My DI told me I could warn you the investigation was to be reviewed, but I'm not allowed to discuss it with you again until it concludes one way or another. My colleague, DS Pamela Ballantyne, will liaise with you for the initial discovery phase of the review.'

Gourlay took long seconds to reply. 'OK, mate. If you think this is for the best, I'm fully supportive.'

'Thanks, Callum. I'd better go. Take care, aye?'

'You too, Malkie. Give my best to your dad.' Then he was gone.

If I think this is for the best? How could anyone know what's best in a shit-show like this?

He grabbed his coat and headed for the exit. The front exit, now that Thompson had already collared him.

He needed some Deborah time.

EIGHT

Sophie came home at her usual time, dumped her jacket and her bag in the usual spot, mumbled her usual minimalist reply to Elizabeth welcoming her home, then pounded up the stairs to do whatever she usually did until dinner time.

Elizabeth sighed, massaged her eyeballs through her eyelids. She reminded herself no parent did what they did for their kids expecting any kind of payback. With Sophie about to hit her teens and big school, and with her hormones already tormenting her, Elizabeth had no trouble excusing her darkest moods and most dismissive attitude. She drew strength from her unquestioning commitment to her daughter. She intended Sophie to look back on her childhood not with embarrassment at youthful naivete and a cruel tongue, but with a capacity for understanding and compassion that too many so-called parents were incapable of. If Elizabeth did her job right, Sophie would never suffer like she had at the hands of— She derailed that train of thought.

If Elizabeth could teach her daughter never to become a victim, then she'd have served her well.

She glanced at the carriage clock on the wall, a gift for

twenty years' service in her previous career, before her self-confidence and her self-respect had been replaced by the pervading sense of worthlessness and guilt that had been her constant companion ever since. What was it those officers had asked that made her withdraw the charges rather than face the ordeal of seeking simple justice? *How were you dressed that evening? How much did you have to drink? Is it true you were seen kissing him before leaving the nightclub and getting into a taxi with him?*

She felt her stomach tighten, felt nausea swamp her. Andrew, bless him, had spent years working through that nightmare year with her until she'd been able to accept the love she'd missed for so many years. For giving her Sophie – and much more – she'd never be able to love him enough.

She wondered what Sophie would think if she ever learned about her mum's rotten past. Would she be proud of her or ashamed? Would she want to grow up to be as strong as her mum or would she use Elizabeth's past as a guide on how not to live her own life? Would learning that lesson be worth her daughter loathing her, being ashamed of her?

She shook herself, stood; what she'd done today was to stop Sophie from drowning in the torment of vicious and entitled bullies for a second time. She remembered being called to the school three years ago. Sophie had launched herself, eyes blazing and screaming in rage, at Moira Craig in the playground. It had transpired that Moira had been bullying Sophie for months, had gathered herself a gang of hangers-on keener on staying in Moira's good books than caring about any damage to Sophie.

No, Sophie would grow up to be anything but a victim, whatever sacrifices Elizabeth had to make and whatever abuse she had to take to make that happen. It was her duty as a mother.

'Mum?'

Elizabeth crashed back to the present to see Sophie in the living-room doorway.

'When's dinner? What are we having?'

Elizabeth found no problem with her daughter's top priority being what was for dinner. Better that than why her mum seemed distracted and troubled. She glanced at Sophie's wrists, hoped her blouse sleeves might ride up enough for her to check for marks, but Sophie pulled them down and folded her arms.

'Mum? You OK?'

Love flooded her. Even that small sign of concern lifted her.

'Crispy pancakes and chips OK, sweetheart?'

Sophie scowled. 'Again?'

Elizabeth smiled back. 'Yes. Sorry. I have to work at half five.'

Sophie smiled at her and nodded she understood, then turned to go back upstairs.

Elizabeth called her back before knowing she was about to do it. There wouldn't be a good time so now would do.

'I got you a present, for being my favourite daughter.'

The excitement that returned to Sophie's eyes did much to banish Elizabeth's nerves, but she knew questions would be inevitable.

'There, on the coffee table. I haven't had a chance to wrap it, sorry.'

Sophie sat on the sofa and reached for the jumper. She seemed underwhelmed at first, until she put it on and posed in front of the mirror above the fireplace and spotted the logo.

Her face fell, and she looked horrified. 'We can't afford this, Mum. I have a black jumper from the school supplier already.' All the while she protested her mum's extravagance, she ran her hands up and down the sleeves, stroked her cheek with her upper arm. 'Oh, but it feels amazing, doesn't it?'

She crossed the room and landed on Elizabeth's lap, threw

her arms around her, and squeezed so hard Elizabeth thought she felt her vertebrae click.

'It's OK, sweetie. I've been putting a wee bit aside every week since you started at big school. We can afford it, I promise.'

A surge of shame at lying to her daughter threatened to betray her but she lowered her forehead to Sophie's shoulder to cover her face.

'Oh, it really is lovely, isn't it?'

Sophie's face turned serious. 'Thanks, Mum. I'll feel great walking into class with this on, tomorrow.' Her eyes glistened.

Elizabeth squeezed her again. 'You're more than good enough to dress as well as those other girls, Sophie. Don't ever forget that.'

Some sudden thought had Sophie's eyes wide and her hand grabbing her mum's shoulder. 'Does Dad know? He's always going on at me to switch lights off and shut windows and stuff; he'll flip if he sees this, won't he?'

Elizabeth rested her forehead on Sophie's. 'He's a man, Soph. They don't notice things like that.' She poked Sophie in the ribs with her fingers, and Sophie squealed.

'Stop that, Mum. I'm not a child anymore.'

Elizabeth studied her daughter's face.

'No. You're really not, Soph.'

NINE

Malkie parked outside the Lothian Services Outreach Centre, the LESOC, and gazed up at the window he knew to be Deborah's room. One of only two places he knew his heart slowed and his constant anxiety subsided, the other being the porch of the lochside cabin he and his dad now called home. The blackened patch of land where his childhood home had sat went on the market a few weeks previously and had sold in days; land in the old Livingston village never stayed unsold for long. When they'd discovered that a rare incidence of carelessness on his dad's part had nullified his building insurance, they'd found themselves the proud owners of a piece of land worth more than most people's entire homes but no money to rebuild something on it.

Malkie had suggested a joint mortgage, and his dad had complained about them both being too old to get into that size of debt again, but Malkie suspected the old man just couldn't bear to continue living where his wife of forty-plus years had died.

Had been murdered, his mind suggested, which soured his mood.

He needed Deborah: her positivity and her bravery, her

non-negotiable demand that they face whatever came at them together, whatever and wherever their relationship might be destined to grow into. They'd met when Malkie had hunted a man who attended the LESOC briefly for PTSD therapy. The man was falsely accused of a near-fatal hit-and-run on a young man the previous year. Despite protestations from all who knew him, Malkie would always feel he had let that man down, that he could have done more to save him from an armed response officer's carbine. Deborah had refused to allow Malkie to wallow. They had become friends, recognised the damage done to each other's lives and their mutual struggles to always look forward. In recent weeks, their visits had started to hint at something beyond friendship being not just possible but inevitable.

While he feared the possibility of intimacy with Deborah, he wished for it, too. For the first time in almost thirty years, he wanted someone who seemed to be open to the idea of wanting him, too, and it scared the shite out of him.

He found Dame Helen Reid, the fierce but loveable head of the LESOC, waiting for him in the reception area.

'Malcolm. How lovely to see you. It's been, oh, how long has it been?' Her eyes twinkled.

'Very funny, Helen.' He ignored her mock scowl at his familiarity. 'It's been two days, and you know it. You know everything that goes on here. You miss nothing, do you?'

Dame Helen looked scandalised but ignored his jibe. 'I've told her I saw you arrive, so she's expecting you. Try not to walk in right in the middle of her soaps, though, OK?'

'Wise advice, Helen. Thank you.' He saluted her and headed up the plush carpeted mahogany and brass staircase to the first floor. Outside her room, he listened at the door, heard her TV: two London accents tearing lumps out of each other, something about one knowing what the other one had done and promising they'd go down for it. He forgave Deborah's fascination with soaps and other dreary reality shows because he'd seen the other side of her: the fighter, the bravest woman he'd ever known, too good for him.

He eased the door open.

'Oh. Come in, Malkie. It's rubbish this week, so you're not interrupting much.'

He entered, glanced at the TV, feigned surprise. 'Is the quality of the writing and the dramatic tension not up to its usual high standards tonight, no?'

'Sit down and shut up, Dirty Old Man.'

She'd never let him forget his ridiculous joke about being an undercover copper when they first met, and his heart never failed to glow when she called him that.

'How are you, Deborah?'

She patted the side of the bed. 'I'm good. Twenty metres today, didn't fall once, and I hardly wobbled at all. Helen gave me extra rice pudding at dinner time for my efforts. She meant well.'

Malkie chuckled. 'She always does, doesn't she? Daft old bird.'

He sat on the edge of her bed. She took his hand. He'd learned to love the feel of her scars against his skin, the texture, somehow both rutted and leathery but soft, too. He stroked her skin with his thumb, as he always did.

Her eyes gleamed. 'Kiss me, Detective Sergeant McCulloch.'

Malkie leaned forward, surprised himself with how easy it felt, and planted a long, soft, gentle kiss on her lips. Only one side of her mouth had been left undamaged, so his own lips often touched her teeth, somehow still bright and white and perfect despite the damage inflicted on the rest of her when her RAF helicopter crashed and changed her life.

He rested his forehead on hers and time stopped for long, long, happy seconds. He stood, turned, sat back down, and stretched his legs out alongside hers.

Deborah held one hand out in exasperation. 'Well?'

Malkie feigned ignorance. 'Well what?'

'Don't start, bud. Spill. How did it go?'

Malkie sighed. 'It didn't.'

Deborah's eyes took on a stern cast and her head tilted to one side as if warning him his next words could be his last for this visit.

'I was right outside the shopping centre. Jennifer and her mum were going to meet me for coffee and buns. I was nearly there but some poor sod got smacked by a car on the Almondvale Boulevard. Uniforms were there in minutes obviously, with the station being a short walk away, but I still had to hang around to help control the mouth-breathers with their mobile phone cameras recording everything for their social media, of course.'

'Mouth-breathers? Again?'

'Mouth-breathers.'

'No knuckle-draggers today, no?'

'No, their knuckles slow them down, so the mouth-breathers always get to the locus first.'

'The locus?'

'Where the accident happened.'

He noticed the smile tickling the one good side of her mouth. 'Ha ha. Very funny. That's how us *polis* talk, don't you know?'

She rubbed his arm. 'Aw, bless. Don't ever change, Malkie.'

She turned serious again. 'Anyway, stop changing the subject. Did you see her?'

'No.' He held his hands up as exasperation darkened her face. 'I couldn't just walk away from the... scene of the accident. Not even when the proper responders arrived. We just can't do that.'

'So, you called her and rescheduled, right?'

'Yes, Deborah.'

'So, you're still going to meet her? Soon?'

'Yes, Deborah.'

'Cheeky sod. Just make sure you do. No excuses next time.'

They sat in silence for a while and watched two more East End natives square up to each other for some outlandish reason.

'Were you relieved? When you had to cancel, I mean?'

Malkie's gaze dropped. She took one of his hands to stop him fidgeting with his fingers.

'Aye. Aye, I was. I was excited to meet her, although I was dreading it, too.'

She squeezed his hand. 'Good.'

'Eh?' Malkie turned to her, confused.

Deborah settled back into her pillows with a satisfied smile on her face. 'Means it matters to you.'

You will always, always be too damned smart for your own good, Deborah.

He chewed on this for a while before deciding that – once again – she knew him better than he knew himself. She and Steph were just too annoying for words.

He slid down the bed until his head rested on the pillows beside hers.

'Funny thing. There was a wee woman bumped into me, right before the collision. She looked terrified. I couldn't hang on to her, not with the bloke in the road maybe needing medical attention, so all I could do was memorise what I could of her for my report later.'

'Did the guy survive?'

'So far, aye, but who knows what damage was done to him, sounded like a hell of a smack he took. Mind you, he was a big bloke. Padded, you know?'

'Not nice, Dirty Old Man. Not nice.'

'The guy looked like a security guard, so maybe he was chasing the wee woman, but she had no bag or anything. And anyway, they're not supposed to chase shoplifters out of their own shop premises, let alone outside the shopping centre. They sign a contract agreeing never to pursue runners outside the premises but then get their arses booted if they then don't do just that. He's probably going to find no sympathy and no claim against his employer if he's hurt really bad.'

'All sorts of people get screwed over by the people that should be looking after them, don't they?' Deborah's voice had started to fade to a soft mumble; she must be close to sleep. Her daily meds dictated her sleeping patterns, which was why Malkie always tried to visit her early. Earlier than his job normally allowed.

He turned the volume down on the TV, leaned the side of his head against her, and closed her eyes.

This is enough. This will always be enough.

He smiled to himself, watched her chest rise and fall under the covers, stroked the scar-textured back of her hand with his thumb.

He couldn't stop thinking about the wee woman, though. She'd looked scared and frantic and – he had to assume – had at least been suspected of shoplifting, but she looked nothing like the casual volume criminals he was used to. She'd looked – he fished for the right word – *decent*.

Tomorrow, he'd find out what had been nicked from the security guard's employer. Maybe that would explain the persistent, nagging feeling he had that the wee woman had been just as much a victim, herself.

After a half hour, he eased himself out from an arm Deborah had thrown around him, kissed her on the forehead, adored her for long seconds, then left.

TEN

Malkie stood from the desk – *his* desk – to wander down to the far end of the open-plan office where the Uniforms sat, for another morning briefing. He'd arrived this morning feeling more positive than he had for months. After tearing himself away from a sleeping Deborah he'd found his dad drinking hot chocolate on the porch of their cabin. The sky was clear, the vast black cupola of stars from the northern horizon to the massive silhouette of the Pentland Hills to the south at the same time both stunning and calming, making the already cold February night even more Baltic. They had talked into the early hours and skirted around the subject of reopening the FIU case into the house fire, just enough for both to know the other's mind and to silently agree their mutual decision.

Thompson's voice snapped him back to the present. She waited for a few stragglers to pass on their way to the briefing.

'Are you certain? I mean, like, really bloody sure, Malkie?'

'I am. Dad, too. We can't let it lie.'

Thompson sagged. 'Good. I'm glad.'

They walked again, but she wasn't finished yet. 'You only talk to the FIU if they reach out to you, aye?'

'Yes, Susan.'

She let that one go.

'And if it turns ugly and you need time for you or your dad, you tell me, aye?'

'I promise.'

'OK. Let's get the briefing done.'

Malkie sat between Steph and DC Louisa 'Gucci' Gooch, both of whom he knew would always have his back.

Steph got the first hit in. 'Nice of you to drop by, Malkie.'

Gucci gave him no time to gripe back. 'We assumed you were just your usual fashionably late, so we saved you a seat.'

Neither smiled. Both played it straight.

'Brilliant, nagged in stereo. Lucky me.'

They looked at each other in mock surprise, then both grinned.

Thompson's voice stopped any further hilarious banter.

'OK, troops. I need to keep it short today.' She ignored a happy collective sigh as she consulted a sheet of paper in her hand. 'Another house has been burgled in Harthill. Same MO so probably the same scrote. Who was on that yesterday?' Two hands went up, without enthusiasm. 'Excellent. Same again, thanks. I know, I know, but go through the motions, OK? It's the fifth in a month so we might actually nab this wee shite.'

She continued through who was doing what, who was off sick or on leave, progress on ongoing cases. When she wrapped up, she barely got her 'Take care, people' out before chairs scraped on the floor and officers stood.

As they returned to their assigned workspaces, Pamela Ballantyne fell into step beside Malkie.

'You sure about this, DS McCulloch? Me? You're sure?'

Malkie stopped, made her turn to him. 'Absolutely. Thompson wants it kept low profile until – if – you find something that might make the Fiscal consider reopening the case, and of all the people she could have picked to do the first round of poking around, I can't imagine anyone more... thorough to assign the job to.'

She stared at him. He guessed she'd be looking for the barbed subtext to his comment. Or waiting for a punchline.

Malkie sighed. 'Pam. Pamela, we've had our differences but when it comes to investigating whether some bastard... murdered my mum, I want the best. And you're the best we have. No bullshit.'

She studied him. 'OK. Good. We'll need to work together on it although I'll lead. You'll not be officially attached, obviously, but if someone did kill your mum, I'll find them. We support our colleagues, right?'

Malkie's turn to study her. This was not the Pammy they'd all grown to know and avoid.

'Thanks, Pam–' He stopped himself.

'Oh, good grief, Malkie. I'm OK with Pam. Just not...'

'OK. Got it.'

Her eyes flashed him one more stern warning, then she walked off.

Malkie returned to *his* desk to chew over the conversation he'd just had with her, of all people. She seemed to want to get the answers Malkie, and his dad, needed. Probably only out of her own sense of professionalism, but he'd take that.

Steph turned from the desk that she kept so clean and uncluttered it had become her de facto permanent workstation as much as the mess on Malkie's made that desk his.

'What was all that about? You and Pammy having what looked like a grown-up conversation without sweary words or open hostility? Explain.'

He spotted Gucci watching and listening too, and not bothering to hide her curiosity.

Malkie couldn't find it in him to tell them to mind their own business; both had been there for him often enough when he needed them.

'We're reopening the investigation into my mum's death.'

Both of their faces lost all trace of amusement. Their obvious concern reached inside him and threatened to trigger one of the ever-more frequent and never more unwelcome emotional lumps in his throat.

'You remember Callum Gourlay. The FIU guy?' They both nodded; both had helped him through that episode. 'I re-reread his report, and...'

Both gave him the time he needed.

'The seat of the fire was nowhere near my mum's bedside table. It started on the windowsill. She kept loads of candles there, every one I ever bought her. Imaginative birthday gifts have never been one of my strong points.'

Both smiled. Not at him; for him.

'She never lit any of those candles, not in the twenty years I've been buying them for her. They've accumulated there for two decades, gathering dust and remaining unlit. Next to a window she never closed, even during the winter. Gourlay is positive the fire started there. I only skimmed the FIU report, so I didn't notice it. I stopped reading at *accidental fire caused by candle.*'

'Not surprising, mate. Not sure I'd have read the whole thing, talk about painful.' Steph's voice gentle and her eyes soft. Gucci smiled at him but said nothing.

'You bloody would, and we all know it.' He smiled too now.

'Aye, fair enough. I would have. But you can't blame yourself for taking Gourlay's findings at face value. You had enough on your mind at the time.'

Malkie reached for Steph's hand, but she sat back and folded her arms; she had a reputation she valued.

Malkie shrugged an apology. 'Anything on that RTC outside the shopping centre? Is the guy OK? Gucci?'

'No idea. Hasn't come our way yet. Might end up with Road Policing, if it was just an accident.'

'What about the woman who barged into me? Have we ID'd her yet.'

'No, but Uniforms got a description of a woman who nicked a jumper from the Carla Castaligna outlet shop. Shop staff found the hanger stuffed behind a seat in the changing room.'

'A shoplifter. Same woman? Would explain her hurry and the look she flashed at me.'

'Could be. The description matches the woman you described in your report.'

'Wee woman. Woollen winter coat. Bulky, like she was wearing twenty layers of clothing for a trip to the Arctic? Woolly hat with a thing on top?'

'Aye, same.'

'That guy might die for a bloody jumper?'

Steph stood and locked her PC screen. 'Need to chase up a call that just came in, might be related. Back in a mo.' She headed for the door to the front desk and reception area.

Gucci continued. 'Not just any jumper; a £350 jumper.'

'£350 for a jumper? Seriously?'

'That's not the worst of it. You don't have kids, so you won't know. My sister does.'

I do have a daughter, Gucci, but she's in her twenties and I missed... Everything. I have no idea if she was bullied at school. Then again, she's a Morton, so maybe she was the bully.

'Malkie?'

He returned to the moment.

'Black school jumpers are standard uniform in a lot of schools. Some parents spend silly money because they can, and they tell their kids to make sure their pals don't miss the fact.'

Malkie stared at her, disgusted. 'Seriously? £350 on a school uniform?'

Gucci shrugged. 'Them and us, Malkie. Haves and have nots. 'Twas ever thus.'

'Eh?'

'Rab Lundy said it the other day, claimed he read it in a book. I think he wanted to sound smart. Last week, he was going around correcting people for saying *should of* or *could of* or *would of*.'

'He'd better not try that with me. I'm still struggling to imagine Rab reading anything that doesn't come with crayons.'

Gucci smiled. 'Meany. He's OK. Still a DC in his forties but OK apart from that.'

'Aye, he is. I've met worse. And watch it, DC Gooch. Nothing wrong with taking one's time up the greasy pole.' She turned back to her desk, looking pleased with herself.

Steph reappeared, and looked like something juicy had come in. 'Call to Crimestoppers. Some very leading questions about the RTC yesterday. Caller said she wasn't sure enough to report officially, yet. But she asked if there was a reward for information.'

Malkie shook his head. 'A reward for information on someone she won't admit to being confident was involved? Got to admire the enthusiasm of your typical upstanding citizen, right? I don't suppose she was helpful enough to call from a traceable number, was she?'

'Don't know. She called anonymously. Unless it turns into a much bigger deal, we won't get a warrant for her phone or IMEI number.'

'Aye, I knew that. I did, cheeky sod. So, Uniforms will struggle with it, then it'll go on the *no reasonable prospect of an arrest* pile and disappear into the annual stats we get flogged with every year.'

'Aye, techs are scouring the shopping centre's CCTV but there's only one camera between the shop entrance and the exit from the centre, so if she kept her head down, they might get nothing too.'

'Why are you interested, boss? Uniforms have this one and shoplifters rarely get much time put into nabbing them.'

'Unless that security guard…'

'Martin Jessop. Twenty-four. From Whitburn. Critical but stable.'

'And you ask me why *I'm* interested?'

'I'm thorough.'

He let it go; knew it couldn't end well. 'Unless he doesn't survive or ends up wishing he hadn't. Looked to me like he took a hell of a hit.'

'Aye. He needed immediate surgery, back and legs and ribs. It's his back they're most worried about.'

'So, it could come back to us. If he got run over while chasing a shoplifter, Management might want her caught and made an example of. Retail industry's kicking up a stink recently about us *polis* doing nothing about shop theft, and I can't say I blame them.'

'Aye, well, we do what we can with the resources we're given, right?'

'In other news. Thompson has assigned Pam Ballantyne to re-examine my mum's case, and I'm happy about that.'

Steph raised her eyebrows. 'I think I agree, but I thought your dad might want to just get past it and forget about it?'

'I considered that and I'm sure he did too, but neither of us said it out loud, so we kind of agreed we needed answers without actually saying the words.'

'Must be nice to have parents you feel connected to, and don't look at me like that: my mum's long gone, my stepdad's a waste of oxygen and my real—' She couldn't bring herself to say the next word. 'To hell with them both. I'm not them.'

This time, Malkie reached out quickly, didn't give her time to retract her hand. He gave it one, brief squeeze, then let go again as she looked around, scandalised. 'No, you really are not, Steph.'

She scowled and turned away. He caught Gucci watching again. She smiled at him as only Gucci ever did. She used to make him wonder *If I ever had a daughter...* That spurred him to tackle his next, momentous, task.

Time to reschedule his first ever meeting with his twenty-six-year-old daughter.

ELEVEN

'Davie? That you?'

'Ach, what the fuck do you want, Isa?'

'Nothin'. No' this time. Might have something for you, for a change.'

'Continue.'

'That security guard that got knocked over at the shopping centre – was it Sally Jessop's lad, Martin?'

'How did you know that?'

'Did anyone see it happen?'

'No, why?'

'Just something nippin' at ma brain. Might be nothin'.'

'Spit it out, for fuck's sake. What have you got?'

'Nothin' concrete. Ask around if anyone got a look at a woman who nearly got hit by the same car.'

'Why? How do you know it was a woman? You're no' givin' me much, Isa.'

'Just ask. By the way, what was he doin' runnin' oot the shopping like that? Surprised he can run more than a dozen feet without keelin' over.'

'Some woman nicked a fuck-off expensive jumper frae the

shop he minds in the shoppin' centre. He isnae fit to chase anyone but you know what he's like: any excuse to throw his weight around. He must have been bored. Stevie's ragin'. If he gets his hands on whoever he was chasin', he'll fuckin' kill them.'

'D'ye think Stevie will offer a reward? You know, for identifyin' her?'

A pause, then the voice on the other end turned menacing. 'What the fuck do you know, Isa?'

'Nothin'. Just a wee hunch. I'll let you know. Tell Stevie I'm on it.'

'You fuckin' get back to me tonight, Isa. Dinnae disappoint me.'

TWELVE

Steph listened to Malkie arrange another meeting with his daughter for lunchtime the same day, but by voicemail. He looked relieved not to get through to her, but with thoughts of his mum and the impending raking up of everything he thought he'd got through months previously, she could imagine he wouldn't trust his famously careless gob not to sour a conversation with Jennifer.

She gave him an arm punch, her way of expressing approval.

As he placed his phone back on his desk, Thompson appeared beside Steph's desk holding a manila file. She looked as uncomfortable and awkward as Steph could ever remember seeing her. Thompson struggled to get her words out, opened her mouth, closed it again, then nodded towards an empty meeting room and walked away.

Malkie raised his eyebrows at Steph, but she knew as much – as little – as he did about the reason for Thompson's manner. That wasn't completely true: one recent development in Steph's life had promised to blow up in her face, and Thompson's manner might suggest it had done so.

She shook her head at Malkie. He squeezed her arm, and she was too preoccupied to care who saw him do it.

In the meeting room, she found Thompson seated at the table, the manila file in front of her.

Steph sat. 'Dean? Again?'

Thompson took a second, as if she loathed to confirm Steph's guess.

'Aye. He's claiming someone assaulted Barry Boswell again.'

'And he's accusing me?' Steph couldn't keep a cold sliver of rage from creeping into her question.

'No. But he had the cheek to ask where you were last night. Doesn't take much to see he's hoping you were alibi-free. I have no idea whether he wants to try to drag you into it – again – but he obviously wants you to think about that possibility.'

'Bastard. Sorry, ma'am. I was home alone, as I am most evenings. I watched crap on TV with a spag bol and a couple of glasses of rosé, then fell asleep on my sofa. I went to bed sometime in the early hours. So, no alibi. If he wants to put me in the frame for it, I can't confirm my whereabouts.'

Thompson's brow furrowed. She tapped her fingers on the manila file.

'I take it that's the transcript of his call? Crimestoppers, was it?'

Thompson slid the file around on the table and pushed it to Steph. She opened it and read the few paragraphs.

'Blah, blah, close friend Barry Boswell assaulted leaving my block of flats blah, blah, attacker fled blah, blah...'

She looked at Thompson, who seemed to have been waiting for just this part of the call.

'He's been attacked by Detective Constable Stephanie Lang recently, but I can't confirm she was the woman I saw running away.'

Steph sat back, held two fingers to her lips as if to lock them shut.

Thompson took the file back, read it again herself, shook her head. 'Fucking weasel.'

'You don't believe his hint that he might have seen me? Or at least that he saw some female that looked similar to me?'

Thompson shrugged. 'What can I say, Steph? You know the score as well as I do. You did admit to me that you attacked Barry Boswell, and I'm afraid that as much as – and I'll never confirm saying this to you – that fucker deserved it, you know if Lang—'

'Can we call him The Scumbag, please? No? Just Dean then, please.'

'Of course, for now. If his memory suddenly sharpens miraculously and he identifies you, what can I do?'

Steph knew Thompson would have no choice, but the side of her she didn't like to admit existed resented Thompson's failure to voice unequivocal belief in Steph's innocence. Probably the same part of any mother's brain that couldn't begin to believe even the hardest evidence of her offspring having committed some awful deed. Genetics and defensive instinct trumped reason, every time.

'I know. But come on, ma'am. My word against his?'

Thompson's eyes held on Steph's, but she said nothing.

'Except that I already admitted kicking the living shit out of the rotten bastard once already, right?'

What could Thompson say? Steph closed her eyes and leant back, felt her neck click. It felt good.

Thompson stood. 'I don't have to do anything about this for now, not until – if – he decides to try to drop you in it. Try not to stress too much about it, Steph. Us Pigs are always getting blamed for unreasonable force by idiots who *know their rights*. Comes with the job, right?'

'My attack on Boswell will be on my file though, right?'

'Aye, but after he and your... After he and Dean Lang withdrew their accusation and claimed mistaken identity, it's only recorded but without further action, and it'll stay that way. Unless one of them accuses you again.'

'But I'm not on desk duty or any nonsense like that, no?'

'No. I need you out there, Steph. Fighting the good fight and all that rubbish.'

Back at Steph's desk, Malkie waited with open curiosity on his face. She sat, didn't mean to keep him waiting, but couldn't believe she was about to report Dean's claims out loud. Malkie wouldn't believe a word of it, but her having put herself in this position, and the weight her stupidity now added to the suggestion she might have been responsible, shamed her. How could she have been so stupid. Because the man who had kept her mum addicted to crack throughout her short adult life, and the man who had raped her and left Steph knowing what filthy genes filled every cell of her, had shown her such a red rag she had no chance of restraining herself. Boswell had it coming, deserved it, but Steph should never have been so idiotic to be the person to give it to him.

'Steph? Come back to me, partner.'

She found Malkie's brow creased with worry which turned to anger.

'Him, again.'

'Them.'

His eyes blazed, but he allowed her to speak when she could.

'He put a call in to Crimestoppers, said he saw someone running away from having kicked the shit out of Boswell. Mentioned that Boswell had been assaulted by me recently. Left it at that. Just enough for it to make it to Thompson, but not enough to trigger formal action. Not yet.'

She leaned forward. Steph would never let anyone but Malkie catch her crying but her chest heaved and she released a long, slow, shuddering sigh.

'I really messed up, didn't I, Malkie?' She looked at him, felt tears pushing to be released.

Malkie seemed to crumple, he ran his hands through his hair, stretched his back. 'I suppose so, aye. But no worse than I ever did. You want to talk about messing up? Remember that time I walked into a pub full of people dressed in black, flashing my warrant card and asking where some silly bastard had disappeared to? Then someone explained to me—'

'It was someone's wake. Aye. You idiot.'

'Aye. Now *that* was fucking up in style.'

They sat, quiet, for a while. Malkie turned back to his desk, checked his phone. He grimaced as if unsettled.

'Jennifer?' Steph nodded at his phone.

'Aye. Lunch. Today. Unless something else gets in the way, obviously.'

He turned back to the report he'd been staring at.

The wee woman. She knew what had happened behind her; did she also know she was responsible? She had no bag in her hands and no obvious bulges under her bulky winter coat that he could see before she ran off.

Could she end up triggering the first full investigation in months to nab a petty shoplifter?

He checked the file on the RTC again, no update on the security guard's condition. Martin Jessop. The name rang a bell. He looked him up on the computer. Several court appearances for minor theft and assault, never anything that earned him time inside. He entered a query to search for known associates.

'Oh dear.'

Steph turned to him. 'What?'

'The guy that got hit yesterday, the RTC. He's Stevie Jessop's adopted nephew.'

'So that woman—'

'If it was her fault, if Martin Jessop was chasing her, she'd better hope his rotten family don't find her before we do.'

THIRTEEN

'Davie? It's me again.'
'And?'
'What was it got nicked from that shop?'
'We don't know yet. They won't know until they do a stock check. Why?'
'What shop was it?'
'Fuck's sake, Isa, what have you got?'
'What was the shop?'
'Isa, I'm getting fuckin' bored now.'
'Was it the Carla Castaligna shop?'
'How did you know that?'
'Fuckin' goody two-shoes wee cow. Who'd have thought it?'
'Fuckin' pushin' yer luck, Isa. Who?'
'It was definitely the Carla Castaligna shop, aye?'
'Isa…'
'Elizabeth Dunn. Twenty-eight Ryedale Avenue in Livi.'
'How do you know? You know Stevie's going to go apeshit. Are you really fuckin' sure, Isa?'
'Pretty sure. Anyway, what about that reward?'

'Stevie's in Amsterdam on business, back on Wednesday. I'm in charge until he gets back.'

'Really? So, how much?'

'Fuck all, Isa. We'd have found out who did it anyway, so just fuck off, eh?'

'Davie? Fuck's sake, Davie...'

'Crimestoppers. Can I help you?'

'Aye, ye can. There was woman lifted a jumper from the Carla Castaligna shop in the Almondvale Shopping Centre yesterday. I might know who she is. Is there a reward?'

FOURTEEN

Elizabeth made it through her shift, including one more extra visit Isa sprang on her because – the bloody cheek of her – she had to pick something up from Argos before they closed. Three of her clients had snapped and complained at her for carelessness. Not one of them bothered to say it wasn't like her or ask if she was OK, but she expected that from people whose lives could be as miserable as Andrew's. She'd ended her shift at least fairly certain she'd done all their meds OK and recorded everything the agency demanded in the notebook by the front door, but she still carried a nagging fear she'd let one of them down. Missing even one small detail could mean a night of misery for any of them. A tap not opened on a catheter, painkillers or muscle relaxants not administered, juice tumblers not filled. Anything could cause them ten long hours of discomfort or pain or worse until she returned in the morning. She always ran through her roster on her phone last thing before bed to confirm her early calls for the next day. As long as she hadn't missed something critical because of her scattered thoughts today, she and her clients would be the only ones to know. Of course, a couple of them would be eager for Isa's next shift so they could complain about Elizabeth's stupidity. If they remembered it for long enough.

She collapsed into her chair without taking her coat off. Andrew's voice sounded from the kitchen.

'That you, Liz?'

She bolted upright. Strange to find him downstairs at this late hour. He still managed to get himself to bed most nights, his illness hadn't robbed him of every scrap of dignity. Yet. But on top of Sophie's reaction earlier, and the catastrophising her mind had been tormenting her with all evening, any small change to routine was a worry.

'Aye, it's me, love. Hang on, I'll come through.'

She threw her coat on the sofa and pushed her shoes off her aching feet, then walked through.

Andrew sat at the table, watching the footie on his phone. He'd had to stop sitting on the living-room furniture because of one evening when both Elizabeth and Sophie had struggled to get him out of an armchair quickly enough one night and he'd soiled himself. Bad enough in front of his wife, excruciating to have his daughter witness it. As Andrew had remarked often enough, without a trace of self-pity, the biggest damage from MS was to the dignity.

He spent most evenings at the kitchen table on a hard chair they'd had raised with extensions. They would never be able to afford medically modified furniture beyond the bed and the stuff the carers used, so they improvised while they still could. Although Andrew had never, and would never, add to the pressure his illness inflicted on his wife and daughter, he'd admitted he feared he'd die more quickly if he ever had to go into care.

They'd had too many conversations when ugly truths had slipped out from his mouth or hers. Truths they could never take back, but which wreaked carnage on their relationship however much they consoled each other that brutal honesty would always serve them best.

'What are you doing still up this late, love?'

Andrew paused the video and laid his phone on the table. 'Sophie was acting weird, earlier.'

Elizabeth felt guilt flood her; was she going to have to lie to Andrew too? Did the fact that he said nothing about the jumper mean Sophie had kept it from him? Was she now making her daughter party to her deceit? Could she be screwing up any worse?

'What's happened, Liz? What's wrong?' His voice, worried and scared, stabbed at her heart.

She felt tears threaten to spill and dried her eyes on a tea towel lying on the table. 'It's nothing. She caught me having a wee cry when she came home from school. That's all.'

'Why were you crying? Not because of me, I hope?' Guilt haunted his voice.

'No. Not you. Isa.'

Andrew's eyes communicated a complete lack of surprise. 'What's the wee cow done now? Has she been giving you a hard time again?'

'No. Well, not really. Sort of. Nicola called in sick, again. Isa told me to pick up half of Nicola's visits tonight. She didn't threaten to sack me, but she's wanted me out for ages. She's never liked me, just because I speak in grammatical sentences and don't pepper them with expletives. She seems to think I consider myself better than she is. Which wouldn't be difficult, but I never let it show.'

She paused, swallowed, feared her next words might just add to Andrew's troubles.

'We need the money, and I won't get another job, not with my record.'

'You were exonerated.'

'But I did it and everyone knows I did it.'

'Fuck them. They don't know you. They have no idea what you—'

'No, Andrew. Doesn't matter. I'll never get another job like before, so we'll never be on the same money we were.'

Andrew slumped. 'And, of course, I'm not earning, and my benefits just keep going down. I'm sorry, Liz.'

She didn't try to talk him out of flogging himself. He never listened.

She stood and filled the kettle. 'I need a decaf then bed. I'm on an hour earlier tomorrow to cover if Nicola's still sick.'

'Sick, my arse. She has no idea what being really ill is like.'

She wrapped her arms around Andrew's shoulders and kissed him on top of his head.

'Oh, get a room, will you?' Sophie entered, feigned nausea at having witnessed even that small degree of parental intimacy.

She did a double take, then looked at Elizabeth, appalled.

Yes, her daughter was now party to deceiving her own father.

Elizabeth shook her head behind Andrew, and Sophie crossed to the fridge.

'Your mum says you found her a wee bit upset earlier. You OK?'

Sophie took an age to pour herself a glass of milk and return the carton before she turned. 'Aye, but she explained it, said she was just really tired. She made me cuddle her then I escaped upstairs.'

Elizabeth laughed, too loudly, she feared. 'Rubbish. Not the way I remember it at all. Go to your room, young lady, until you learn not to tell such whoppers.'

Sophie headed through the door back to the living room, but stopped. 'Oh, by the way, Isa appeared at the door earlier.'

Andrew grunted. 'Bloody woman, what did she want?'

Elizabeth's breath caught in her throat. She could get no words out.

'She just wanted to know if Mum had got her message to pick up some extra shifts tonight.'

Elizabeth tried to promise herself she'd not have a right go at Isa when she next saw her, as much as she'd want to.

'Funny thing was... she asked me about school. All sorts of questions about going to secondary school, what it was like compared to primary, that sort of thing. When I didn't tell her much, she looked over my shoulder into the living room and up the stair then wandered away again. Weird.'

Andrew looked up and back at Elizabeth. 'Does any of that make sense to you? What's the wee besom up to?'

Elizabeth shook her head. 'I don't know. She likes to check up on people like Nicola, see if they're really off sick, but I hardly ever call in sick, and she'd have known I was in the middle of my visits at that time. I'm as clueless as anyone.'

Sophie wandered away. Elizabeth followed but made sure she caught up to her at the foot of the stair. 'Sophie. I don't want you to worry, but...' How could she ask without raising Sophie's suspicions? She couldn't.

'Were you still wearing that jumper when you answered the door?'

Sophie's eyes turned fearful, guilty. 'Aye. I kept it on for a while after you went to work because I love it so much. Is that OK?'

Elizabeth felt her stomach turn over and adrenaline flood her. She'd mentioned the car accident to Isa, and then the awful bloody woman had seen Sophie's jumper. With Isa being a short, stocky, wee woman, the logo would have been right at her eye level.

'Mum? What's wrong? You're scaring me, Mum? Should I get Dad?' Sophie took a breath and turned her head back towards the kitchen.

'No. Don't. Sorry, sweetheart. You've done nothing wrong.'

'You've gone white, Mum. What's happened?'

Elizabeth amazed herself with her new-found ability to

concoct a lie from nothing in an instant. A convincing lie, she had to hope.

'Oh, you know Isa. Wee sweetie-wifey, always has been. If she blabs to anyone that I'm having to work seven days a week but buying you a Carla Castaligna jumper, she'll have the benefits people on me. She'd do that.'

Sophie's eyes told Elizabeth two things: that she didn't believe a word of it, and that she feared to know the truth.

'It's fine, Soph. I promise you.'

Lie upon lie.

Sophie gave her a fierce hug, looked her in the eye one more time, then trudged up the stair.

Elizabeth waited until she heard Sophie's bedroom door close, then sat heavily on the bottom step.

'What's up, Liz?' Andrew would take an age to lift himself to standing and navigate his way to her, so she took a moment to pinch some colour back into her cold cheeks and dab at her eyes with her blouse sleeve. He had enough to worry about.

Isa was foul-mouthed and rude and would never win any awards for her cerebral abilities, but she would know an opportunity when she saw it, regardless of the damage she might do in taking advantage of it.

What was she dragging herself, and Sophie and Andrew, into?

FIFTEEN

'DS McCulloch. A call came in that you're flagged as interested in.'

A woman Malkie didn't recognise appeared beside his desk. She handed him a sheet of paper which trembled in her fingers. He took it with as warm a smile as he could muster and she wandered off. She might still suffer the common misconception that CID officers were to be treated with respect, or career-limiting emails to her boss could result.

He scanned the sheet, picked out the keywords. 'Shoplifter. Almondvale Shopping Centre, Carla Castaligna fashion store. Potential ID for perpetrator.' He saw nothing of note.

'Miss?' She turned back to him with a look of apprehension. He waved her back to his desk. 'Nothing to worry about. What's your name?'

'Sally, sir.'

He let the *sir* go, suspected she was nowhere near ready for familiarity with an actual detective. 'This is for the Uniforms. The man that got hurt might yet survive, so it might not come down this end of the floor.'

She squirmed. 'Last paragraph, sir.'

He kicked himself inside; same as that damned FIU report – when would he learn to read documents in their entirety before forming opinions?

'Caller advised that family of injured party are known to be dangerous and considered highly likely to search for the shoplifter and punish her.'

Malkie's radar pinged. 'Thanks, Sally. Good spot. I missed that bit. Good job.'

She seemed uncertain of his sincerity before smiling and nodding, then heading back to her side of the office.

How did this caller know the shoplifter was female? Was she there and had witnessed the accident, or did she know the wee woman? Amongst certain kinds of people, friendship rarely stretched to missing out on a reward for information leading to etc. Did their community-spirited caller to Crimestoppers know her personally? He logged in to the PNC database and ran her details, now that she'd been named in a call to Crimestoppers but, yet again, he reminded himself to stick to his own side of the job until events or evidence warranted closer involvement.

He sent an email to the duty Uniform inspector, gave her the Crimestoppers call reference, suggested her lot monitor it. Something about the whole incident itched in his mind but he'd only narrowly escaped total career-implosion before by poking about where he shouldn't have been.

He went back to his in-progress report on his minimal involvement in the hit-and-run. He wanted to write 'Collided with woman, thirties, medium height, black winter coat. Heard collision of Adrian Burns's vehicle, woman fled, I attended to the injured party' and be done with the damned thing. However, he knew from painful experience, and even more painful lectures in front of an entire morning briefing, the preference of Senior Management for painfully accurate descriptions of every occurrence, observation and action in wordy Police Scotland officer-babble. A copper never saw anything, they observed it or identified an occurrence. Malkie had never mastered the art of corporate-speak that pervaded every document, email, report, HOLMES file and even telephone conversation that went on in the station. Even Rab Lundy seemed to be learning proper grammar, and something called the passive tense from those books he read that didn't come with crayons. He'd tried to explain to Malkie that the passive tense avoided pointing fingers specifically at anyone whose arse it might be considered wise to cover.

He finished, decided it was his usual shite quality of report, then submitted it anyway. He dragged the job out until noon, then grabbed his jacket and coat and headed for the door to the reception area.

The short walk across the grounds of the Civic Centre to Almondvale Boulevard took him only a minute, but he used it to gaze around himself, watched people stroll along pathways beside frosted lawns glistening in the midday February sunshine. Some, he hoped, were content and enjoying the day as he tried to. Some, he knew, would be waiting for a court appearance or a meeting with the social, and shitting themselves they'd get sent down or told to quit the booze or drugs or lose their children.

He scolded himself for his negativity. He was on his way to meet his daughter.

His daughter.

The more he said the word to himself, the more comfortable he felt with it. Even Sandra Morton, her mother and subject of Malkie's disastrous first – and after that, his only – serious relationship, seemed to have mellowed with time. He found himself wondering if she really might have estranged herself from her rotten family for her own sake and her daughter's.

Not hers. Their daughter? *Fuck's sake.*

He and Sandra would never be close again and even co-parenting might be a stretch, but he could agree to some kind of arm's length civility for Jennifer's sake. The last thing the poor girl – woman – deserved was to suffer for the blood that ran in her veins. His thoughts triggered a pang of grief for Steph; neither woman could change the genes that made them. He chose to believe that Jennifer's efforts to grow beyond her birthright and all its ugly connotations would be every bit as hard-fought as Steph's struggles to see past her own ugly history.

As he passed the crossing where Martin Jessop had been hit by Adrian Burns's Volkswagen, he scanned the road. Cleared already: no tape, no lane closure to preserve evidence, only a standard sign detailing the date and time and main details of the RTC and the Crimestoppers number. He wasn't surprised; the fact that the security guard had been chasing a shoplifter when he ran out into traffic didn't elevate it beyond a Road Traffic Collision. It would probably go down as Accidental, nothing to do with CID. Even if the victim died, unless some indication of premeditation was suspected on the part of the driver, it would stay with Road Policing.

So, why did the look on that wee woman's face bother him so much? He scolded himself; if it came their way he could take an interest, otherwise he needed to put his stupid gut feelings away where they couldn't cause trouble for him or anyone else. He'd learn that for real one day. He'd bet his pension the wee woman was no career shoplifter.

He realised he'd reached the coffee shop already on autopilot. He scanned the tables and spotted the one person in the shop that had to be her, watching him with what looked like both excitement and trepidation.

She stood as he approached her table and held out her hand.

'Hi... Malkie.' She grinned, sheepish.

He took her hand, found her grip firm and warm. They held on to each other for a second, and he suspected she enjoyed this first, tangible, physical, moment of contact, as much as he did. Emotion flooded him. He'd expected awkwardness, a failure to form any kind of greeting that wouldn't sound hollow and trite. But the right words came without effort.

'Hi, Jennifer. I am so, so happy to finally meet you.' A lump formed in his throat, and her eyes teared up.

'It's lovely to finally meet you too, Malkie. Mum's told me loads about you.' She stammered after 'Mum' as if not sure of Malkie's feelings about what that small word encapsulated or possibly because it drew attention to the fact that she couldn't say 'Dad' yet. If she ever could.

Fuck's sake, think how difficult this must be for her, you idiot.

He flapped a hand at her, smiled, felt warmth spread through him. 'All bad, I'm sure.'

She flashed an uncomfortable look at him. 'She said you'd say something like that. No. She's never said anything but good about you, actually.'

Two minutes in and lectured by my own daughter, already. Maybe I'm Dad material after all.

'Fair enough.' He held his hands up in mock surrender. 'Your mum and I, we... Before the last couple of months, we hadn't spoken for a long time. Well...' He chuckled, tilted his head at her. 'For about twenty-five years, I suppose.'

She smiled. 'Twenty-seven. I'm twenty-six now.'

He did the maths in his head. Ugly sex and near murder shortly after his seventeenth birthday, nine months plus twenty-five years. Yep, sounded about right.

Fuck's sake, I needed to check?

A silence followed; Malkie's born of a guilt attack that his own daughter hadn't known who he was until her twenty-seventh year.

'Have you ordered yet?' He clapped his hands together,

eager to escape to the counter for even a few minutes to gather his thoughts.

'No. I waited.'

I know you did, Jennifer.

'What are you having?'

'Mint tea, please. Two bags. Sean will know my order.' She nodded to a twenty-something barista with a ponytail and what Malkie believed was called a soul patch.

'Are you a regular here?' He'd rarely stepped inside the shopping centre or anywhere else crowded for more than two decades in case he ran into one of the rabid Morton brothers, but to think he'd spent nearly every working day of his adult life sitting a half mile away from where she got her teas...

'Malkie? Hello?' He returned to the present, saw concern on her face.

'Mint tea. Two bags. Ask Sean. Right.' He dithered for one more second; he felt unsure of the ground he walked on, let alone his grip on this situation.

Sean had Jennifer's tea and a curious grin ready before Malkie reached the counter.

'Thanks. Latte for me. Large. And stick an extra shot in, please.'

When he returned to the table, Jennifer was shaking her head but smiling at her phone. Malkie sat, passed her tea to her. She showed him the display: a message from *Mum*, saying '*Well?!?!?*'

Malkie saw a look of mischief on Jennifer's face. He grinned back. She placed the phone on the table.

'Nosy sod. Let's make her wait.'

And with that, any remaining unbroken ice shattered and fell away.

'So, Sandra told me you work in Advocacy? In the Civic Centre?'

'Yes. Seven years already. They want me on the management fast-track but I'm resisting because I prefer front-line work. I don't want any kind of buffer between me and doing concrete good for my clients, you know?'

Like father like daughter, already?

'Aye, I know exactly what you mean.'

'Is that why you went from DI back to DS?'

He took a mental note to expect brutal candour at any time and found himself delighted.

She gaped at him. 'I am *so* sorry. Sometimes I have zero filter, and I forget. That was so rude of me.'

He laughed, leaned forward, beckoned her in with his eyes. 'I love people with nae filter.' He toasted her with his coffee beaker and took a long drink.

Relief washed the panic from her face. 'Oh, thank fuck for that. Shit! I mean—' She blushed, flapped a hand between them, floundered for a way to save one hell of a character-revealing half-sentence.

Malkie snorted, expelled coffee from his nose, and coughed. Jennifer produced a pack of tissues from her jacket pocket, peeled off a few and thrust them into his hand.

When he thought he'd cleared the last of the coffee from his nostrils, he laughed again. She looked sheepish, as if expecting a fatherly lecture.

'Jennifer.'

Her eyebrows lifted, as if dreading whatever might come next.

'Please, don't ever change.'

The rest of their time passed comfortably until a warning of Malkie's next meeting pinged on his phone. Jennifer looked disappointed; she'd been in the middle of asking why he suffered so many '*over-promoted and under-talented arseholes*' in his job. He learned that she – like he – suffered an inability to tolerate anything but complete candour and honesty from all, and the inevitable professional challenges that attitude caused.

He cited that shared streak of bloody-minded refusal to pander to bullshit and office politics as the primary reason he'd allowed himself to be – and he assured her he accepted the word – demoted to DS; sitting behind a desk just didn't do it for him.

Jennifer's parting words as they stood to go their separate ways would live rent-free in Malkie's mind forever.

'I know I have Mum's looks and her gob; now I know where I got my endearing personality from.'

They hugged. No half-hearted, testing the waters, sounding each other out cuddle with a polite air space. They shared a tight, unabashed wrapping of themselves around each other. When they separated, both walked away quickly, and Malkie wondered if she, like he, had needed to flee before tears embarrassed them both.

SIXTEEN

Elizabeth was ripped from her afternoon horizontal shift on the sofa by an insistent banging on the door. The kind of banging that people did on TV shows that made you shout, 'Give her a bloody minute, will you?'

She almost swore; she needed her afternoon kip more than ever today, covering double shifts because repeat hypochondriac Nicola had called in sick. She could have cursed Isa's name for dumping so many extra hours on her despite her clear protest she was already overloaded. But she refused to swear, always, like she refused to lose her temper, for any reason, ever.

She heard Andrew's chair push back on the kitchen floor then a pause as he braced himself to stand; while still semi-able and certainly OK to look after Sophie in Elizabeth's absence, it seemed like he struggled more every day.

'Stay where you are, Andrew. I'll get it. You doing your crosswords, aye?'

'OK. Thanks, Liz. Feeling it today.'

One more reminder of the burden on their lives they never asked for and Andrew never deserved.

The banging had stopped. She sat up and came face to face

with a man outside the window to the street. He looked angry, and he looked mean. He nodded his head towards her front door with a look that dared her to defy him.

At the door, she fastened the security chain. She rarely did so because the neighbourhood they'd been forced to downsize to when Andrew's illness hit them all was low income and in the catchment area of an at-least average-performance secondary school, but also, somehow, relatively low crime, too. In her previous incarnation as a professional person, she'd made countless visits to a website with maps of Scottish Deprivation indices and other sociological statistics, which had then become a necessity for her to move her family somewhere they could afford but wouldn't regret.

She dragged herself back to the present, reached for the door handle. With the door open the four inches the chain would allow, a face appeared in the gap. Bad teeth, stubble, acne scars and bad attitude written all over it. She could almost taste his breath as it funnelled through the gap.

'Are you Elizabeth Dunn?'

Panic flushed through her. This had to be related to the hit-and-run she'd caused. Indirectly, she pleaded to herself, but yes: she'd caused it.

'No. Sorry.'

She pushed the door to close it, but she saw the man take a step back then it exploded inward. It smashed into her face as the security chain was ripped from the wall. She felt a blast of searing pain in her gum then tasted blood.

She staggered backward.

Andrew's voice called from the kitchen. 'What's going on, Liz?'

She screamed for him, fear making her forget how little chance he'd have against someone younger and stronger like the man who now stood in the doorway. She heard Andrew's chair on the floor again.

The man reached down and grabbed her by the neck, pulled her to her feet. His strength terrified her.

He stared at her, took a photo from a pocket in his jeans and compared. He nodded.

'Lying bitch. You're coming with me.'

As he dragged her backwards to the door by her hair, she saw Andrew appear in the kitchen doorway. He screamed at the man as he lunged forward on his walking stick. 'Get off my wife, fucker.' Then he fell over. He landed face down, but his head glanced off the coffee table as he fell, and he went still.

'Andrew!' Elizabeth screamed, tried to tear herself from the stranger's hands but couldn't. He hauled her away as Elizabeth stared in mute horror at her husband, unmoving on the floor, blood seeping from the side of his face.

She lashed out at the bastard, nearly tearing her hair out by the roots. He punched her. She felt pain like she'd never known since giving birth to Sophie and the world spun.

Fighting to hold on to consciousness, she saw the inside of a van, the floor covered in a blue tarpaulin.

She tried to scream, but the impact as she was thrown onto the tarpaulin winded her, then the door slammed behind her.

She sobbed. Tried to push herself up. 'Shut the fuck up.' Something stamped into her back and slammed her back down onto the floor.

She passed out, terrified Andrew was dead, and horrified at what Sophie would find when she got home from school.

SEVENTEEN

Malkie had barely set foot inside the station reception area when Bernie Stevens shouted at him through the security screen.

'DS McCulloch. Urgent message for you.' She held a slip of paper in the air.

Malkie swiped his card and pushed through the door to the long, wide, scruffy, open-plan office of Police Scotland J Division, diverted right behind the reception desk, picked up the note Bernie had left on the desk and had already turned away from.

A 999 call had come in fifteen minutes earlier claiming to identify the previous day's shoplifter and advising of imminent danger to her. Elizabeth Dunn. Twenty-eight Ryedale Avenue, here in Livi. He walked the fifty or so metres to the area of the offices cordoned off by filing cabinets for CID use. No sign of Steph. DC Rab Lundy spotted him. 'She's gone to attend that 999 shout. About the shoplifter. Why did a shoplifting come in on a 999 call?'

Malkie could only guess why, and none of the reasons he could come up with ended well. 'It won't be for the shoplifting.

It'll be because the security guard who got run over is one of the Jessop family.'

'Was.'

'What?'

'Was. He died an hour ago.'

Malkie's stomach sank.

'Fuck.'

The face of the woman from the day before flashed across his mind. She'd been terrified. Did she know who had just got run over behind her? Did she realise how much danger that might put her in? Did she have the faintest clue how much shite she would be in now? He doubted even the Jessops would risk abducting a woman who'd done nothing more than nick a jumper, even if one of theirs had been hurt. But now he'd died? Still a reach. Could there be another level to this? Did Martin Jessop know the woman? Was that why he'd chased her all the way out of the shopping centre let alone out of his own place of work and all the way to the road outside? And Jessop hadn't looked the athletic type. What the hell had made him keep after her despite him sweating and gasping for air so badly he could probably barely see straight.

Something else... There was some other reason. Something that made this personal.

He printed off mugshots of Davie and Stevie Jessop, then sprinted back to the reception area. 'Bernie, can you please let Steph Lang know I'm en route to Ryedale Avenue, please? Thanks, Bernie. Appreciate it.'

As he charged out the front door to the car park, he noted that Bernie nodded and held a thumb up rather than glare at him as she usually did.

That wee woman had killed a Jessop. She probably hadn't meant to but that would matter nothing to them. If she was running from him, and there was some personal connection there, modern science couldn't measure the amount of shite she'd brought down on herself.

Ryedale Avenue was one of those odd suburban streets that most large towns had at least one of. Run-down and scruffy, dirty and half the properties in need of refurbishment or demolition, next door to a sink estate or heavy industry, enough to make property cheap but somehow relatively untroubled by crime and drugs. In modern times, even many low-income households could afford fifty-inch TVs and the latest PlayStation, so these properties should have been as much rich pickings as Murieston, so no one knew why mouth-breathers who profited from other people's misery left this one neighbourhood pretty much alone.

He couldn't miss number twenty-eight. An ambulance and Uniform responder vehicle stood outside, plus the usual mob craning their necks for a glimpse of blood or worse, and a constable looking like he'd had a bellyful of questions lobbed at him that he wouldn't be allowed to answer even if the poor sod knew what was going on inside.

A message pinged at him from his phone. Steph.

> Elizabeth Dunn, 34, care worker, attacked at home, missing. Husband Andrew Dunn, 38, found unconscious inside property but no further info, yet. Get here quick.

He patted the Uniform on the arm as he passed him on his way into a garden barely bigger than the bathroom in his cabin. He noted, though, that unlike many in this neighbourhood, some effort had been made to cultivate the small area beyond just knee-high grass and weeds. Pots lined the ground at the front of the property, most of which contained plants he suspected might flower nicely in a few months' time. A pair of heavy wooden chairs sat under the front window. He noticed they were chained together, though.

Inside, he found Steph standing in one corner of a small living room. Two paramedics worked on a man stretched out on his back on the floor. The man kept trying to get up and the paramedics kept pushing him back down. One of them put a hand on the man's arm.

'Andrew, you've taken a hell of a knock to your head. We need to make sure you're OK to stand, OK? You'll need to go to St John's but not until we think we can move you safely. OK? You hear me, Andrew?'

Andrew lay his head back down. Tears sprung from his eyes. 'What time is it?'

The paramedics looked at each other. 'Nearly four. Why, mate?'

Andrew renewed his fight to sit up. 'Sophie. She mustn't see me like this. Get me up. Get me up, for fuck's sake.' His voice took on anger and frustration as he pushed the paramedics' hands away and forced his way up to a sitting position.

Steph stepped forward and crouched beside him. She held a hand up to one paramedic. He relented but watched Andrew's eyes.

'Andrew, I'm Detective Constable Stephanie Lang, from Police Scotland. Who's Sophie? Your wife?'

Andrew focused on Steph, seemed to relax; Malkie couldn't see her face from behind but knew she'd be doing that amazing thing she did that comforted anyone who didn't already know what a stroppy and dangerous wee shite she could be.

'My daughter. School finishes at half three.'

Steph placed a hand on his shoulder. 'We'll tell the officer at the door to reassure your daughter you're alright, OK?'

One of the paramedics insisted on interrupting. 'Hang on. We haven't finished assessing him yet.'

'The officer will tell Sophie you're conscious and being

given the best possible care, OK?' She stared at the paramedic as she reassured Andrew. The paramedic nodded, presumably satisfied he couldn't be misrepresented later. Steph turned her attention back to Dunn. 'Is someone coming who can look after your daughter while you go to St John's, Andrew?'

'Me.' A short, serious woman in some kind of work tabard appeared in the kitchen doorway with a steaming mug in her hands. She handed it to Andrew, who sipped it two-handed. Malkie smelled tea.

'I'm Theresa Dunn, Andrew's sister, Sophie's aunt. Sophie will be home – she glanced at her watch – any time now.'

The paramedics helped Andrew up from the floor and guided him towards an armchair. He seemed wobbly, his legs ready to fold under him at any time.

'No. A kitchen chair, please. I can't get out of these chairs anymore.'

A key Person of Interest in his previous case had suffered from MS, and Malkie felt certain he recognised the symptoms.

'Is it MS, mate?' He'd learned during previous cases to develop an instinct for those who preferred to just be asked outright.

Andrew looked at Malkie, appraised him. 'Aye. MS. And it's a bastard.'

'Aye I know, mate.'

They shared another look.

'Do you think you can give one of our officers a description of the man you saw?'

'Aye, I can. You catch the bastard, aye?'

A voice from the door made everyone turn, a girl's voice, frantic.

'Where's my mum? What's going on?' Steph and Theresa Dunn darted for the door rather than leave the Uniform to deal with both the still-abundant crowd of spectators and a conversation Malkie would never wish on any twelve-year-old. Theresa reappeared with a girl in school uniform and pointed to Andrew, sitting on the kitchen chair with a paramedic still fussing at his bandaged head. The girl ran to her dad and stood in front of him, her hands on his shoulders. She scanned him, looked appalled at the amount of blood seeping through the bandage applied across his scalp. Her eyes glistened.

That look. She's terrified for her dad. Terrified. Is that what being a good dad is like?

Tears poured from her. 'What happened? Where's Mum? Where's my mum, Dad?'

Steph stepped beside her. 'You must be Sophie, aye?' Malkie never failed to be surprised by how gentle Steph could be when she wanted to.

The girl nodded. 'Aye. Where's my mum? What happened?'

Her voice started to creep towards strident again, so Steph steered her towards the sofa. After one more look at her dad, Sophie sat beside Steph.

'Your dad's OK. He fell and hit his head on the coffee table, that's all.'

Sophie seemed to relax a little. 'Have you called Mum?'

Andrew stared at her, appalled and clueless. He opened his mouth then closed it again, then looked to Malkie.

Malkie sat on the armchair next to the sofa, leaned forward on his knees, made himself casual and unintimidating. He nodded to Theresa to sit on the other side of the girl.

'Someone attacked your mum, Sophie. Your—' Before he could continue, Sophie collapsed. She sobbed and moaned and fell sideways into the waiting arms of her aunt. The girl's arms seemed to fit, flailing in front of her, as if she had no control over them. She screamed 'Mum' over and over until she exhausted herself and cried quietly into her aunt's chest.

Malkie cringed inside. Every so often he got a reminder of

how words that became matter of fact to police officers often took on a catastrophic weight to the ears of those they were delivered to. He glanced at Andrew, who cried too, but quietly and abjectly.

How did it feel, mate? You must have seen your wife abducted and you could do sod all about it. That's brutal.

Andrew's eyes fell to his lap, and Malkie gave him the time he needed.

Theresa started to pull Sophie's coat from her shoulders. Sophie allowed her for a second but then yanked her arms away and pulled the coat closed in front of her. A look she flashed at her dad started Malkie's Columbo brain off: the girl was wearing a black jumper. Could Elizabeth Dunn be the terrified wee woman who had run into him the previous day?

He scanned the room, spotted a cabinet full of framed photos behind an armchair. In one of the biggest, he spotted her. Elizabeth Dunn, Andrew and Sophie, smiling, Sophie in her school uniform and holding some kind of framed award.

It was her. Elizabeth Dunn was the mystery shoplifter. The man who'd been run over – and had now died – was a member of one of the most notorious and vicious families ever to blot the West Lothian social landscape.

He pulled the mugshots of the Jessops from his inside jacket pocket and laid them on the coffee table.

'Mr Dunn, the man you saw attack your wife, was he either of these men?'

Dunn took a second to dry his eyes then focused on them like a man determined to do all he could to get his wife back. After an agonising few seconds, he shook his head and Malkie's stomach turned over.

'I only really saw him from behind, as he took her. This guy' – he pointed to Stevie Jessop– 'is too big. The guy I saw was tall but kind of lean and wiry.' Malkie itched to point out that Davie Jessop looked to fit just that description, but he was no stranger to the carnage and confusion of confirmation bias and all the damage it could cause.

Dunn took a few more seconds, then shook his head again. 'I'm sorry. This guy, the slimmer one, he *could* be a match but I couldn't swear to it. I'm sorry.'

He hung his head; he'd had a chance to contribute and had given them nothing. Malkie couldn't remember ever seeing a man look so wretched.

He thanked Dunn and stood to leave, assured him they were doing all they could, but he doubted he'd sleep one iota until they found Elizabeth.

Was it enough? A Jessop killed? The Jessops' reputation for violence? But still, what made Martin Jessop chase Elizabeth Dunn so far beyond what anyone would expect of him?

EIGHTEEN

When the van stopped and roused her from exhausted semi-consciousness, Elizabeth enjoyed only a few seconds of blessed confusion before her memory battered into her with the reason behind her situation.

Andrew. Oh God. Andrew. He'd fallen and hit the coffee table on his way down. Sophie would be home by now, so he'd be taken care of even if all Sophie did was call Theresa, but what effect would all that have on a twelve-year-old?

The doors at the back of the van opened and a brutal white light blinded her. Fingers grabbed her hair and dragged her out. Before she could clutch at the hands, she felt pain burn across her scalp and feared she felt chunks of her skin ripped away.

She landed on ground thick with mud, but hard enough underneath to wind her. A shadow against the blinding lights – someone massive – fell on her and she felt a knee land hard on her chest. The man stuffed a rag in her mouth, and she gagged on the taste of oil or something else bitter and choking, then pulled what felt like a rough hessian bag over her head and dragged her to her feet by one arm. The man yanked on her with such power she almost feared her shoulder might dislocate, turned her away from the lights and dragged her forward.

Dust from the weave of the bag choked her. She coughed, stumbled, fell over. The man kicked her in the stomach then yanked her to her feet again.

While she struggled not to throw up, especially with her mouth blocked, she felt herself dragged, almost too quickly to stay on her feet. Desperation urged her to make no noise, anything to avoid another kick. She felt the temperature change, warm up, and saw softer lighting appear through the weave; she'd been taken indoors.

She babbled, tried to say, 'Please. I'm sorry. I didn't mean any of this to happen. Please don't hurt me.' But got nothing intelligible out through the lump of cloth in her mouth.

A fist slammed into her face. She barely saw the shadow pass in front of her before it impacted. It slammed into her cheek, high on the right side, on the edge of her eye socket. Pain seared through her, felt twice as severe for her not having seen it coming. She screamed through the manky knot of cloth that clogged her mouth.

'Fuckin' shut it.' A slap on the back of the head. A warning that the next reminder might come with as hard a blow as the first?

She cried, felt the skin around her right eye tighten and swell.

After long seconds of falling over and being dragged back to her feet, and of further slaps through the hessian bag, she heard a door open and was pulled forward again. Her feet hit some obstacle, and she pitched forward. Other hands grabbed her from behind.

'Fuckin' stairs, you dumb twat.'

She fell forward and collided with the first man's legs. He kicked her, lifted her to her feet, then dragged her further upward. After two more stumbles, the ground levelled out.

After several seconds of silence, the bag was ripped from her head and the gag from her mouth.

An upstairs room. Filthy floor, peeling and stained remains of paint on the walls. Wooden planks across the windows, barely slivers of light penetrating the gloom. A light bulb flickered into life above, and she saw the same man who had kidnapped her from her home.

He leaned in, brought his face inches from hers.

'There's a mattress and a bucket and a bottle of water. Don't make a fuckin' sound.'

She reeled from both his breath and from the look in his eyes that suggested he *wanted* her to give him an excuse.

The second man stepped round in front of her. Just as massive as the first, bald, tanned, piercings in both ears and his nose, and the same eager look in his eyes. These men loved to hurt people.

Elizabeth crumpled, dropped to her knees and dipped her head, hoped her complete surrender to them would stop any further assault.

The second man grabbed her hair and pulled her head back. He studied her face, tutted, and shook his head.

'Stevie said no damage, Davie. That eye's already half shut.'

Davie checked it for himself, scowled. 'Fuck it. There's still plenty left for Stevie. He'll let me off.'

'You better hope so, mate. You know what he can be like, and he was right fond of Martin.'

They left her. She heard the door slam shut and a lock slide into place with a heavy, metallic *thunk*.

Elizabeth crawled to a mattress in the corner. She guzzled some of the water from the bottle, then stretched out to find the least painful position she could.

She sobbed quietly in case they meant what they said about any sound from her.

She felt her bladder loosen. She pushed herself off the

mattress, her muscles screaming their agony at her as she lowered her trousers and panties and squatted over the bucket. She wondered if she'd ever felt less dignity in her life.

As she waited, she admitted two creeping realisations to herself.

First, something about those two names troubled her. Stevie and Davie. She'd heard of them, somewhere. Not well, not personally, but by reputation, and she felt with sickening certainty that their reputation was one of violence.

Second, they'd talked about Martin – who she assumed to be the security guard – in the past tense. She'd killed a man. Not directly, but she'd caused it. For a bloody woollen jumper. No, she did it for Sophie. To give her a chance. She'd been self-harming, for God's sake. What if she went on to do worse? Elizabeth stuffed a finger between her teeth to stifle a furious and terrified sob.

Sick fear coursed through her. She shivered, whimpered, wrapped her arms around herself, as she fought not to surrender to a screaming urge to throw herself at the door, maybe knock herself senseless and escape this nightmare she'd brought on herself.

Stevie and Davie. Stevie and Davie who? Why did their names tickle her mind more with dread than curiosity? What did she know about them that she wasn't remembering? How bad were they? What might they do to her that could be worse than she'd suffered already?

And her family. What might they do to Sophie and Andrew?

What kind of a rotten excuse for a mother was she?

NINETEEN

Malkie stepped out into the street again; he knew his mouth, even in professional mode, wasn't something Elizabeth Dunn's family would find appropriate.

'Rab? Malkie. If Gucci's with you too, put me on speaker, mate.'

After the click, he continued.

'You heard about Elizabeth Dunn's attack and probable abduction, aye? I'm fairly confident she's the shoplifter that the security guard, Martin Jessop, was chasing yesterday, so if she *has* been abducted, we need to find her quick before the Jessops do what we all know they do best, OK?'

Malkie waited a few seconds while – he guessed – Rab wrote everything down. For a man who professed to read a book a week, he always seemed slow to take information in when it mattered.

'Rab, you start all the usual searches on Elizabeth Dunn, plus Andrew, Sophie and Theresa Dunn. I assume you already asked the shopping centre security for their CCTV recordings. Gucci, get the IMEI number from the phone that called in to Crimestoppers, see if you can trace where and when it was bought. I want to know as much as we can about who made those calls. Steph and I are going to pay the Jessops a wee visit, which will be about as much fun as it sounds.'

Malkie wrapped up the call and returned inside to find Steph comforting Sophie, who still clutched her coat closed over her black jumper. He nodded to Aunt Theresa, who stepped over and allowed Steph to leave with Malkie.

They headed outside to the doorstep but found several phone-wielding ghouls still waiting to capture full-colour money-shots for their Snapchat feeds. They stepped back into the hallway and pushed the front door nearly closed.

'If the Jessops go after her for what she's "done" to one of their own, then she's in trouble. Idiots like them care more about picking someone – anyone – to go after than they do about finding the right person. Remember that poor sod in West Calder? The paediatrician?'

Steph scowled; she'd struggled not to let that incident get to her. 'He had to move to East Lothian, poor sod.'

'What happened to the guy that did get sent down for it?'

'Did his time, moved up north. He sold his house for a fortune and built himself a log cabin on Skye, far enough from any neighbours so he didn't have to do the door-knocking and "Hello. I'm a pervert" thing. Last I heard he's happy enough; was close to retiring anyway.'

'Fuck's sake.'

'Aye. Sick, eh?'

Malkie shook himself; that way a deep, dark hole waited.

'So, we give them a poke, see if we think it's worth taking a closer look at their properties, aye?'

'Aye. They'll admit nothing, obviously, but if we do them together, maybe one of us might spot something. None of that family, except Stevie, are the sharpest knives in the cutlery drawer, so one of them might slip up. What reasonable grounds will we cite?'

'Condolences for the loss of their son/brother/nephew/cousin/whatever and an assurance we'll do all we can to bring them justice?'

Steph snorted. 'Not one of them will believe a word of that.'

They stepped out the front door to head for Malkie's pool car. 'They don't have to believe it, so even a crap story like that will suffice.'

Inside the car, she turned to him.

'Suffice?'

'Aye, suffice.'

'Fair enough. Where first? Stevie Jessop's palatial residence?'

'Aye, let's go visit the knuckle-dragger-in-chief, shall we?'

The Jessop family home stood at one end of Slamannan Road, a street on the scruffiest side of Livi. Where Elizabeth Dunn's neighbourhood home was shabby but at least borderline civilised, this was the kind of area that coppers went into only in pairs and never for long.

Stevie Jessop's wife, Paula, had produced so many offspring they'd managed to blag themselves both semi-detached sides of one building, knocked the walls through, and got themselves a six-bedroom detached property in a neighbourhood where one working car was considered affluent. The place was a toilet like many of its neighbouring properties, but it was the only six-bedroom toilet in the whole estate.

Malkie gazed in wonder at their surroundings. 'Fuck's sake. How this lot never rose to the heady heights of the Fieldings is a mystery to me. They must make a packet out of the cheap coke they sell round this estate, so why aren't they minted?'

Steph made a show of examining the property and those upwind and downwind of it. 'They seem to make enough of a margin to feed their habits and their sumptuous lifestyles but have no desire for more. Any thoughts of getting themselves organised and making some serious dough is beyond them.'

'Except for Stevie. If he had two others in his rotten family with a brain between them, we'd have one more big fat file in the PNC.'

'Let's hope that never happens, mate. They're in the system, just not on a big-enough scale to make any real noise. Lots and lots of small-scale, volume stuff, plenty of collars for assault and battery, drink driving, shoplifting, but somehow they've never been caught actually *handling* any pharmaceuticals, only using for personal consumption, etc., etc.'

Malkie reached for his door handle. 'Let's get this over with, then we can both go home for a hot shower.'

Steph sighed but opened her own door.

The Jessops' front garden was a mess of rubbish: beer cans, fag ends, empty tobacco pouches, Buckie bottles, and all the other detritus any seasoned copper or social worker would expect to accumulate in a place like Chez Jessop.

Malkie pushed the button on a brand-new-looking Ring doorbell. He leaned back, scanned the front of the building and spotted two cameras. He stepped back down to the footpath, didn't want to catch anything.

A child answered, no more than five or six years old and wearing only a manky T-shirt and mankier joggers. Nothing on its feet. Snot filled and protruded from one nostril. Malkie hadn't seen a brat like that since a treacherous wee shite called Donald Wagstaff jumped him from behind one day after school and his nasally afflicted wee brother had laughed until he nearly unclogged himself.

My mum was there for me, that day. Where's this wee guy's parents? Christ, suddenly everything I see and hear is about bloody parenting.

The child before him stared, no trace of curiosity or intimidation; a child well used to the roughest kinds of people coming and going with a regularity that must be a constant source of woe to overworked Social Services.

'Is your mum or dad in, er, son?'

The child scowled at him. 'I'm a girl. Are ye blind?'

A lesser copper might have cringed, but Malkie was so used to opening his gob and fucking up he'd developed an instinctive ability to file such events away under '*Another classic Malkie moment*' and continue without blinking.

He waited for the child to turn back into the property to yell for one or other parent.

The child did nothing.

'Can you fetch someone, you think?'

The child stared for a second longer, then, without turning her head, yelled, 'Dad. *Polis*,' then continued staring.

A man appeared behind her, a massive slab of a man with a bad complexion and greasy hair, whose shoulders brushed the wall either side of the hallway. He wore a T-shirt and joggers like the bairn, but he also had trainers on his feet that Malkie would bet his pension cost more than he made in a month. The man wore a look of disgust that Malkie thought might never leave his pockmarked face.

The man pushed the child behind him. 'Go inside. I don't want you catching something off these... people.'

The child ran inside. The man stepped out and pulled the door closed behind him, as if hiding something, although all Malkie had seen was a bare chipboard floor and grubby, once-white, wood-chipped wallpaper.

'What d'ye want?' The man's breath caught Malkie unawares and he had to cough to cover a gag reflex.

Does a phobia for personal hygiene run in the family?

He rallied but stepped back further. 'We were hoping to talk to Stevie Jessop, to express our condolences about the death of your...' He realised he didn't actually know how the man standing before him was related to the victim.

'Martin's our adopted nephew. Was.' The last word delivered with clear undercurrent of '*So what are you pigs doing about it?*'

'Which would make you...'

Steph spoke from behind him. 'Davie. Sir.'

Davie Jessop looked over Malkie's shoulder. 'Aye, what your wee sidekick said. I'm Davie, Martin's uncle and Stevie Jessop's brother.' He paused as if waiting for a reaction.

'Anyway, we'd like to express our condolences on—'

'Aye, you said. What else d'ye want?'

Malkie enjoyed the moment for a second but kept it from his face, he hoped.

'We'd like to talk to Mr Jessop – Steven, I mean – about a lady who appeared to be running away from Martin immediately before the accident.'

Davie's eyes narrowed, and Malkie put him straight onto his internal '*up to his fuckin' neck in it, somehow*' list.

'We simply need to understand if the woman is known to any of you, if you might be able to fill us in with more information on the incident.'

'Why would we? We weren't there, were we? How would we know who she – you did say it was a woman, aye? – might be. She was just some shoplifter, no?'

'Fair comment, but it's standard procedure to interview anyone who knew the deceased in case they can offer any insights given the limited information we have at the moment. Where is Stevie, so we can have a word with him?'

'He's oot the... he's out of town.'

'Thing is, Mr Jessop, the same woman was attacked in her home and has gone missing. We're very concerned for her safety, as I'm sure you can understand. Have you met the woman personally?'

Davie was having none of it; apart from Stevie, he was known to be the least blunt of the otherwise intellectually challenged family. His eyes narrowed, barely enough to be noticed but unmistakable at this close distance. 'How can I know her. You didnae tell me her name. I'm no' an idiot, mate.'

Debatable, Davie. Debatable.

'Ach, sorry. Aye. Her name is Elizabeth Dunn, lives on Ryedale Road. Do you know her?'

Davie's eyes relaxed. 'Never heard of her. Next question?'

Malkie grinned at him. 'Aye, mind if we have a look around inside?' He heard Steph sigh behind him.

Davie laughed. 'Fuck's sake, how stupid d'ye think I am, copper? The answer is no, spelled F-U-C-K-O-F. He grinned back, seemed chuffed with his witty riposte.

'F.' Malkie corrected him.

Confusion knitted the huge man's thick brows. 'Eh?'

'Three Fs in Fuck Off, mate, not two.'

Malkie turned away before Davie could get a further genius jab in. He stopped when Steph didn't follow him She stared at Davie, looked like she found a specimen like him too fascinating to stop studying.

Davie leaned out and over her. 'Go on. Fuck off, doll. Run after yer boss, like a good wee police bint.'

Malkie would wonder for evermore how Steph maintained her composure, a look of bored disappointment even, but she did.

The woman was a pure phenomenon.

TWENTY

'Is that Isa?'

'Aye, who's this?'

'It's Stevie, Isa. You've been stirrin' a lot of shite up, Isa. Davie's just had the polis at our door.'

'...'

'Nothin' to say? Isa?'

'I wisnae tryin' to cause trouble, Stevie. I promise. I just wanted to help. Honest.'

'Aye, but for a price, right?'

'...'

'Isa? Fuckin' answer me.'

'I thought there might be a wee thank you for identifying her so quick, ye know. That was all. I would have telt ye anyway, Stevie. Honest.'

'Stevie?'

'I'll be back in the country on Wednesday, and you and me are gonnie huv a wee talk, Isa.'

'Wh... Why?'

'Because I want to know why the Pigs were at my door today, already asking about that same woman. I wonder how they managed to link her to Martin's death as quick as you did. Any idea, Isa? No. Cat got yer tongue, Isa?'

'Martin's died? I didnae know that. I huvnae got a clue how they found her so quick. Honest. Security cameras in the shoppin', maybe? Or someone that was there recognised her?'

'But how did they work out that a woman gettin' battered on her own doorstep was the same woman who nicked that jumper? And so quick after you asked my Davie for money and he told you to fuck off? Can you explain that, Isa? Who else did you tell?'

'Naebody. No' a soul, Stevie. Promise.'

'The morra, Isa. Eight o'clock. If ye dinnae call me, I'll send someone tae bring ye.'

Click.

'Mornin' or night, Stevie?'

'Stevie?'

TWENTY-ONE

Back in Malkie's pool car, Steph spoke first.

'If we ever get to nick that guy—'

Malkie finished for her. 'Let you make the arrest?'

She shrugged her shoulders as if she resented being so predictable. 'Aye. That.'

'Did you notice when he caught me out trying to trip him up?'

'Aye, but it was a bit clumsy, even for one of his mental capacity, wasn't it?'

'Oh, aye. Defo. But did you notice how seriously fucking happy he was that I didn't trip him up?'

'Meaning?'

'Meaning, almost like he felt like he'd dodged a bullet.'

'He's on one of your lists now, isn't he?'

'Fuck, aye. He's—'

Steph held a hand up, cut him off, stared out the window and up at the roof line of the house.

'Did you hear that?'

Malkie shut his gob and listened. Second time, he heard it. A muffled banging from somewhere inside the upstairs floor.

Both exited the car in seconds. As they sprinted up the garden path, an upstairs window slammed shut and they saw Davie Jessop's face staring out at them for a second, he uttered what looked like the F word, then disappeared. He opened the front door, stepped out and closed it behind him before Malkie could do his special *do not fuck me about polis*-knock.

Davie breathed hard, not exactly athletics material. 'What... what the fuck do you want now?'

Malkie didn't bother trying his special *don't fuck me about polis* hard stare on him; that would require the man to possess some ability to '*read the room*'.

'We heard some noises from upstairs. Sounded bad. Is everyone OK? Can we help?'

Malkie made a move for the door.

Davie leaned back on it and to the side, folded his arms across his chest in a classic defensive tell.

'Kids. Wee bastards are always knocking stuff over.' He swallowed nothing down twice while he waited for Malkie to continue.

'Maybe better if we check the weans are OK, aye? What do you think?'

Davie's face took on a note of relief as the typical knuckle-draggers go-to flash of genius eventually occurred to him. 'No' that we've got anythin' tae hide, but ah cannae let you in without a—'

'Warrant?' Malkie sighed as Davie's relieved expression turned to one of smug triumph.

'Aye. It's not my house so I can't let you in without a—'

'Warrant,' Malkie finished for him.

'Aye. That. Sorry, like.'

Malkie glanced at Steph. Could they get away with it? They'd claimed they'd only visited to offer condolences and ask about the deceased. Steph returned an almost imperceptible shake of her head. They returned to the car, but both leaned on the outside and watched the upstairs windows. Steph noticed that a communal passage ran between the Jessop home and next door.

'That's not private property,' she muttered, then headed for the rear of the property.

When Malkie caught up with her, she was staring at an upstairs window. Boarded up from the inside.

'Don't know about you, boss, but that looks like a lot of wood to cover up a broken window.'

'I would agree, but not unusual or troubling enough to force entry on public-safety grounds.'

She sighed. 'No.'

They returned to the car again, and Malkie called the station.

'Who's this? Gucci. Good. Get all over the Jessop family of Slamannan Road. I want to know everything worth knowing about a pair of right rotten fuckers called Stevie and Davie Jessop, and Martin Jessop, OK? Oh, and a Paula Jessop too, OK?'

He listened, then winced. 'Sorry, Gucci. You're right: bad language *is* a weakness. Can you start on this right away, please? Thanks. I know I can always rely on you, Lou.'

He grimaced at Steph as he hung up. 'Too much?'

'Far too much, old man.'

TWENTY-TWO

Elizabeth reeled from the door when she heard heavy footsteps thunder up the stairs outside.

Light exploded through the doorway as the first man – Davie, she thought his name was – threw the door open and charged across the room. He'd already gagged her again when she heard the doorbell; he started to rip it from her face, had second thoughts and left it on.

'What bit of don't make a fuckin' noise was too complicated for you, you fuckin' stupid wee cow?'

She felt his booted foot slam into her stomach again and she retched. She felt her stomach empty itself up her throat despite the gag in her mouth. It burned the back of her throat, then the inside of her mouth and her tongue. She coughed and choked, tried to swallow it back down, but only succeeded in breathing the muck back down her windpipe. She thrashed on the floor, the agony in her gut eclipsed by the sensation of drowning in her own vomit. She barely felt the man grab her, turn her round so hard she thought he might break her arm, and rip the thick black packing tape and gag from her mouth.

She coughed and retched, her guts racked by violent

spasms, her eyes and nose streaming, her mouth and windpipe burning.

She sucked in huge breaths of stale air from the dank and filthy room. Then she cried.

Another pair of feet thundered up the stairs. The second man she'd seen earlier paced the room, his hands on his head. 'Aw, for fuck's sake, Davie. Stevie's go fuckin' freak, man. What were ye thinkin'?' His accent sounded Eastern European with a heavy Scots layer on top of it.

Davie stood away from them both, looked terrified of what the second man might do to him.

'Ah didnae mean to hurt her that bad, Stan, but she's a fuckin' nightmare. Those Pigs that were at the door, they heard her, I know they did. Fuckers might come back, you know?'

Stan stopped pacing, held a hand up as if to warn Davie that one more word might be his last.

'Davie, you know I your brother's man and always be, but I swear...' He tailed off, clenched his hands at his side as if holding in a fury Elizabeth was terrified might be taken out on her. She cried, miserable and terrified.

Stan crossed the room to her. She scuttled back, pushing with her legs and scrabbling with her hands to the disgusting mattress. She covered her head with her arms and waited.

No further blows came. She opened her eyes to find the man called Stan staring down at her, his face stiff with concentration. 'You pretty. Like my wife before she die.' He seemed to drift for a second; did he have a softer side? Could she play on that?

He grabbed her by the hair again. He didn't pull on it, but she moaned and grabbed his fists anyway. 'Davie. We need to move her. Where can we move her?'

Davie held his hands out, his face at a total loss.

'Fuck's sake.' Stan scratched the stubble on top of his scalp. 'You and Stevie have sister, no? Lives outside of city?'

Davie's face lit up. 'Aye, Andrea. She hates him so he likes turning up there and leaving her hot tub full of piss and beer and fag ends. But she's as scared of him as anyone, so she'll keep her gob shut. Brilliant idea, Stan.'

Stan sighed, and Elizabeth heard him mutter something about a 'fuckin' moron' as he dragged her to her feet. She yelped as he yanked on her arm. Stan lifted the half-full bottle of water from the floor, shoved the neck in her mouth so hard she felt sure her gums would bleed, then squeezed the bottle.

'Drink. All.'

She choked on the first mouthful, clamped her throat shut to get a hold of her gag reflex, then gulped the rest of the water down.

Stan threw her back down on the mattress. 'I hear you again, I hurt you, again. Nod you understand.'

Elizabeth nodded. The humiliation of debasing herself hurt more than the kicking she'd taken.

Stan left the room, called Davie after him. Davie flashed Elizabeth a look that promised more violence, then followed Stan. As she heard the heavy metal bolt slammed into place on the outside of the door, she wept. Quiet and miserable.

She'd really thought those police officers would do more.

She knew they heard her because they came back.

They'd have to come back, wouldn't they? She cast her eyes around the room and spotted a screwdriver, half-hidden under a paint tray. They must have missed it. She forced the blade between the boards and the window frame and heaved with all her strength. It barely moved. She tried again, and again achieved nothing. For all she did an active job that involved a lot of lifting, she found her hands and wrists inadequate to loosen even a single board. She threw the screwdriver on the mattress and lay down again.

Stan's words came back to her. 'You and Stevie have sister.' Stevie and Davie. Brothers. It wouldn't come clear in her mind.

She had heard of them, but what the hell had she heard *about* them? She needed to remember, needed to prepare herself for what this Stevie man was like. He sounded worse than Davie and Stan put together. How bad might it be if she was still here when he came back from wherever he was?

And if those police officers came back too late, or not at all…

TWENTY-THREE

'Tell me we've got *something*. That poor woman's daughter is in bits.'

Malkie took his coat off as he walked, threw it over the back of the chair at *his* desk.

'The bloody Jessop bastards are up to their necks in this. I'd bet my pension on it. Now, as much as I must be careful not to allow my feelings to influence our investigations because we all know the folly that confirmation bias can cause...'

He glanced at Steph, who nodded her approval.

'Those fuckers *are* involved. Davie Jessop just about shit himself telling me he had no clue about Elizabeth Dunn.'

Gucci and Lundy shared a look. As fellow DCs along with Steph, they had become accustomed to Malkie's habit of getting himself too emotionally involved too early and would – Malkie knew – be bracing themselves for a bumpy ride. Malkie prided himself that working a case with him was at least never boring.

'Oh, calm yourselves. This one doesn't have my panties in a bunch. Not yet. But, Steph, you have to agree Davie Jessop looked just a bit too relieved I didn't manage to trip him up, aye?'

After a second, she nodded. 'Aye. I saw it. He did look relieved, and desperate not to drop himself or any of the other Jessops in it. But I'm confident he already knew the shoplifter was a woman.'

'OK. Let's agree they stink to high heaven, in more ways than one. Anyone got something to cheer me up?'

Rab made sure he was first to demonstrate his obvious – to himself, at least – competence for the job. 'Door-to-doors in Ryedale Avenue proved fruitful. Video doorbell caught Elizabeth Dunn getting bundled into the back of the van and caught a fragment of its registration. It had a carrier bag over it, would you believe? But it had worked loose so half of it was visible.'

Malkie nodded, pretended to be impressed by Rab's ability to take credit for a scrap of intel handed him on a plate by the Uniforms. Rab did try hard. He was the only other officer in J Division happy to languish at a lower grade than they were capable of, in their forties, Malkie being the other. He had refused to contest his own demotion from DI, such was his loathing of desk time and paperwork.

'Well done, Rab. Keep up the good work, mate.'

Malkie saw a smile touch Gucci's lips as Rab checked all present, in turn, for signs he was having the piss ripped out of him. Malkie wasted no time in moving on.

'Gucci?'

'Eh? Aye. Right. All I got is Elizabeth Dunn's electoral-roll entry, her employment history and credit rating and bank account details – her bank are getting approval to send us her account history. I'm still working through it all, but I've managed to confirm she's currently a care worker for a company called Isa's Angels, would you believe. Been with them for a couple of years. But the interesting thing is where she worked before.'

'Where?'

Gucci flashed a look at Malkie, and he held up a hand. 'In your own time, of course.'

'She held a senior managerial position in a financial services company. And...'

This time she made it clear she paused for effect. 'She resigned under a very large, very dark cloud. A nasty one. I'm still digging into that, but it looks like she accused a fellow manager of inappropriate behaviour, took it all the way to a tribunal, won, then resigned anyway.'

Steph grunted. 'Probably had no other choice, the poor woman.'

Rab glanced at her, a question in his eyes.

'Rab, if she won her tribunal – especially if she won it – staying in their employment would have become untenable. Gucci, was it an old school tie kind of company? City centre offices, awash with MBEs and OBEs? That kind of place?'

'Aye. Gleann Darragh. Irish. Investments and stuff like that. Been around since the eighteen hundreds but diversifying recently into more modern interests to improve their image. Government and private-funded projects, urban renewal, sort of thing.'

Malkie clapped his hands together. Rab had been focused on his screen, possibly hunting for some useful finding he could add to the mix to catch up with Gucci. He jumped in his seat and swore under his breath.

'Gucci, hand all your routine stuff over to Rab, please. I want you to poke about in this inappropriate behaviour thing at Elizabeth Dunn's old job, see what happened. And find out what kinds of stuff they're into. How they make their money. I know, Steph; it's not directly related but I want to find out why a woman who held a position in financial services with probably a six-figure salary ends up living in Ryedale Avenue and too skint to buy her daughter a jumper.'

'A three hundred and fifty quid jumper.'

'Aye, fair point. Gucci, get what you can.'

Rab scowled. 'I could do that.'

'Aye, but we need tact and discretion for that, Rab. No offence.'

'Lots taken, boss.'

'Ach, well. I'll lose some sleep over that, right enough. Steph, can you find out as much as you can about where Stevie Jessop is at the moment? I'm positive his genius brother, Davie, started to say he was out of the country, then stopped himself. We won't get a warrant for ports and airports yet but see what you can dig up, eh? If they're involved and Davie's running things then Stevie will be shitein' himself. I want to know why Davie Jessop looked as twitchy as a nun at an orgy. Sorry, Gucci.

'I need to check in with Pam Ballantyne on something, then I'm going to talk to Andrew Dunn again. See if he can shine any light on this mess.'

Steph flashed him a look. He chose to believe he saw love and support there. Either that or a warning to watch his mouth with Ballantyne, of all people.

She opened her mouth to say something, but her phone rang. She glanced at the display and her face turned angry.

Malkie braced himself. 'Dean?'

Steph closed her eyes and sighed. 'Aye.'

Malkie gave her shoulder a squeeze. 'Need me?'

Steph patted his hand. 'No, but thanks. I'll be OK.'

Malkie stared at her for a few more seconds. He didn't expect any further reaction, but he wanted to leave her in no doubt he'd be there any time she needed him. She stood and headed for the reception area and the doors to the grounds of the Civic Centre.

Malkie headed for Pam Ballantyne's desk. She looked up as he approached, and sighed. 'Oh, give me a chance will you, Malkie?' She did him the favour of keeping her voice down and going easy on the scorn she usually saved up for conversations with him.

'Sorry, Pam. I just hoped maybe you'd had time to give it an initial skim, maybe enough to form a preliminary opinion? Even just a feeling?'

She stared at him for long seconds, then pulled a manila folder from her leather briefcase, stood, and nodded towards a meeting room.

As Malkie sat, she closed the door, then sat beside him. Not opposite him; beside him.

She took a moment to scan the document in the folder. Malkie saw copious amounts of red ink scribbled all over it; Pam was ever thorough, if nothing else.

'The candles, Malkie. On your mum's windowsill. Are you absolutely and unequivocally certain that...' – Malkie had already started nodding – 'they were never lit? Never? Can you be beyond certain of that?'

'Positive, Pam. Zero doubt in my or my dad's minds. If they hadn't all melted in the fire the investigator—'

'Callum Gourlay.'

'Aye. Good man, Callum. He would have seen the thick coating of dust on them. Mum was house proud but for some reason never touched those candles.

'That's how I know some fucker killed her, Pam.'

TWENTY-FOUR

When he parked outside the Dunn family's home, Malkie took a few moments.

He needed to bear in mind that Martin Jessop's death had still – technically – been accidental. The fact that he'd been chasing a shoplifter who increasingly looked to have been Elizabeth Dunn didn't change the fact it was an RTA. Any decent prosecution lawyer would cite the shoplifter's actions as instigating Jessop's death, but any decent defence lawyer could counter-argue for separation of the two actions in order to convince a judge or jury that Dunn – if it was her, he reminded himself – might be guilty of shoplifting but nothing more. After all, Malkie knew as well as any other copper that although most shop security guards would get their books for not pursuing a shoplifter beyond the store entrance, their contracts absolved the retailers of all responsibility for any injury sustained if they did. Hence, the argument that – legally – Martin Jessop stopped being an employed and insured security guard and became just another member of Joe and Josephine Public the instant he set foot outside the shop, and certainly when he pursued his quarry outside of the whole shopping centre.

All of which promised to become messy, so he needed to be more careful than he might normally be capable of not to muddy the issue further by over-stepping the bounds of his investigative authority.

But one thing that fell well within his remit was to establish the facts and the background to the incident, until and if it managed to fall between the cracks and become just one more road fatality, regardless of the contributing factors.

He yearned for the days, two decades ago, when right and wrong could be relied on to be obvious. When nabbing someone who'd '*done it*' was driven more by a sense of moral justice than by what the Fiscal's office thought could lead to a successful prosecution.

If something awful happened to Elizabeth Dunn, then regardless of her culpability for the theft or the circumstances that drove her to it – whether morally understandable or even condonable – Malkie would have to be the person to break the news to her family.

He stopped his own train of thought. If her actions were understandable or condonable?

She's scared to death for her own flesh and blood. What would I already do for Jennifer? And I've only known her a day.

When he climbed from his car, he slammed the door closed with more anger than he'd intended. He took a breath and held it before opening the Dunn family's garden gate.

Sophie Dunn opened the front door before he could ring the bell.

'Mr McCulloch. I heard you get out of your car. My dad's in.' She plodded up the staircase, misery coming off the poor girl in waves, and disappeared around a corner to the upper floor.

Malkie stepped inside, closed the door behind him. He saw no sign of Andrew Dunn in the living room, but remembered the poor sod was limited to hard, upright kitchen chairs;

anything like an armchair or sofa he'd struggle to get out of without help.

Andrew sat at the kitchen table; his hands clasped around a mug of what looked like tea. He looked up as Malkie entered. A brief surge of some kind of emotion flashed across his face. A copper's appearance at a time like this tended to engender hope in people, or despair. News they dare not pray for or news that would tear them apart for the rest of their lives.

Malkie put the man out of his misery. 'No news yet, Mr Dunn.'

Andrew's face lost all emotion again, crowded out by the exhaustion and despair Malkie would bet his pension had wrecked the poor bastard.

Malkie sat. 'We have Uniforms out looking for her and we're monitoring all the CCTV we can find within a half mile of here, as well as recordings from inside the shopping centre. Detectives are checking out witness and door-to-door statements and loading it all up into the database for analysis and cross-referencing.'

Malkie realised he wasn't trying to reassure Andrew that all was being done that could be. He was defending himself from the feelings of uselessness that always racked him in these situations. He could do his job, try to find the fucker that had abducted this poor man's wife, but nothing he could do here and now could touch the sides of the fear and torment Andrew must be feeling. Him and his daughter.

'How's Sophie doing, Mr Dunn?'

Andrew shrugged. 'I have no idea, Detective—'

'Please. Malkie.'

Andrew managed half a smile and a nod. 'She hasn't come downstairs since...' He took a few seconds, sipped his tea. 'Damn it. Freezing.' He pushed his hands down on the table and rose to his feet with a grimace and a moan of pain. 'You want some?'

Malkie found he did. 'Please. Strong, milk and two, thanks.'

Andrew limped to the kitchen sink. Malkie noticed that all the most commonly used small kitchen appliances sat close to the sink. Andrew leaned his stomach against the edge of the worktop, steadied himself, then filled the kettle and grabbed another mug, all without moving his feet from the same spot.

Malkie didn't offer to help. If the man wanted help, he'd ask for it. 'I wanted to ask you about Sophie and Elizabeth. Is that OK?'

Andrew's hand stopped halfway to a jar marked *sugar* for a second, then he continued.

'Sure. If it'll help.' Malkie heard the doubt in the man's voice, the despair.

'I wanted to ask about Elizabeth's day-to-day life. Her work. What she does for relaxation. Any friends she socialises with regularly, that sort of thing.'

Andrew spooned sugar into two mugs. Malkie saw the tremor in his hands and the fierce concentration on his face as he focused on not spilling any.

'Elizabeth has no life, Detec... mate. She's up at dawn getting Sophie's school stuff ready, then does four hours at work, then she makes us both lunch and takes a nap in the afternoon before making Sophie's dinner and spending what time she can with her, then she does another four hours' working. By the time she gets home in the evenings, she's too exhausted to do any more than make us some hot chocolate, watch some telly, then she crashes. I'm usually in bed before she comes home because my carers can't work that late, so Liz gives me my meds before getting to bed herself.'

Andrew turned from the counter. 'Can you get the mugs, please. Safer for both of us.' He cracked a smile but Malkie saw embarrassment behind it. Andrew returned to his chair and dropped backwards into it. Sweat beaded his forehead.

And he's only early-stage MS by the looks of him, poor bastard.

'That's Liz's life five days a week. Saturdays she works, but Sophie helps her with breakfast and other meals. Sundays, she cleans this entire house from top to bottom.' He swallowed and Malkie saw tears appear in his eyes. 'Sometimes I think she's scared to stop in case she notices what a shit life she has. Wasn't always like this, you know?'

Malkie silently thanked the man for giving him a way in to discussing Elizabeth Dunn's earlier life and the bad end to her previous career.

'You mean her tribunal and resignation?'

Andrew glanced at him, sharp and bitter. 'No, mate. I mean me. Well, what those bastards did to her, aye, but mostly I think it's me that's dragged her down.' His head slumped, his chin nearly on his chest, and he wept. Malkie gave him time until he dragged a slow and weak arm across his eyes and looked up again.

'See, when you get married. When they get you to say *in sickness and in health?* Most people who say that have no fucking idea what that can mean. Sorry for the language.'

'Nae fuckin' problem, mate. Us Pigs swear like troopers all the time. You let rip, mate.'

Andrew laughed, just once, then sagged against the back of his chair, looked more exhausted than when Malkie had arrived, if that was possible.

Malkie raised his tea mug, held it out towards him. Andrew lifted his too, slow and careful, and returned Malkie's silent toast to... didn't matter. The moment did.

'I believe Elizabeth was in financial services, aye?'

'Aye, but what does that have to do with what's happened to her? Should your lot not be putting APBs out on the van and getting her photo up on *Crimewatch*?'

'*Crimewatch* stopped years ago, and APBs are American,

mate. We put BOLOs out on people. Be On Lookout For. And we'll have an alert up on the Police Scotland Facebook page by the end of today. For now, I need background. People tend not to get abducted from their homes and bundled away in white vans for shoplifting. Is there anything else you can think of that might explain what happened to her?'

Malkie watched as a look came over Andrew's face he was too used to and would never stop hating.

Andrew's eyes turned cool. 'She's a care worker now. For old people living at home. The shit in her old job was twelve years ago and she's heard nothing from those bastards in seven years, so it's not related to that.'

'What happened? At Gleann Darragh, Andrew?'

Andrew's eyes narrowed. 'You did your homework, didn't you? Don't you know?'

'There were no criminal proceedings initiated against anyone, only the Industrial Tribunal, so we can't get much without a lot more digging and form-filling than I suspect it merits. I just want to know the broad strokes of what happened, if that's OK?'

Andrew sighed, took a moment to gather his thoughts, or to decide how much he wanted to tell a copper.

'She was doing really well, climbing the greasy pole, nicely, you know? She was senior in their business financing department, final sign-off on all agreements. Lots of responsibility so a healthy salary, you know?'

He paused. Malkie fed him a prompt. 'What kind of investments did she deal with?'

'Leisure projects. Cinemas, bowling alleys, gyms, skating rinks, swimming pools, that sort of thing.

'Then one of the senior partners, Struan Monahan, thought his position entitled him to come onto her in the coffee kitchen after hours one night. Pushed her up against a wall, rubbed against her, the manky fuckin' bastard. She complained, of course. She was sacked and her reputation ripped to slutty little shreds. She took it to a tribunal and won, but her career and her self-confidence took a hammering.'

Andrew squeezed his fingers into his eyes, took a few seconds before he could continue.

'We downsized so she felt no pressure to go back to that kind of job. I carried on working – I'm a delivery driver – until this...' He indicated his legs with his weak and stiff left arm. 'When I had to stop working, she had to start again. Benefits people made me fill out a form and because I answered all the questions honestly, they said I wasn't badly-enough affected to qualify for full disability. She took the care job because her hours let her look after Sophie and me, and her clients are all local.'

'It was that bad?' Malkie felt rage smoulder in his guts. A woman's life ruined because some wealthy old pervert thought himself entitled to everything, including a woman's dignity. Would things never change?

'She could have gone back into financial services if she'd wanted to. Enough people knew how good she was and would have risked cutting ties with Gleann Darragh to let her back in. But Liz couldn't bring herself to believe any organisation would be different. She was convinced that her reputation – the one she didn't deserve – would follow her. One side of her mind knew that wasn't true, but the other side, the one that could never forget the feel of that fucker's hands on her... She'll never get past that, I don't think.'

Andrew's head drooped again. No tears this time, but a low voice that chilled Malkie to his core.

'I thought about finding him and hurting him. But I put it off longer and longer, then this...' He indicated his legs again. 'I couldn't give him a slap hard enough to hurt now.'

Malkie felt hatred sluice through him. Too many men like Monahan shrugged off even tribunal findings against them, comforted by serious lawyers funded from massive offshore accounts and even more massive egos fuelled by armies of sycophants with varying shades of brown noses.

'I know she's being visiting food banks recently, even though she tries to hide it from me, but I know for a fact, Detective, that she would never, not in a million bloody years, steal from a shop.'

Some kind of realisation dawned on him. 'Come to think of it, what the hell was she supposed to have nicked, anyway?'

This won't end well.

'A jumper.'

Andrew's expression betrayed his disbelief, almost anger, as if the accusation offended him.

'A jumper? A fucking jumper? No. She wouldn't. Food, maybe. A birthday present for Sophie I could understand, but a bloody jumper?' His voice became strident with denial.

Malkie held his hands up until Andrew calmed himself and seemed ready to listen again.

'It was a £350 Carla Castaligna jumper. Black, wool, V-neck.'

Andrew gaped at him and confusion creased his eyes. Then the penny dropped. He sagged forward onto the table, his arms bunched under him as if he wanted to close himself up, deny whatever realisation had hit him.

'Oh, Christ, Liz. No.'

He sobbed, then. Malkie placed a hand on his upper arm, put enough pressure on to remind the man he was there but not enough to intrude. The level of this man's grief must be unbearable and had to be private until he decided to let Malkie in.

When he raised his glassy and bloodshot eyes again, Malkie helped him back to a sitting position.

Andrew sat for long moments, shaking his head and moaning.

Malkie drank his tea and waited.

When Andrew spoke again, it was quiet and frightened, as if dreading the answer.

'For Sophie. For school. Bloody rich kids. Sophie's been bullied at primary school already, but...'

Malkie nodded. 'I don't have kids, mate, but one of my colleagues has nephews and she thinks it might be that, aye.'

Andrew took long seconds to get his next words out.

'I didn't know it was so bad. I had no idea.'

Malkie almost recoiled from the agony on Andrew's face.

'What was, Mr Dunn?'

Andrew looked appalled and ashamed.

'Her arms, Detective. We caught her self-harming but just once. I thought it stopped months ago. Oh Christ, Sophie. I'm sorry.' He hung his head.

Malkie left his tea mug on the table and let himself out. He heard Andrew sob quietly behind him.

TWENTY-FIVE

'Chicken wire, you useless shit. Remember?'

Steph pushed past Dean Lang, her nominal stepfather and a man destined to remain forever on Steph's 'give me just one excuse' list. She took a seat at a table for two and barked at him. 'Nothing for me. Tell me what you want then fuck off.'

Dean smirked. He knew she rarely swore, thought it a weakness in herself, a failure of her normally non-negotiable grip on her emotions.

He ordered himself a glass of tap water, ignored the scowl from the barista when she asked what else and he told her, 'Just the water.' He sat opposite Steph, took a drink, then leaned back in his chair.

'Was he serious, your boss? About the chicken wire? He didn't look the type.'

Steph held on to her disgust for the man, channelled it, fed it into her determination to never again let him pull the worst out of her and land herself in as much trouble as she'd nearly been in before. Springing her biological father, the rapist Barry Boswell, on her had overcome her will, crushed her self-control, triggered rage that to this day still scared her. She must never let Dean Lang do that to her again.

'He would. For me, he would. He's ten times the man you'll ever be.'

'But chicken wire and rocks? Would that really work?' He grinned, pushed Steph's temper to breaking point.

'And dropped in a big, fucking-deep loch. Aye it would work. You want to find out?'

She regretted the cheap threat as she said it. She redoubled her grip on her fury.

Dean's grin slipped. Steph hoped he was reconsidering how well he knew his stepdaughter, after all.

Steph leaned forward. Dean cringed as if to make himself a smaller target, but his eyes remained defiant.

'Tell me what you want and do it quickly. I really don't like being this close to you.'

He licked his lips, and even that disgusted her.

He seemed to deflate. To lose all trace of his previous bravado. 'I'm in trouble. Barry blames me for you kicking the shit out of him And he thinks it was me who attacked him a couple of nights ago. You need to talk to him.'

Steph gaped at him. 'You. Are. Fucking. Kidding. Me.'

He stared back at her, licked his lips again.

'You want me to tell that... animal that... What? What exactly do you want me to tell him, because I'm struggling here?' She folded her arms to fend off an almost overwhelming urge to grab his manky hair and slam his face into the table.

He shrugged; then – and this had Steph tightening her grip on her arms – seemed to plead with her.

'You have to. He came to my door the other night, wanted to punch my lights out, says I ambushed both of you that night.'

'You mean the night you asked to come round to talk, then sprang my rapist fa... that bastard – on me? You mean that night?'

'Aye. I did it for both of you, trying to rebuild bridges, like, you know?'

She stared at him, incredulous and appalled. 'You fucking liar. You useless, despicable shite-stain of a liar. You sprung Boswell on me to push my buttons, and it fucking worked and now I'm on a warning. You happy?'

He considered his response for a second. 'No, I'm not. I still can't stand the sight of you but I need you. Just this one favour then you never hear from me again. I promise. I need you to talk to him, make him believe that night was a bad mistake and I feel rotten about it.'

He slumped back in his chair, let out a long sigh, ran his nicotine-yellowed fingers through his greasy hair. 'I fucked up, but I need him to—'

'What? Forgive you? No. You can fuck off. You and that pig come nowhere near me again or...'

He waited for her to finish her sentence but she couldn't. Wouldn't.

'Are we done here? Because I really don't enjoy being this close to you.'

Dean's eyes took on a panicked look and he sat forward, clutched his hands in front of him as if feeling for inspiration. The way his face changed, Steph figured he found desperation instead. He recovered himself, braced himself for something.

'I saw you.'

Steph swallowed a furious outburst; the bastard meant to cause her more trouble. 'Where, Dean? Where did you see me?'

Dean swallowed. He blinked three times. His fingers fidgeted with his jacket sleeves. 'When Barry got attacked outside his block of flats. I saw you. Running away.'

Steph's temper broke. She managed to keep a rein on it, but hated herself for letting an animal like Dean see even that reaction in her. 'I've been nowhere near that bastard since you ambushed me in your squalid, filthy wee flat. And you know that. Do not test me; you will regret it.'

Dean snorted. 'You sound like that lard-arsed boss of yours. What was it he said? *"You will suffer an unfortunate accident"*? Is that supposed to be scary? Fuck's sake, there's nothing of you.'

'And yet I hospitalised your pal.'

A vicious gleam appeared in Dean's eyes. 'You mean your dad, Steph?'

She was across the table and clawing for his face before she knew what had happened. He lunged backwards, fell off his chair sideways, scrambled away from her, screamed as if in fear of his life.

Customers turned, some frightened, some fascinated. A barista stepped out from behind the bar but couldn't bring himself to help Dean to his feet. He took one look at Steph and backed off again.

Steph considered pulling her warrant card before realising how badly that could backfire. She brought her breathing back under control with a massive effort and left the coffee shop.

She made it twenty yards down the street, her breathing deep and controlled, before she heard him.

'Fuckin' psycho. That's what you are. A stuck-up brat, a wee miss smart-arse goody two-shoes, just a nasty wee fuckin' thug. That's what you are, you wee fucker.'

Steph turned, fast. She pushed Dean against a shop window, stuck her face in his and with one hand around his throat, under his chin, forced his head backwards.

'You come anywhere near me again, you call me, you even text me, I will kill you. You got that? Have you got that?' Her last words screamed into his appalled face, her spit flying into his terrified eyes.

She removed her hands, left them in the air between them as if fighting an urge to finish him.

'Stay away from me, Dean. If I have to hurt you, trust me, I will, and it'll be the worst hours of your sorry, pathetic little life.'

She breathed, let her hands fall to her sides. She fixed him with a gaze that she knew had scared the shit out of bigger and worse men than him. 'Do you understand?'

Dean nodded, his eyes wide, his lips clamped shut.

'I was nowhere near that bastard Boswell at the time you claimed he was assaulted. Yes, Dean, I know it was you that called it in. I was at home, watching TV, and my internet streaming provider will be able to confirm that.'

She walked away, prayed he would say nothing more.

'I didn't tell anyone, you know.'

She kept walking, feared what she might do if she turned around.

'That it was you that put Barry in hospital. I didn't tell anyone.'

She carried on walking.

'But I got the whole fucking thing on video, you dumb bitch. You want to see how your alibi holds up when your bosses see that?'

She stopped and hated herself for doing so.

'Thought that might grab your attention, Detective Constable Lang. If anything more happens to Barry, you're right in the frame for it, you smug wee bitch.'

She turned.

His face blanched. He ran.

Only then did Steph notice how many pedestrians had stopped to enjoy the show, and heard her tell Dean Lang she would kill him.

One had a phone pointed her way.

TWENTY-SIX

Elizabeth only realised she'd managed to sleep when the man called Stan threw the door open, crossed to the stinking mattress she'd eventually managed to bring herself to stretch out on, and grabbed her by her hair. She reached for the screwdriver she'd hidden behind her, but Stan was too quick for her. Another chance wasted, or another excuse for the man to hurt her averted?

Davie appeared in the doorway too. 'Where are we takin' her?'

'Stevie said to take her to your sister's place.'

Davie grinned like a wee boy told he's going for McDonald's. 'Aw, brilliant. Huvnae been in a hot tub for ages.'

Stan stared at him. Davie seemed to shrink and shuffled his feet.

Elizabeth's mind went into survival mode. If those police officers came back to search the house after hearing her banging on the window boards, could she leave something to tell them she'd been here? No, if a moron like Davie didn't think to sanitise the place, Stan would. Stan scared her far more than Davie ever could, and he was also much smarter than Davie. She needed to leave some trace of herself outside the house.

Stan dragged her from the room by her hair. She screamed, and clawed at his huge, meaty hands. In the upstairs hallway – bare floorboards and stained, peeling wallpaper – three small children wearing only underwear and T-shirts watched her without a shred of fear or even interest in their eyes.

Stan stood her up at the top of the stair then pushed her in the back. She walked down to Davie, who was waiting by the front door. Davie checked the gag was still secure then opened the door. It was dark outside, late. He scanned the street, then stepped outside.

Stan grabbed her hair from behind and dragged her outside, her feet kicking and dragging through the muddy and rubbish-strewn front garden to a white van, manky with road grime. Davie opened the back doors, also scanning the street as he did so.

She saw her chance. Letting go of Stan's hands left no support for the pull on her hair and pain erupted across her scalp, but she managed to rip off the only thing she could think might still save her. She threw it into the hedge. Then she grabbed Stan's hands again to stop him from tearing her hair out.

Stan dumped her in the back of the van then got in with her. He sat on a pile of what looked like decorator's blankets and rested his feet, crossed at the ankles, on her back.

She cried. Quietly so as not to earn herself more bruises. They'd seemed content to hold her in the house to wait for the guy called Stevie. Were they now taking her to him? Stan had seemed scared of Stevie, so what kind of animal was he? Worse than these two?

All this for a jumper? No, for her daughter. Whatever waited for her at the end of this drive, Sophie was worth it.

Then she wondered was it worth Sophie growing up without a mother, and a father who might not live another ten years?

She sobbed, then. Moaned.

Stan ground his heels into her back. 'Shut fuck up, bitch, or I hurt you.'

She clamped her lips down on her weeping. Survive this drive. Then worry about what comes next.

After a long drive, the van stopped again. She could form no idea of how long a drive: her mind fought all her attempts to listen for sounds outside that might later help trace their route. She'd seen that on TV once. Those programmes, she knew now, came nowhere near close to reality.

Stan stood and the doors opened from the outside. Hands grabbed her and a sack was pulled over her head, again. She was dragged out, stumbled as she stepped from the back of the vehicle. Stan lifted her back to her feet, his hands like crushing steel bands around her arm.

'Oh, God. Take her somewhere else. Please?' A woman's voice, angry but fearful, too.

'Shut it, Andrea. We—'

'Names, fuck's sake.' Stan's voice, angry and despairing.

'Fuck. Sorry, Stan. Inside, Andrea. Stevie will be home the day after tomorrow, so be a good girl until then, aye?'

Stan's voice again, furious now. 'Davie. How many times? Shut mouth.'

Silence for long moments, then Stan dragged her again. Just like last time – was it only earlier today? The biting cold of the night air and the darkness turned to the warmth and soft lighting of an interior. Stan pulled her through one room, through a doorway she bumped into, then down a staircase.

The sack was ripped from her head. No light on in this room. A cellar? This, at least, had a bed and what looked like a chemical toilet. On a table beside the bed sat bottles of water, packs of sandwiches, and bags of crisps. Beside it, in a basket on the floor, Elizabeth saw packs of wet wipes and a folded towel.

Stan gazed around him. 'What the fuck's all this?'

Elizabeth saw the woman now. Late forties, she guessed. Slim and well-groomed, her hair a stylish pixie-cut, she wore jeans and a long cardigan, looked luxurious, cashmere or something as expensive. The woman's eyes met Elizabeth's then darted away again. She bowed her head as if ashamed, turned to Davie who had appeared in the doorway to the cellar.

'I'm not treating her like an animal, Davie. I'm not you. Or Stevie.'

Davie grinned at her, an ugly and mean leer. 'You were always too soft for your own good, Andrea. Now fuck off, aye? With all of this shite laid out for her, there's zero reason for you to come down here again, right? So, I'll take the key.'

Andrea glanced at Elizabeth again, and Elizabeth thought she saw an unspoken apology, a *please don't blame me for this*.

Andrea pulled an old, heavy key from her cardigan pocket and handed it to Davie. She held on to it as Davie's fingers closed around it. 'This is the last time, Davie. You tell Stevie, this is the last time. I don't care what he threatens to do to me. No more, OK?'

Davie pulled the key from her hand. 'Aye, whatever, sis. Good luck wi' that.'

Davie hustled Andrea out of the door. Stan gazed around him, then back at her. He walked to her, loomed over her, lowered his face from his towering height, down into hers. She was surprised to find he smelled clean and wore aftershave.

'You make all noise you want, lady. No one hear.' He ripped the tape from her head and pulled the gag from her mouth. Then he grinned at her. Even his teeth were perfect.

He booped her nose with one meaty finger. 'You be good for Stan, yes? I don't want hurt you. I had wife. Pretty like you. Dead now. Bad wife.'

Quicker than she could have believed, he slammed a fist into her stomach. She felt all breath forced from her and a gaping, brutal lump of pain exploded through her. She went down, gasping for breath and fighting not to give the bastard the satisfaction of seeing her throw up.

He left, and she heard a heavy mechanical clunk as he turned the key in the ancient-looking lock.

When the agony faded so she could breathe without pain, she crossed to the table, gulped down half a bottle of water, then lay down on the clean, quilted bed.

She stared around her new prison. Old, stone-built walls. Massive stone floor tiles. The door looked like thick wood, not MDF. An old building?

Where the hell was she? How long until she'd get whatever was coming to her?

She cried again, didn't bother trying to suppress it. She felt certain no one outside would hear a thing from her from down here.

TWENTY-SEVEN

When Malkie signed his pool car back in, he wandered through to the CID area. Just in case anything major had developed and needed his attention, he told himself. He ignored the side of his mind that knew Rab or Gucci or Steph would have called him sharpish if something noteworthy had come in.

As he passed the ladies' bathroom, he heard sobbing. *Again?*

Instead of heading for his desk, he ducked into a meeting room. He left the light switched off and closed the door. Through the glass wall, he saw Pam leave the bathroom. She cast her eyes around the length of the open-plan office. Some Uniforms stood outside the duty inspector's office near the door to the front desk and reception area. He checked his watch. Shift change.

Pam sat at her desk. She leaned her elbows on the table and held her head in her hands, seemed to lose herself in the scratched and scuffed wooden surface. Malkie saw her shake her head. She heaved in a huge breath, crossed her arms in front of her, and leaned over them as if bracing herself on the hard wooden desktop. He saw a tear drop from her nose and felt no better than a cheap voyeur.

When she wiped her nose, stood, and walked away, he breathed a sigh of relief. He'd had no reason to fear she'd catch him watching her from inside a darkened meeting room, but he was glad to escape and stop feeling so shoddy. As he headed for his own desk, she reappeared with a bottle of water he assumed she'd fetched from the shared fridge in the staff rec room.

She stopped when she saw him, stared at him as if he were the last person she hoped to bump into.

'I don't have anything for you yet, Malkie, so don't ask. You were warned your mum's case would be low priority.'

She seemed to realise what she'd said and looked shocked at her own insensitivity.

'I'm sorry. I didn't mean...'

Malkie waved a hand at her as he approached her. 'No worries, Pam. I know what you mean, and I didn't expect anything else. Not when we have live cases backed up like we always do.'

He sat on the edge of her desk. She frowned but said nothing.

'Are you OK, Pam? If you don't mind me asking?'

She glanced at the bathroom door but only for an instant. She sat, rolled her chair back from the desk and from Malkie, crossed her legs and clasped her hands in her lap, every inch the disciplined professional.

'I'm fine, thanks. Why do you ask?' Her question sounded almost like a dare.

'No specific reason. I just thought you seemed a bit...'

She lifted one eyebrow.

'I mean I thought you seemed a wee bit tense. That's all.'

To Malkie's amazement, she softened. He'd never seen her soften.

'I'm fine. Just got things on my mind, as do we all, right?'

He studied her for a second, hoped more would be forthcoming, realised he'd heard all he was going to.

'Well, you know where I am. I mean, I know we're not pals, only colleagues, like, but...'

He fished for the right words, felt himself on the cusp of something, a chance to build some kind of relationship with the woman who many considered his archenemy. He could never handle people hating him. Not people he held in respect – even if only grudging.

'I hope you don't think you need to butter me up, Malkie. I hope you already know any opinions I may hold about you will have no bearing whatsoever on the diligence with which I'll review your mum's case. You know that don't you?'

Another dare dressed up as a question?

'I know that, Pam. I wasn't. I just... I care about every colleague. Well, most. Gavin McLeish won't make me lose any sleep. Not after...'

Her reaction told him she thought as much of her ex-DI's behaviour on the Walter Callahan case as he did.

Pam raised both eyebrows. Had he reminded her what a massive idiot she once used to depend on for her career prospects?

When you're in a hole, stop digging, you idiot.

'Anyway. Home for me. Dinner.'

As he grabbed his coat and pulled it on, a question popped into his head that he couldn't leave unasked, even in a situation like this.

'What about Pamela?'

She frowned at him. 'Pamela who?'

'You. You said you don't mind Pam but never—' He cut that off as her face darkened. 'Do you mind Pamela? I'd like to know.'

She considered him for a second. 'Only my mother calls me

Pamela. I prefer Pam. Are we done here, Malkie?' She bent her head to paperwork on her desk.

'Aye. Thanks. G'night, Pam.'

As he walked out to the car park, he looked forward to whatever his dad had left for him to warm up for dinner, and to a hot chocolate on the deck of his – he'd started to appreciate – beautiful wee cabin on the shore of Harperrig Reservoir. He wondered who and what Pam had to look forward to. Maybe she went home only to an empty flat, maybe a dog or a cat. Might that explain her infamous prickliness, her severe and intimidating demeanour? Malkie knew how miserable loneliness can be, but he also knew how a life alone could be a blessing.

By the time he sat behind the wheel of his car, he was already dialling a number.

'Dad. I'm fine, nothing to worry about.'

He took a breath.

'How do you feel about meeting your granddaughter?'

TWENTY-EIGHT

As Malkie parked outside the LESOC, he realised that three visits a week had become the norm. Any reluctance to believe his luck had turned when he met Deborah had evaporated. He now found himself able to think of himself and Deborah as an item.

His train of thought – as usual – took him straight to a place where hard questions waited. What difficult practicalities might their relationship bring?

Was Deborah capable of physical intimacy? Was he? Was he capable of overcoming the emotional scars and lasting trust issues inflicted on him by his car crash of a relationship with Sandra Morton? Granted, even after just one meeting he'd decided the product of that relationship, his daughter, Jennifer, would bring him joy like he'd once thought beyond his reach, but the damage Sandra had done to him now threatened his future with Deborah. He fought a surge of fury at Sandra; the past was the past and he found himself believing she really was the most different person possible from the toxic wee girl he remembered.

He berated himself. What was he thinking? Deborah still

had months, maybe years, of long, painful and exhausting recovery to get through. She'd promised herself and others that she would one day ride her horse, Indie, again. That, he told himself, was a goal worth aspiring to, rather than getting it on with him.

He had a word with himself.

If it happens, it happens, and I'll deal with it if it does. When, not if. No. If.

'Grow up.' He growled at himself as he exited the car.

Dame Helen Reid's office door was closed; she'd have retired hours ago to the granny-flat that the founder of the LESOC had stipulated as a condition of donating the family home to the charity, over fifty years ago. She had lost her husband and then her son to other people's wars, been left with no one, and had made the LESOC possible.

Malkie climbed the stairs to the first-floor corridor. He still felt like some scruffy intruder when he came here. No property he'd ever own would have carpets as thick as these or even a scrap of real mahogany. He couldn't stop his mind from wondering where Elizabeth Dunn was right now, and in what state.

Outside Deborah's door, he tucked his shirt back in – why did the bloody thing never stay in? – and knocked.

'Not tonight, Sven. I think I heard my boyfriend's car.'

He pushed the door open. 'Funny. No, I mean it. Hilarious.'

Deborah's smile vanished. 'Oh dear. Another one of those days?'

'Sorry. Aye. Stick some crap telly on and budge up, will you?'

Deborah switched the TV off. 'No. Talk to me. I'm a flight lieutenant and you're just a DS, so I'm pretty sure I outrank you, so out with it.' She sidled over with only a small grunt of pain and Malkie stretched out next to her. She leaned sideways and rested her head on his shoulder.

'Spill. Leave nothing out, and that's an order.'

Malkie sighed. He wanted to hear how her physio had gone that day; her reports of her small successes and her continuing recovery never failed to fill him with pride and love so intense he thought he might burst. But he knew she could be as merciless as Steph when it came to Malkie-maintenance. He decided, this once, to share his day with her so he could then enjoy the reports of her own victories.

'A woman's gone missing. I'm pretty sure she's the same woman who shoplifted from the Almondvale Shopping Centre, and the shop security guard chased her all the way out to the street. He got hit by a car and died. His family are bad news, and now she's been abducted from her home. Poor woman used to be a big deal in financial services, apparently, but she got royally shafted by the Patriarchy and now she lives in a two-bed terraced box on the scruffy side of town, cares for elderly people in their homes for the minimum wage, and has been reduced to shoplifting. Life is so damned depressing sometimes, Deborah.'

She tried to reach over with her hand but couldn't make the move, her face contorting with the pain and the effort. Malkie reached over and wrapped his gingers in hers, rested both their hands on his chest.

'I don't know how you do it, Malkie. I mean, every day?'

Well done, mate. Drag her down, too, why don't you?

'Ach, we'll find her. She'll not even do time for the shoplifting. Prosecution KC will try to pin the security guard's death on her, but he was way beyond his legal and contractual authority chasing her out into the street like he did. It'll get ugly, and she'll suffer for it, but I doubt she'll get done for his death. I don't think so, anyway. I should probably know that, shouldn't I?'

She snuggled closer. 'How do you manage to get through a day on your job when you often don't have a clue what you're talking about, old man?'

He turned to give her a trademark *polis* hard stare, but the grin on her face disarmed him as it always did. As ever, he marvelled at how the brutal damage done to half of her face had left her teeth in perfect condition. He often wondered if she'd had dental work done since her accident but never felt he had a right to ask.

'I don't know. I know how to investigate, and I know how to catch bad people, and I seem to have a better knack than most coppers for empathising with PoIs, even the mouth-breathers. Maybe that helps me think like them and nab them.'

'PoIs?'

He scowled at her. 'How many times, Miss Fleming? Persons of Interest.'

'Sorry, sir. Will remember next time.'

'But I just can't seem to hold all the regulations and SOPs and sentencing guidelines and form numbers and all that kind of shite in my head. It's all I can do to say the formal caution right, and that can cause no end of problems if we get even a single word of it wrong.'

'SOPs?'

'Standard Operating Procedures. Long-winded and incredibly boring documents meant to help us coppers do our jobs right. Very useful on nights I have trouble sleeping.'

She laughed, and the sound lifted him.

'Thing is, the family of that security guard, I said they're bad news. They're the worst kind, way worse than the Fieldings. That lot that got Walter Callahan killed, remember?'

'I do. That poor, poor man. I wheel myself round to his wee granite memorial in the LESOC graveyard most days, say hello to him, you know? I wish I'd got to know him. He sounded like a really nice bloke underneath all that horrible PTSD he suffered, from what you've told me.'

'He was. Damaged goods but that was never his fault.

Damn it, I don't think I've stopped for a chat with him for a couple of weeks.'

'I'd tell you not to flog yourself, but we both know there's no chance of that. Visit him before you leave tonight. There's enough light shines down from the cafeteria to see where you're going and you know exactly where he is.'

Malkie mulled over in his mind how he'd allowed Walter to slip from his memory. He'd worked several cases since Callahan's death, but he felt he owed him more than most of the other victims he'd been too late to save.

We do what we can, as Mum always told me. Walter would kick my arse for being such a snowflake.

'Anyway, tell me about your day, Flight Lieuey Fleming.'

'Wasn't great today, actually. Had my monthly physio assessment. Didn't get the news I was hoping for.'

Malkie squeezed her. Heard her groan as her recovering body protested but knew they'd both got to a place, together, where the occasional ache or pain was to be expected, and so was ignored.

'I've been working my bollocks off. My proverbial bollocks, I mean. Shut up. But the doc said my recovery slowed this month. He said it happens and that it's not anything I need to worry about, but it made me realise how much I've been living my life – such as it is – from month to month, probably been focusing too much on just that one day every month: assessment day.'

'*Such as it is.*' Almost as bad as another classic Malkie loathed: '*How are you? Oh, not too bad, you know?*'

'Malkie. Pay attention when I'm moaning.'

'Sorry, Deb. Just that kind of phrase, you know? "*Such as it is.*"'

They endured a mutual awkward silence. Deb spoke first.

'Was I feeling sorry for myself? I hate self-pity.'

'No, I don't think that was self-pity. I do far better thumb-sucking than that. I have a black belt in thumb-sucking, Deb.

No, that was frustration, and you turn your frustration into determination then into discipline which becomes action.'

She patted his chest. 'Thank you, Doctor Malkie. How much do I owe you for that session?'

'Oh, sod off.'

He felt her giggle into his chest.

'Is it that bad? Are you starting to go stir-crazy? You know, become institutionalised? I watched it happen to a friend of mine and it changed him completely. Barney. He was such a good man at heart: kind and funny and cared for people utterly, despite his own progressive misery. But after more than ten years needing every humiliating little thing done for him, he couldn't help but start to see people as being there just to serve his needs. The day he barked at me for forgetting to put sugar in his tea was the day we had a serious talk and the day I left his house feeling like a complete shit for making a man with an already miserable life just feel more awful. He was furious with himself, ashamed, poor bastard. I told him it was inevitable given he'd become institutionalised in his own home, but he was having none of it. He never barked at me or any of his carers again.

'I forget how much I miss him. He used to have a wooden thing beside his bed that said *Don't count the days. Make the days count.* Over the years, it got pushed further and further back on his bedside table until it eventually fell down the back. I never saw it again until the day we emptied his house out. I think I still have it in a box, somewhere in the cabin.'

'You still haven't unpacked everything? Mind you, I suppose not, in that tiny wee place.'

Malkie cast his mind over the various boxes stacked in the third bedroom, tried to remember which one he'd tossed the thing in when he moved from his rental house in Linlithgow.

How easily we let our most prized possessions and our fondest memories fade.

'Oi. Stop that. You're drifting again. Pay attention to me, Dirty Old Man.'

He laughed. 'Will you ever stop calling me that?'

'You said it first yourself, buster.'

'I was joking, and you know it.'

'Mud sticks.'

Don't I just know it, Deb.

She pushed into him, tried to turn towards him. He raised a hand to push her back, couldn't bear to see how much pain twisted her face. She batted his hand away and managed to turn fully towards him. She stared at him. No, he realised she was gazing at him. Different.

She leaned up and kissed him, gently at first, then insistently. As ever, he felt his tongue touch her teeth where her lips had been burned away in the accident, and he embraced that feeling, loved it, treasured the fact that she would let no other person on earth so close to her injuries.

He responded, found himself desperate to give in to her. Despite her younger age, he held no doubt she'd have had more intimate partners than he ever did, and he hoped she'd forgive any clumsiness on his part.

He leaned toward her, eased her onto her back, propped himself on one elbow and stared at her. She looked as uncertain as he felt; had she enjoyed any kind of love from a man since her injuries redefined her, in her own mind, at least? He felt tears prickle in his eyes and wondered if he'd ever want more than this moment, to let go, to immerse himself in her, lose himself in her, give in to her.

He kissed her back. Her arm snaked around his neck and pulled his face hard onto hers. Her lips crushed his, hungry and desperate, and he let himself fall into her.

He felt tightness and heat. The last time a woman had made him feel that way he'd rejected any thought of giving in to it. This time, he welcomed it.

He kissed her lips, then her forehead and her cheeks, both the unharmed side and the leathery, scarred, side. He kissed her neck, and she gasped. She lifted one leg and laid it across him. She moaned. Malkie had no idea whether from pain or from something more intense and he didn't care. She was the arbiter of her own limits, and she pulled at him for more and more.

As he kissed her shoulders, exposed where she'd pulled the stringy strap on her top down, she reached for him. He felt her hand wrap around him and squeeze, gentle but firm. She moaned again. Louder, demanding now. She tried to bend at the waist, to lower her head to take it all the way.

She screamed, cried, wailed, then fury took over. She collapsed onto her back, slammed her fist into the mattress again and again as she raged.

He recoiled, unaware what he'd done that could have hurt her but appalled at himself anyway.

He yanked on a red emergency cord that hung by her bed, then stood, paralysed by his ignorance of what to do.

It took a nurse seconds to run through the door.

'Deborah. What's happened?'

Deborah managed to squeeze four words out. 'Give me drugs, Pauline.' The nurse disappeared again.

Malkie stepped back because that's what you did when nurses or doctors needed to work on someone: you gave them space. Deborah flapped her hand on the other side of the bed at him. He sat in a chair on that side and took her hand. She squeezed it so hard he feared she'd break his fingers.

The nurse reappeared with a white dish containing a syringe and vial of liquid and a strip of tablets. She took seconds to half fill the syringe and inject what Malkie guessed to be morphine into Deborah's arm.

Deborah's grimace faded to be replaced by exhaustion. Her face was pale and beaded with sweat. She closed her eyes and laid her head back on the pillow. The nurse checked her pulse and blood pressure and various other things Malkie had no clue about, then smoothed the sheets over her.

'Ten minutes. No more please, Malkie. OK?'

Malkie nodded, mute and still terrified he'd done this to Deborah. 'What happened? Was it me?'

The nurse smiled. 'No, just Deb being a stubborn old cow.'

Deb raised a single middle finger at Pauline. The nurse nodded. 'Abuse is good. Abuse means she's coming back to her usual self.'

Deborah lifted her other arm and raised what remained of her middle finger on that hand.

Pauline grinned at Malkie. 'Ten minutes.' Then she left.

'What did she mean? Stubborn?'

Deborah looked embarrassed but defiant. 'I don't want morphine. I've seen other officers given morphine during surgery, and in one case it was nothing more than a way to help the poor bastard on his way.'

She paused, sighed. 'I thought I could manage my pain without it. I was wrong. I'll never hear the end of this from Pauline.' Her eyes widened, appalled. 'Or Dame Helen.' She groaned.

'So, it wasn't anything I did?'

She glared at him. 'Why does it always have to be your fault, Malkie? Why do you insist on taking responsibility for everything, even if you don't know anything about it? I bloody hate when you do that.'

Her words stung. Even while being told not to feel so guilty for everything all the time, he felt guilty for having to be told that.

Get a grip. She's right. Grow up.

She seemed to deflate, sag down into her bedclothes.

'I'm sorry, Malkie. Pain makes me cranky, you know?'

He squeezed her hand but could find no words.

'But yes, it was your fault that it happened.'

His panic-meter went straight to red. 'Eh? How? What did I—'

She laughed.

'You got me horny as hell for the first time since my accident, Malkie. And that's no mean feat. I haven't even—'

'Too much information.' He blushed, felt heat fill his cheeks. She laughed even harder.

Ten minutes later – to the second, he'd bet – Pauline eased the door open again and poked her head through. She scowled at them both and lifted her wrist to indicate her watch.

Malkie tried to remove his fingers from Deborah's for the third time in the past minute. She seemed to remain in a deep sleep, but her fingers clamped on his. He used his other hand to demonstrate to Pauline.

The nurse grinned and shook her head.

'Ten more minutes, Deborah, then I throw him out, physically if I have to.'

Malkie feigned offence. 'Hang on, I'm a *polis* officer. You can't talk to me like that.'

'I was talking about you Malkie, not to you. Ten minutes.'

She disappeared again.

Malkie leaned forward, rested his forehead on their joined hands, and did all he could to make the next ten minutes feel like an eternity.

TWENTY-NINE

Steph piled through her front door and slammed it shut behind her. Normally, she'd scold herself for losing her temper, for letting an evolutionary throwback like Dean get to her, but today, right now, her rage wiped out any hope of self-awareness.

She threw her jacket on the armchair and dropped into her sofa, one arm over her eyes, her legs crossed at the ankles, her other arm grasping at air beside her as if clutching for something to hold on to.

She breathed, long and slow, but hated the juddering of her chest as she released each lungful of air.

'Rotten, rank, disgusting, vile, manky, fucking, wee, cu—'

Having used up what felt like twice her normal self-imposed allowance of swear words she permitted herself every month – although she'd recently stopped counting – she tested her temper, pictured Dean's face, his leering grin, his greasy and pockmarked skin, his lank and oily hair.

'Fucking.' She screamed it this time, so hard her voice broke and turned to tears, to racking, furious, helpless sobs.

She let the rage run its course. Slammed the side of her fist into the sofa cushions over and over, until the message got through that her ridiculous pity party could not benefit her one scrap. She invested so much effort every working day in maintaining her professional composure in the face of often-staggering provocation that she found herself suddenly sick of it; if anyone deserved the daddy of all attitude failures, she did.

Daddy. The word soured in her mind. She had two choices for who she could consider her father and both turned her stomach. One, the rapist who took advantage of her drug- and drink-addled mother. The other, the misogynistic waste of oxygen who kept her mum out of her head for years on cheap coke and vodka then forgave his best mate for sleeping with her and refused to recognise it for the sexual assault of an unwitting victim that it really was.

Unwitting victim. Bland words, easy to ignore when said about some stranger; a brutal kick in the guts when applied to her own mother.

When had Dean learned that Barry had raped her mum? The answer came to her and sickened her. Neither Dean nor Barry would believe that he'd had committed rape; if she didn't say no then it had to be OK, right?

The thought of her mother in that state, having that kind of thing done to her – she must have had some idea when she sobered up, hadn't she? – she wanted to scream again, to throw anything within reach through the huge glass windows of her Linlithgow flat, just to see *something* destroyed by her rage. Like kids vandalising bus stops, sick of being told to move on all the time and having nowhere to move on to but another place where they'd be told exactly the same thing. What chance did the poor sods have? Was their behaviour nothing more than quick fixes for tethers they'd long since reached the end of, and tunnels whose lights had long ago been extinguished?

She sat up, turned, planted her feet on the floor. She noticed she still had her DMs on. She unknotted the laces in one and pulled it off, felt glorious relief rush back into her foot after such a long day. The laces on the other boot tangled, and the more she pulled at them, her fingers impatient with irritation, the tighter they knotted. She had to force herself to a calmer place, where she could stop, analyse the knot, choose the place to pull. As the knot loosened and she pulled the boot off, she failed to fight another wave of rage. She threw the DM across the room with another 'Fucker', the loudest and most savage yet. It hit her meagre DVD collection and knocked some cases out onto the floor.

She wiped her eyes, breathed in and out, then headed for the kitchen. She made straight for the drinks cupboard that held a dozen different flavours of gin, and pulled out the first bottle her fingers fell on. She grabbed a glass from the draining board, a bottle of tonic water from the fridge and a handle of ice cubes from the freezer, sat back on the sofa and filled her glass with more gin than tonic.

She held her glass up towards her reflection in the TV screen, then realised she had no idea what she could be bothered toasting to. She downed half the glass before coming up for air, felt it soothe her mouth then her throat and down into her stomach.

She closed her eyes. Listened to the silence of the room, interrupted only occasionally at this late hour by the sound of vehicles passing on the Linlithgow High Street outside. Many of these old tenement flats still had old sash windows, and unlike in some adjacent properties, Steph had never had the heart to replace them with white uPVC. Copious application of draught excluder around the frames helped, but she had to draw the heavy blackout curtains when the temperatures outside really bit.

Dean's words echoed in her head: 'If anything more happens to Barry...' Did the bastard plan to hurt Boswell and frame her for it? They'd been pals for longer than Steph had been alive but an animal like Dean would throw any number of friends under the bus to get what he wanted. And what he seemed to want, right now, was her career ruined and her broken beyond repair.

They had to be dealt with.

She played a thought experiment for purely hypothetical purposes: how to deal with Dean and Barry together, at once. And not get caught, of course. Threats about chicken wire and boulders and deep, deep lochs were – she hoped – purely wishful thinking on her part. Even as she imagined Dean's pale and lifeless face sinking beneath the dark surface of some body of water, of which Scotland had more than the rest of the UK put together, she recoiled from the idea in her mind. It was beyond her. She'd joined the *polis* to stop bad people from hurting good people. As much as removing the DNAs of two atrocities like them from the Scottish gene pool would be doing the country a service, dealing with them in any way less than one hundred per cent legal would demean her and lead her down a path from which every part of her recoiled.

The law had its flaws, but it did its best to separate the decent – even the barely saveable – from the irredeemable animals, didn't it? Despite its fallibility and the insanity of many of its results, in general it served to uphold some vestige of justice, even though too many cash-rich but morally bankrupt lawyers made a mockery of the relationship between it and justice on a regular basis.

No, as much as – she allowed herself just one more before bed – fuckers like her nominal 'fathers' deserved an ugly and unpleasant seeing-to, that way anarchy lay, didn't it?

She downed the rest of her gin, headed for the bedroom without detouring to the bathroom to brush her teeth. A decision she knew she'd regret in the morning but tomorrow wasn't now. Now, she needed sleep and the oblivion she had to hope would come with it.

As she stared at the ceiling for two hours, she tried to work out what the hell the bastard was up to. He hadn't named her during his call to report the attack on Boswell. And it all seemed too convenient; Boswell attacked again so soon after she kicked the shit out of him, and now Dean admitting Boswell wanted his blood, too? Was she being set up? Did Dean attack Boswell himself? When they'd ambushed her previously, in Dean's flat, she hadn't picked up much in the way of brotherly vibes. They'd been friends for longer than Steph had been alive, but now? Was Boswell nothing more than a casualty of Dean's campaign to ruin Steph's career? A handy punchbag still too feeble and injured from Steph's assault on him to put up much of a fight?

She punched the side of her head, felt a banging headache coming on. She was going to feel shit all day after this.

She recalled Malkie's admission that he'd attempted an intervention, remembered how amused Dean had claimed to be at Malkie's attempts to play the hard man. Bless him; his heart was always in the right place even if his brain misfired too often, too.

Chicken wire. And rocks. They could do it.

No. Too far. Breaking the law would forever be a step too far for her, but bending them in the interests of dealing with two stains on society like Dean Lang and Barry Boswell would more than justify a modest degree of latitude in her actions to serve up some natural justice to a pair of the most deserving scumbags she'd ever met.

No, not just scumbags.

Fuckers.

Another lazy reliance on an overused word, another breach of the demanding standards she expected of herself.

But no other word quite did the job, sometimes.

THIRTY

When he reached home, he found his dad, Tommy, had waited up for him. He made them both a hot chocolate then sat and stared at the beautiful, calm, black waters of Harperrig Reservoir until his dad put his mug down and turned to him.

'I've thought about it.'

Malkie could think of only two subjects his old man might mean, and one of them – they both knew – was already happening and too late to stop now. Which left only one subject to discuss: how he felt about meeting the daughter of the woman who'd nearly got his son murdered, three decades ago. The granddaughter he never knew existed.

Malkie put his own mug down. 'Jennifer.'

'I wish I could tell you I can handle meeting her, but I can't promise that, son. I'm sorry. And that other woman...'

'Sandra?'

Tommy grimaced, as if the very sound of her name hurt him.

'No, that's fine. Even I can't be bothered spending any more time with her than I have to. But Jennifer didn't ask to be born into the Morton family. She's turned into a fine young woman, Dad. I'm already damned proud of her, even though a part of me doesn't have any right to feel that way. It's weird.'

Tommy's face had taken on a look Malkie could rarely remember ever seeing: anger. 'You can't be bothered with her, Malkie? She tried to kill you. You should hate her with every fibre of your being, no?'

Malkie chewed over his next comment. He'd never heard his father speak such venom about another person. It shook him.

'I don't want to fight about this Dad, but...'

Tommy bristled, looked appalled at what his son might want to say that could possibly drive a wedge between them.

'Even Sandra is a changed pers—'

'No. I won't hear that, Malkie. She tried to have you killed.'

Malkie squirmed. 'No, Dad. She didn't try to do anything to me. She just didn't intervene when she knew her brothers wanted to. Not the same thing. She *has* changed, too, but I still can't be bothered with her.'

'Can't be bothered with her? Seriously, Malkie?' Tommy sounded incredulous. Almost scandalised.

They lapsed into a guilty silence. Had they ever raised their voices to each other before? Had he ever heard his dad shout at anyone? He couldn't remember a single occasion. After a few minutes, his dad rose and headed inside. At the doorway of the cabin he sighed, paused, seemed about to say more, but then shuffled away without another word.

Malkie closed his eyes and reached out across the reservoir, as if he could commune with his mum in desperation if the situation called for it.

'What have I done, Mum? What else could I have done? He doesn't deserve any more pain.'

Malkie hoped he'd remember his mum's kind face, always smiling even if only with her eyes, sometimes. He felt nothing.

No reassuring memories of her wisdom, no soothing recollection of her ever patient and calming manner.

Nothing.

THIRTY-ONE

By the time Malkie dragged himself from sleep, dreading more of yesterday, changed his clothes, sprayed on some deodorant, and hauled his miserable arse into the station, he'd missed the first five minutes of morning briefing. It usually took place at the Uniform desks, closer to the entrance from the foyer, so he tried to sneak in the back way via the charging bar and the custody suite.

But of course, Thompson had to be standing facing his way, didn't she?

He gave up any hope of joining surreptitiously and strode, head held high, to the back of the standing-room overflow leaning over filing cabinets.

Thompson did him the favour of not thanking him for joining them, but she didn't need to. He did notice, though, that Pam Ballantyne's expression as she looked at him, while disappointed, held no trace of her usual scorn which sometimes bordered on open disgust.

No nasty sneer? Again, Pam?

'Malkie. Elizabeth Dunn. Abduction of?'

Malkie tore his eyes from New Pam.

'Andrew Dunn's description of her abductor could be a match for Davie Jessop, Stevie Jessop's brother and Martin Jessop's uncle. Andrew Dunn has MS and spends most of his time sitting at the kitchen table. By the time he got himself to his feet and staggered through to the living room, he only saw the back of the man as he bundled his wife into the hallway and out the front door. He fell over and lost consciousness.

'On that basis, we visited the Jessop home, said we were there to offer our condolences and to ask for any info that might be pertinent to his "accident". Davie Jessop told us Stevie is *away* and wouldn't elaborate but I'm certain he was about to say Stevie is out of the country. As we walked back to the car, we heard banging from behind the property; we checked it out and found one bedroom boarded up. Quite thoroughly. I'm going back there today, and if I still smell anything off, I'll be asking for a warrant.'

As he said the words, he realised he should have asked yesterday. Even if refused on the basis of only one coincidental family link to the deceased and an unreliable partial description of Dunn's abductor, at least he'd have got it on the record that he felt sufficient suspicion. Had he been too keen to get to Deborah and hide?

Must do better, old boy.

Thompson's expression turned cautious. 'It's not much, though, is it, Malkie? Any news on the vehicle she was taken away in?'

Rab Lundy raised his hand. 'A Mercedes Sprinter. Was found burned out on an unfinished road in the new Heartlands development outside Whitburn. Responders have it taped off and SOCOs will attend this morning. Responders said whoever tried to burn it did a crap job and left enough surfaces undamaged that they might be able to lift something, but the plates were removed and the VINs been scratched off so we can't ID it that way.'

Thompson flashed him a look that to Malkie, and he suspected everyone else, said, '*And you're telling us this now?*'

Rab looked around him, held up one finger. 'I only just saw the note this morning, two minutes before the briefing.' His look dared anyone to say more.

Thompson held a placatory hand up. 'OK. Fine, Rab. Thank you.'

Rab nodded as if to acknowledge his vindication.

'OK, pay them another visit today. Let's hope the SOCOs lift something from the van that'll get us a warrant. And find out if either of the Jessops owns a white van.'

'He does, but it's a Transit. First thing I checked.'

Malkie ignored Rab's petulant tone. 'And if Elizabeth Dunn is at the Jessop place? She might not be by the time we get the warrant. You know what the Forensics workstack is like.'

Thompson flashed him a look. 'I'll expedite it. For now, try to push Davie Jessop's buttons, maybe find out where his brother is and when he's expected back, but don't push too hard for now.'

Malkie nodded. He didn't need to articulate his frustration and could admit in the privacy of his own mind that Thompson was right. The link between Elizabeth Dunn *possibly* being involved in Martin Jessop's death and her abduction by someone who *might* resemble Davie Jessop, but only from behind, didn't clear the justification threshold for a warrant by much, if at all.

Malkie zoned out of the rest of the briefing and was relieved when Thompson wrapped it up without calling on him again.

Back at their desks, Gucci wheeled her chair over between Malkie and Steph. Her face promised something juicy.

'I poked about a bit in Gleann Darragh. Found this.' She placed a sheet of paper on Malkie's desk. Steph sidled over and leaned in.

A copy of an online news article concerning abusive calls

made to an employee of the Gleann Darragh Livi offices. The employee wasn't identified, but the idiot who made the calls was named as one Steven Jessop.

Malkie and Steph and Gucci stared at each other.

Malkie broke the spell. 'That'll do. Well done, Gucci. You want to come with me, Steph? Maybe Davie will give you an excuse to use reasonable force? I wouldn't get in your way.'

Steph considered this. 'No, but I'll assist if only to get a second pair of eyes and ears on the place, maybe spot something we can use?'

'You mean make sure I don't miss anything?'

She stood, pulled her jacket from the back of her chair, and pulled it on.

'Malkie, you're unfit, scruffy, wouldn't know an arse from an elbow even if they were labelled and you've come closer to losing a healthy pension than any other copper I ever met.'

He scowled at her. What the hell kind of an answer was that?

'But you are one of the sharpest bosses I ever worked for. You... Your brain doesn't miss things. If anything, you see stuff lots of us don't, stuff we just don't *get*, sometimes. So. Please. Stop being so bloody defensive and let's go and irritate the tits off Davie Jessop, OK?'

He stood, didn't have to pull on his coat since he'd not had a chance to take it off yet, and nodded. 'Aye. Let's go poke a Jessop.'

'What a revolting thought.'

At the Jessops' home, they found the door wide open behind the same grubby brats from before, one focused with serious intent on jumping high enough to reach a fat wee arm into a hedge to retrieve some toy or other, and another trying to push in. They screeched at each other. Whatever crappy object they both wanted, it couldn't be worth the almost open warfare he saw brewing. Three more sat, their hands gripping gaming consoles and their heads bowed. He suspected nothing but the smell of chips would distract them.

Steph nudged Malkie. 'Nintendo Switches. Three of them. They're not cheap.'

'If they're even paid for.'

Malkie stared at them, wondered if they'd ever gone burn-jumping or played cops and robbers, and decided that at least they were getting some fresh air.

He nodded towards the dingy interior of the house. 'Is anyone in, kids?'

Only one responded. 'Aye.' He didn't look up from his screen.

Malkie rang the doorbell, which looked out of place to him: shiny and clean against the cracked and manky render that clad the property.

Davie Jessop appeared. A look of panic crossed his face, but he replaced it with an arrogance that made Malkie's stomach drop. If Elizabeth Dunn had been here, she wasn't anymore.

'We just wanted to ask a few more questions, Mr Jessop, if that's OK?'

'Aye. Sure.' He grinned at them, pleased with himself for something. 'Come in.'

Malkie shared a look with Steph; neither would relish the thought of entering the place without vaccinations but the chance to see the inside couldn't be passed up.

Jessop led them to a living room on the right. Grubby, yellow-stained wallpaper and too much sofa and armchair for the size of the room, in front of a tiled fireplace full of beer cans and takeaway boxes.

Jessop dropped himself into the armchair and indicated the sofa. Malkie took one look at it and decided even his supermarket suit was too good to inflict the various stains on.

'We're fine, not planning to trouble you for long, but thanks.'

'Suit yersel'. What dae ye want this time?'

'I heard banging from behind your home yesterday, as we left. We've also had a partial description of Elizabeth Dunn's abductor from her husband. A description which, I'm afraid to say, could be considered a close match to yourself. I need to ask where you were yesterday evening. So we can hopefully eliminate you from our enquiries, you know?'

Something like concern passed over Jessop's face. 'I was here, watchin' the weans. And no, ah cannae prove that. You can ask them if you want, but good luck getting' anythin' oot o' them.'

Steph spoke from behind Malkie. 'Do you mind if I use your bathroom please, Mr Jessop?'

Jessop beamed at her, almost as if he'd been hoping she'd ask just that. He looked like he was enjoying himself, which pissed Malkie off to a quite extraordinary degree.

'Aye. The downstairs bog is rank, needs a clean but the wife isnae in. The upstairs one should be OK. Top of the stairs, first door on the right, doll.'

Steph lifted her eyebrows at Malkie then excused herself. Jessop seemed to find this hilarious and didn't bother to hide his delighted grin.

'So, Mr Jessop, has anything else come to mind that might be relevant to the fact that the woman who we believe your adopted nephew, Martin, chased out of the shopping centre was abducted from her home the same day? Anything you can help us with?'

Malkie maintained as calm and unconfrontational a professional demeanour as could be expected, but he also knew from the look in Jessop's eyes that a game was being played. Each would know the other was talking shite, and each would reply to shite with more shite, but punching a mouth-breather in the face until he coughed up where Elizabeth was would not go down well with Thompson and might threaten his pension.

'Naw. Nothin'. Ah told ye yesterday. If one o' Martin's pals has decided she's got somethin' tae answer for, I know nothin' about it.'

'But if you do hear something, you'll let us know immediately, of course?'

'Of course, Mr McCulloch. Always happy to support you boys.'

'You mentioned that your brother Stevie is away. We'd like to talk to him too, see if he can assist our investigation in any way. Can you tell me when he'll be back?'

Jessop's eyes took on a wary look. 'Wednesday.'

'Is he on holiday? Away on business?'

'Nae idea. He doesnae tell me everything, ye know?'

'Aye, fair enough. You must have heard from him, though. You'll have told him what happened to his nephew? Your nephew? Is he coming home early, considering?'

'No. Wednesday. Like I said.'

Malkie knew better than to hope for more, but he needed to give Steph time.

'I suppose it's too expensive to book different flights, aye?'

'I never said where he is.'

'No. You didn't. But it would be better for you if you did. Withholding information from a police officer conducting an investigation can be seen as obstruction if the requested information later turns out to be relevant to said investigation.'

'You Pigs are all the same, aren't ye? Why use five words when twenty will do? Do you lot do that on purpose? To make us wee people feel stupid?'

'No, Mr Jessop. We—'

'Call from the station, DS McCulloch. We're needed.' Steph stood in the living-room doorway and nodded towards the outside.

Malkie turned to go. 'Thanks for your help, Mr Jessop. Please ask your brother to call us as soon as he's back in the country.'

'Fine. I will. Bye, then.'

Malkie suppressed an urge to remind Jessop of the wisdom in not pissing a copper off too much, but he knew that would just earn him a talking-to from Steph in the car.

Outside, Steph pulled the door closed behind her and they stepped past the brats on the doorstep, still lost in their own wee cyber-worlds. 'Upstairs back bedroom. The one with the boarded-up windows. Stuffed full of decorating gear but I didn't see a scrap of new paint anywhere in the dump, did you?'

'No. Nothing else worth reporting?'

Her eyes gleamed. 'Oh yes. A lock on the door. Big, ugly sliding bolt like you'd expect to see on a garden gate. On the outside of an interior door.'

'Really? That's odd, isn't it?'

'Aye, but not enough for a warrant, boss?'

'Hmm. Fifty-fifty, I'd say. But did you notice he let me say "back in the country" without correcting me?'

'Aye, and he seems to think his brother's not coming home early, despite his nephew just dying.'

As they returned to the street, Malkie spotted the hedge-scavenging kids now poking at their hidden treasure with a stick. He peered closer, spotted something glinting.

He reached over the shoulder of the child and plucked a gold bracelet from beyond its reach.

The child screeched at him. 'That's mine. Ah saw it first. Gie's it, ya bastard.'

Malkie mumbled something about evidence and respect for one's elders and turned to Steph, who produced a plastic evidence bag from one of the magic pockets inside her jacket. Malkie dropped it in, and they examined it.

Thin gold with one charm on it. Too clean and bright to

have hung there for long. A love heart with a single white gemstone and two initials inscribed.

ED

Steph's eyes, when they met Malkie's, sparkled. 'So?'

'First, we invite Davie Jessop to the station for a proper chat. You book this into evidence and show a photo of it to Andrew Dunn. Get him to identify it. Belts and braces, etc.'

'Then a warrant?'

'Fuck, aye.'

THIRTY-TWO

Elizabeth woke from a tortured sleep to hear voices from upstairs, muffled through the heavy wooden cellar door. She heard a door slam, then a vehicle engine start and drive off. Ten minutes later she heard a key turn in the ancient lock and shrank back into the corner of the bed, against the walls. She moaned, felt fear course through her, felt the ache still knotting her stomach from Stan's punch.

The woman appeared in the doorway. Andrea. She wore trainers and fitness clothing and had what looked like an old iPod strapped to her upper arm. A light sheen of sweat glistened on her forehead.

Andrea held one finger to her lips, her eyes fearful. She listened back up the stairs for a moment, then entered and locked the door from the inside. When she turned to Elizabeth, shame radiated from the poor woman.

She pocketed the key again. 'They think I just have the one key. I'm so sorry I can't stand up to them. They'll even hurt their own flesh and blood if I defy them.' She hung her head. 'They've done that before.'

Elizabeth stood, crossed to the woman. Andrea panicked

and stuffed the door key deeper into her jogger pocket. A hug seemed far from appropriate or even safe, but she placed a hand on Andrea's arm.

'Please. Let me go. We can go to the police together. I can tell them you're as much a victim as I am.'

Andrea looked up at her. Elizabeth saw what she thought was hope, a consideration of her suggestion, an escape from an unwanted association with a family she suspected couldn't be more different to the terrified woman standing in front of her.

She saw Andrea come to the wrong decision before she shook her head, miserable and beaten.

'I'm sorry. I can't risk it. They leave me alone, mostly. The last time they came here was two years ago. I thought – I hoped – they'd got tired of me. But I was stupid. It was never me they came for. It's this place.' She gazed around the ceiling at the property above them.

'I thought moving out here would put them off bothering me, but it just made me more useful to them, and I think now I'll never be rid of them.'

Tears spilled down Andrea's cheeks. She wiped them with her hand, harsh and angry. She turned to leave.

Elizabeth held on to Andrea's arm, felt tears of her own spill from her eyes. 'Please. Andrea. Please?' Her last word was barely audible, little more than a whisper.

Andrea removed Elizabeth's hand and backed away. She opened her mouth and closed it again, turned to the door, unlocked it with hands Elizabeth could see shook so hard she almost dropped the key, and left. When she heard the lock turn again from the outside, she collapsed back onto the bed and sobbed. She wailed and screamed in rage and fear, hammered at the pillows with her fists.

She noticed the absence of the bracelet from her wrist, the one Sophie had saved her pocket money for two months to buy for her mum's birthday.

She prayed to a god she realised only now she'd not spoken to nearly often enough that she'd see that bracelet on her wrist again, one day. Unless those animals found it first.

No. For Sophie. She would survive for Sophie. And Andrew. For the life she still believed they deserved together.

She would survive this, like she survived the destruction of her previous life.

Andrea had considered her suggestion. She had *wanted* to do what Elizabeth said. She'd seemed desperate to. But then, Elizabeth could imagine only too well how terrified she must be of her own brothers if they'd hurt her before. Men like them knew no limits. No decency. They never saw the harm they caused, the suffering.

For herself, and for Sophie and Andrew, and even for a woman she had only just met, she would survive this.

THIRTY-THREE

It took them an hour to get Jessop back to the station and booked in.

Davie Jessop had bleated about not being able to leave the weans alone. After lengthy and time-consuming consideration, he'd decided it would be OK to call Stevie's wife, Paula, to come home early. She had no doubt taken all the time in the world to appear and then argue with them about police victimisation as they dragged her cuffed brother-in-law to the car. Malkie's temper had risen to punch-someone-in-the-face levels, and Steph's lips were compressed into a thin line, about as much evidence as she ever let slip that someone had got to her.

Jessop made his booking-in as unpleasant as his arrest. He even managed to piss off Sergeant Deke Lambert, a bear of a man with a handlebar moustache and a normally unshakable calm and placid manner which belied the controlled violence he'd been known to bring to bear on deserving scumbags, learned from eighteen years in the Paras.

Jessop got stuck in a custody-suite cell, but only after the customary call for a doctor when he claimed to feel unwell, then his discovery that he seemed to suffer from undiagnosed claustrophobia, so that two Uniforms had to sit at the open door and endure his grinning kisser without being able to do a thing to wipe it off his face.

While Malkie waited for a duty solicitor to arrive, Steph headed for the Dunn home, more eager to get a warrant than Malkie could ever remember. He headed for the desk which nobody had yet dared clean up and so still constituted *his* desk. He emailed Thompson to warn her a warrant request was incoming, then spent a half hour updating the case file until he noticed Pam Ballantyne watching him. After a moment, she stood and nodded towards the pair of glass-walled meeting rooms at one end of the open-plan office.

Inside, she closed the door behind Malkie. He went to pull a chair out, but she stopped him.

'That's one of the Jessop brothers, I believe?'

'Aye. We found a bedroom boarded-up at his house. Yes, we had permission; the bloody idiot invited us in and told Steph to use the upstairs bathroom, right beside the open door of that room. Then we found a necklace snagged in a hedge outside with the letters ED engraved on it.'

'Elizabeth Dunn.'

'Seems like a no-brainer, aye, but you know I never let confirmation bias cloud my judgement, Pam.' He grinned.

She sat forward, her face serious, and Malkie's grin fell away. His heart sank; usually a quick decision meant the easiest decision, the path of least resistance and he – and his dad – needed this not to be swept under any rug under any justification.

'I think there's sufficient reason to test the finding that your mum's death might not have been accidental.'

She sighed, folded her arms over her chest, either to protect herself from a fear of whatever career damage might result from her decision to pursue justice for Malkie, or perhaps to fend off some ill-judged physical manifestation of gratitude from him.

He didn't care: Pam agreed with him. Whether a reopening of the case and a deeper investigation turned up anything that might lead to collaring the bastard who did it was an open and difficult question, but he'd take what he could, when he could.

He sat anyway, released his breath.

'I needed to be sure, Malkie, hence the two days I took to come to even this initial opinion.'

Hence? People still say hence? Give her a chance, damn it.

'I know. It may go nowhere. I know that. The damage done to the place. I doubt we'll ever get a conviction, but—'

'You doubt *I'll* get a conviction, you mean.'

'Sorry. Aye. I'll leave well alone and wait for updates from you.'

'And I promise I'll keep you appraised. I can't imagine how upsetting this must be for you.'

She seemed to drift off, lose focus. Malkie saw trouble wrinkle her forehead and shadow her eyes.

'Pam, what's up? I heard you in the bathroom. Both times.'

She straightened in her chair. Defiance and a fake smile didn't fool Malkie for a second. He tilted his head, poured all of the genuine concern he felt, even for someone as acidic as Pam, into his expression.

She seemed to sag in front of him. He watched her argue with herself for a moment before she leaned forward on the table and laced her fingers.

'Gavin McLeish wants me to apply for a place on an MIT with him.' She held her hands out as if to say, *'There, now you know.'*

Malkie shook his head. 'He thinks he can engineer a move for you? Does the idiot think he can do that without you applying through the normal channels?'

Pam's face turned severe. 'I wouldn't take that kind of shortcut even if he thought he could.'

Malkie held his hands up. 'No, I know you wouldn't, Pam.

But he might think he can do something like that. The man's over-inflated sense of his own importance has always been staggering.'

'I know that. You think I, of all people, don't know that?'

'I didn't mean anything by it, I promise.' He suspected her irritation came less from Malkie's comment as what it said about the calibre of the man she'd once chosen as the boss to hitch herself and her career to.

'So, what do you think you'll do? You could probably sail through your DI exams. Just think the opposite way to everything McLeish thought he was teaching you.'

She smiled at that. 'Oh, don't remind me.' Her eyes came alive as she seemed to catch some momentum. 'Do you have any idea how bloody embarrassing it was for me to defend him, especially after that debacle with Liam Fielding? I mean, what the hell was he thinking?'

'He was thinking the rules only applied to him when it suited his ambitions, Pam. Any side effects on you or me or the Force – aye, I know we're not supposed to call it that anymore. Any damage he did on his way up the greasy pole mattered not one tiny iota to him. He's the very definition of the word *utilitarian*.'

She studied him. 'Is it true he engineered that boy-band-party drug-bust? The one where you got a bunch of dirty needles in your arm because he charged in against all protocol and nearly screwed up the whole job? Is it true the dealer was coincidentally one of his informants?'

'It was my wrist, not my arm, but basically, aye. Did I ever tell you he apologised to me?'

'Sod off. No way.'

'Aye. In private, and it was like he'd rather have had his fingernails pulled out, but he did, technically, apologise.'

'And got an easy leg-up into a DI job out of it. Bastard never apologised to me.'

'Did he owe you an apology for something? Or apologies?'

'You have no idea, Malkie. Why do you think I was always in such a foul mood? Sorry about that, by the way; you were always just too easy a target.'

'Fair enough. McLeish was welcome to it, Pam. I hated being a DI.'

She studied him, again. He hoped she was learning as much about him as he was about her.

'Why is that? Why do you let people think you're lazy and incompetent and won't ever amount to much?'

She seemed to realise how much she'd just said. 'I mean, that's what I've heard people say about you. Just in passing, you know?' She had the decency to look sheepish.

'Ach, I'm none of those things, really, but I can just never be bothered making the effort to change the opinions of people whose opinions don't matter a toss to me. My arrest record is as good as any of theirs, it's just the perception of how I go about making those arrests that people want to talk about. Human nature, really. Bernie Stevens hates me more than anyone else, I think.'

'No. She doesn't.'

Malkie gaped at her. 'How do you know that?'

'She told me over coffee. Ages ago.'

She made him ask.

'And?'

Pam failed to keep a small smile from her lips. She was enjoying this. 'You frustrate her, Malkie.'

'How?'

'She actually likes the way you talk to people. She enjoys seeing you pissing off Senior Management. She bloody loved the way you talked to McLeish by the way, thought you put him back in his box nicely on more than one occasion.'

Malkie's mind reeled. 'So, what's her problem with me then?'

Pam leaned forward, locked eyes with him. He felt something unpleasant coming.

'She hates whiners, Malkie. And she loathes people feeling sorry for themselves.'

Malkie's penny dropped. With a resounding and unpleasant thud.

'I'm not as bad as I used to be, am I? Steph's worked hard on me, as painful as that is to admit. I can't help the fact I sometimes just want the world to stop so I can get off. And I struggle dealing with the shite we see every day, can't understand how we can do the kinds of things we do to each other. But I thought I'd been cutting back on being so vocal about it. I guess I was wrong.'

Pam patted his arm, but only briefly and without real conviction.

'You do moan a lot less these days, but we can all see it in you, Malkie. We all see when you're struggling. I know some, like Steph and Gucci, look out for you, but some of us just can't be bothered with it. Like me, I admit. I don't have the capacity for other people's business as well as my own at the moment.' Some steel crept back into her posture. 'If that makes me selfish, then so be it.'

Malkie considered her. He wanted to wrap his arms around her and give her a huge hug, but he knew how badly that would end. He also feared the possibility that they were both getting carried away and would later regret their mutual over-sharing.

After a knock on the door, it opened. Steph's head appeared. She looked at them both, would feel that she'd interrupted something. 'Andrew Dunn confirmed that bracelet is Elizabeth Dunn's, a gift from her daughter Sophie. Warrant's on its way for the Jessop place. Shall we go ruffle some feathers?'

Malkie stood and clapped his hands together. 'Aye, and kick some arse.'

At the door, he turned back to Pam. 'Thanks for the update, DS Ballantyne, very useful and much appreciated.'

'You're welcome, DS McCulloch, glad I could assist.' She also stood, and waited behind him as Steph backed out.

He heard her mutter '*arse*' behind him, and he replied over his shoulder with a muted '*cow*'.

She walked away from him and Steph like a woman with important places to be and important things to do, but Malkie would bet his pension she was having to suppress a highly uncharacteristic smile.

THIRTY-FOUR

After picking up a couple of Uniforms on their way out, Malkie and Steph drove, with enthusiasm, back to the Jessop home.

After complaining long and loud about Davie's arrest, Paula Jessop swore like a navvy when she saw the warrant but – and this troubled Malkie – she didn't seem as worried as he'd hoped she'd be.

Steph led Malkie straight to the upstairs back bedroom. As she'd described, the windows were boarded over with enthusiasm behind filthy curtains, piles of decorating equipment lay around the periphery.

Malkie wandered around, let his eyes stray over paint tins and trays, brushes and rollers, a ladder and wallpaper table, plastic sheets and paint-stained blankets, all piled on a grubby mattress, and paint-stained rags hanging from nails.

Why on a mattress? It's hardly a quality hardwood floor, just exposed chipboard. Where did the paint come from on those rags hanging on the nails? Nothing he'd seen of the house had been redecorated for years. Decades, possibly. Nicotine yellow the prevailing aesthetic throughout the place.

He kicked the mattress with his toe and raised his eyebrows

at Paula. She'd been standing in the doorway, arms crossed over her chest, ankles crossed, her face a mask of too-bored indifference, but a look at the mattress caused a flash of irritation, possibly concern, to narrow her eyes.

'To protect the floor. Davie can be clumsy.' She sounded about as convinced as Malkie was.

Malkie continued. He scanned everything, poked about in plastic crates and buckets, searched between the paint cans and other containers on the mattress.

He found nothing. The scene was ridiculous but didn't cross the line to suspicious.

He sighed. Paula Jessop folded her arms and beamed at him, smug as fuck.

'I told youse. We're decorating.'

Malkie made an obvious act of looking around the grubby and polluted walls.

'Any day now.' She shrugged and her infuriating, complacent grin had Malkie itching to look the entire room over again.

He stepped to the door and Steph followed. When he stopped she had to put a hand on his back to not collide with him.

Something... His Copper-Sense screamed at him. *Look again.*

He turned back, ran his eyes methodically over every item, one by one, forced himself to name each thing to himself before moving on.

He saw nothing, found nothing, and yet knew he was missing something. Nothing specific, nothing as juicy as Elizabeth's bracelet but some small thing, something off, something not quite right...

He needed the SOCOs in here.

'Seen enough? Can youse leave now? I think youse should leave now.' Paula stood in the doorway, hands on her hips, her foot tapping a staccato rhythm on the floor.

'Can you let Stevie know we were here, aye? This might bring him back sooner, and we need to talk to him, too.'

She glared at Malkie like she wanted to hurt him. Steph moved beside them and stared up at her. Paula stood a full head taller than Steph and yet somehow seemed to shrink in front of them. Steph could have that effect on people even when she didn't mean to.

Leaving Paula staring at the floor, they stepped outside to fetch a Uniform to stand guard until they could summon a SOCO.

In the car, Malkie called Thompson to request a basic SOCO sweep for prints to begin with. After persuading Thompson that yes, he was aware she had already blown her forensics budget for the month and yes, he believed any evidence found there could well be worth the expense. He hung up and settled back in his seat.

Meanwhile Steph left instructions with the remaining Uniform to alert them the instant Paula made any phone call or looked about to leave. She joined Malkie in the car.

Malkie called Gucci. 'Are you at a desk, Gucci? Good. Run a search on the Jessop family. Aye I know, so start with Stevie and Davie and Martin, then Stevie's wife Paula, then expand. OK? Immediate call back if you find any kind of painter or decorator. Aye, I know it's specific but do it, please. Thanks, Lou.'

He felt Steph's eyes on him. 'Aye, I know, I'm presupposing.'

'Presuming, but near enough. Did you notice how much of that dump has been decorated recently?'

'Aye. None of it.'

'And did you notice the state of most of those paint tins?' He already knew the answer, but he was enjoying himself.

'Aye. Not a single one looked unused.'

Malkie continued. 'Ergo – that means *so*, Steph – the likelihood of the Jessops having experienced a sudden desire to swank up their palatial accommodation falls far short of the likelihood that those tins and that gear were dumped there without any intention to be used.'

She sighed. 'Wordy, but fair, yes.'

'Those Jessop fuckers had her there, Steph. Only a genius like Davie would leave her locked up with lots of sharp, pointy tools she might cause some damage with.'

Steph pretended he'd woken her. 'Sorry, boss. Nodded off waiting. What were you saying?'

'Cheeky sod. Nae respect.'

Malkie chewed over his options. Would it be enough to charge Davie?

'Yes.'

He returned to the moment. 'Eh?'

'Yes. It's enough. It was a Jessop that got run over while chasing a woman we've confirmed was Elizabeth Dunn. The man who abducted her bore more than a passing resemblance to Davie Jessop, which was enough for us to interview him at home. He invited us in then as good as told me to use the upstairs loo, where he'd have known I couldn't help but see that room. And that bracelet...'

She held her hands out as if to say *What else do you need?*

'So yes. It's enough.'

He nodded, slow and thoughtful. 'Aye, it is, isn't it?'

THIRTY-FIVE

Someone left breakfast inside the cellar door while Elizabeth slept. Had to be Andrea because either of the neanderthals, Davie or Stan, would have dumped a bowl of milk and a box of cereal on the tray. They wouldn't have gone to the trouble to toast some chunky bread and leave her butter and jam, and they wouldn't have given her a whole cafetière of coffee with milk and sugar.

Anything to alleviate the shame the poor woman seemed to feel at being forced to imprison Elizabeth. She ate the breakfast despite the fear in her gut and the aches in her ribs from where Stan had claimed to hate punching her. She couldn't work out why she ate. The best she could come up with was an obsessive need to do all she could to end up safely back with Sophie and Andrew. Or was it that she needed to *know* that she'd done all she could, to mitigate her guilt at having set this whole sorry sequence of events in motion in the first place?

No. Her own shame and ignominy, she could stomach. Further upset – or worse – for her daughter she could never risk being even a small part of.

She placed the breakfast things back on the tray and left it by the door. When she heard footsteps on the stairs, she imagined she could already tell the difference between Andrea and either of the two men.

When the door opened and Andrea's hand appeared, Elizabeth said her name.

'Andrea. Please. Sit with me for a while. If those animals are out, I mean. This is horrible.'

The hand withdrew the tray, and the door started to close.

'Please, Andrea. Have a heart?'

The door opened again, and Andrea stood there. The distraught look on the woman's face, her broken and miserable posture, sent a shard of guilt through Elizabeth; this too was her fault.

Andrea pulled a chair from beside the door and sat, but she looked ready to spring for the open doorway at the slightest provocation. She sat with her knees and feet together, her hands in her lap, her eyes downcast. She wore the same outfit as yesterday but its wrinkles and crumples told Elizabeth that the woman had slept in them. That, Elizabeth found herself certain of, was out of character, a sign of the depth of her own worry and distress.

'Was breakfast OK?' She sounded as if she added a tacit *'Did I at least do something decent for you?'*

'Yes, thanks. The bread was lovely. And the coffee.'

Andrea looked up and managed a weak smile. 'Freshly ground. Only way to make it.'

Elizabeth smiled back and found herself surprised to realise she meant it. This woman was – if not as terrified as Elizabeth – fearful for her own safety at the hands of her brothers.

'They wouldn't really hurt their own sister, would they?'

'They already have. More than once. I always end up apologising to them, though. For upsetting them or making them angry or getting things wrong.' She faded for a few seconds. Somewhere bleak. 'That's even worse than the actual... what they do to me. Humiliating. Apologising to a man for having hit you. That's all wrong, isn't it?' Her eyes held a glimmer of hope, a need to hear Elizabeth tell her yes, they're to blame, not you.

Elizabeth trusted her own eyes to communicate her confirmation, and the tears that welled in Andrea's eyes told her the woman had understood.

Elizabeth recalled her treatment at the hands of the wealthy and entitled men who had ruined her life, her previous life, her good life. She remembered women, too. Women who she'd thought would have defended her, taken a chance to form a united front, demand retribution for the chronic toxic misogyny rife in the crusty old financial services firm of Gleann Darragh. One young girl, barely in the door, had spoken to Elizabeth in private and only once about inappropriate comments and looks from a senior partner, and agreed something needed to be done. Elizabeth saw her summoned to the boardroom a few days later. She hadn't made eye contact with Elizabeth as she left, and all other attempts to broach the subject with the girl had been met with denials, and protestations that she must have misinterpreted the situation.

'Elizabeth? Did you hear what I said?'

'Sorry, Andrea. I'm a bit distracted at the moment.'

That seemed to remind Andrea of her part in Elizabeth's ordeal, albeit under duress.

'You've been mistreated by men too, haven't you?'

'Yes, Andrea. I have. Both professionally and... physically.'

They sat in silence for a minute, each lost in their private miseries.

'Andrea, can I get out for just five minutes? Please? This cellar is awful.'

Andrea considered the request for only a second before fear crowded out any chance of it happening. 'I can't. I'm sorry. If you run away—'

'I won't. I promise.'

Andrea's eyes spoke volumes; of course she'd run, but who could blame her?

Elizabeth saw the answer coming before Andrea spoke, and she had to wonder just how awful her brothers had been to her in the past to make her so fearful of disobeying them.

'It's fine, Andrea. I shouldn't have asked. Forget it.'

Tears spilled down Andrea's cheeks, and Elizabeth congratulated herself on having done no more than pile guilt upon guilt on the poor woman.

Andrea stood and turned to leave. In the doorway she didn't look back but spoke over her shoulder.

'Am I a bad person?'

Elizabeth considered piling on more guilt; more shame. Maybe she could emotionally blackmail her obviously tortured conscience into releasing her.

But she didn't have the heart.

'No, Andrea. You're as much a victim of those bastards as I am.'

Before the door closed, Elizabeth asked the question she dreaded hearing the answer to.

'What's your surname, Andrea?'

'Jessop. Why?'

Elizabeth felt her stomach lurch and she had to suppress a rush of nausea.

The Jessops. Davie and Stevie. She knew them. By reputation. Everyone did.

Andrea's expression turned soft. Apologetic. 'Yes, those Jessops. I'm sorry, Elizabeth.'

Elizabeth choked back vomit that rose in her throat.

She wept.

Those Jessops...

THIRTY-SIX

On returning to the station, Malkie threw his coat over the back of his chair and clapped his hands together. His coat slid off and landed in a heap on the floor. He ignored it.

'Right. Gucci, Rab. Me and Steph have had a productive morning. We—'

Rab held a finger up. 'I, boss.'

Malkie scowled at him as much in annoyance as confusion. 'I what?'

'Steph and *I*, meaning you, have had a productive morning.'

'That's what I said.' His eagerness to crack on started to edge his voice with irritation.

Rab opened his mouth again, but Gucci threw a scrunched-up sheet of paper at him. He closed his mouth again, but with bad grace.

'As I was saying, Steph and I have had a productive morning.'

Rab huffed, folded his arms and rolled his eyes.

'We found an engraved gold bracelet hanging on the hedge outside the Jessops' property. Aye, I know, nothing's ever supposed to fall into our laps, but it has, this time. Elizabeth

Dunn's husband, Andrew, has confirmed it's hers, so a warrant was a no-brainer.

'Inside, upstairs, where we heard banging from on our previous visit, we found a shitload of decorating equipment but not a scrap of new paint anywhere in the house, and a dirty great bolt on the outside of the door. Looked to me very like somewhere the Jessops didn't want someone getting out of.

'Those Jessop fuckers – sorry, Pam – the Jessops are up to their manky necks in this. Their nephew gets fatally run over by a car while chasing Elizabeth Dunn, then she's abducted from her home by someone who resembled—'

Steph cleared her throat.

'Someone who shared similarities, from behind, with Davie Jessop. And now we find Elizabeth's bracelet hanging from a hedge right outside their house and a bedroom sealed up tighter than a camel's arse in a sandstorm. Sorry, Pam.'

Pam tutted but didn't raise her head.

'So, Rab, all known friends, relatives, colleagues and other associated lowlifes, please.'

Rab unfolded his arms and sat up. 'Started.'

'Really?'

'Aye.' Rab looked affronted.

'Well done, mate. Vehicles, businesses, other residential and commercial properties owned?'

Rab deflated. 'Next on my list.'

'Knew it would be, mate.'

Rab opened his mouth again, but Malkie cut him off.

'Gucci.'

She flashed him a warning look.

'Would you be so kind, Lou, to see what you can find on Stevie Jessop's whereabouts, please? I'm pretty sure he's abroad, somewhere, but with a warrant already issued to search his home, I doubt you'll have much trouble getting info out of airports and ports, etc. I'm sure he's out of the country. The fact that he's not rushed back even though his nephew just died might indicate he's on a schedule. Which might suggest he's engaged in one of his dodgy import businesses. Which means concentrate on ferries first, aye?'

Gucci finished scribbling in her notebook then nodded.

Malkie turned back to his desk.

Rab wasn't finished. 'I was trying to tell you, boss. Davie Jessop has a mate – Angus Campbell, an ex-cellmate – who owns a white Mercedes van. Same kind, a Sprinter.'

Malkie reappraised him. 'Nice one, Rab.'

Rab turned back to his own work. 'I was trying to tell you.'

Malkie shared an '*oops*' look with Gucci and Steph.

All four spent the next two hours trawling databases, checking in with forensics and being told they're working flat out, cross-referencing intel, and raising actions for detectives and Uniforms alike.

Gucci was the first to break the industrious silence. 'The Jessop brothers have a sister. Andrea. She's a retired teacher, lives in Glasgow city centre.'

'Good. Get started on—'

'Background checks on the sister? Vehicle details? Personal and business connections? Get the registration of Davie Jessop's mate's van and do a search on ANPR from his home address and work outward? Ask Glasgow to send a Uniform to her address? That sort of thing?'

'Show off. And?'

He folded his arms like a hopeful schoolteacher. He smiled regretfully when Gucci came up with nothing more.

He shook his head. 'Oh dear. Check ANPR for Stevie Jessop's Transit in and out of Hull or Newcastle ferry ports for the past week, too. I think he's out of the country and bringing some import goods back by van. He wouldn't have been expecting all of this to blow up in his absence so he may have used his own vehicle.'

'Yes, boss.' Gucci feigned annoyance, but no one would believe it for a second.

Malkie turned back to his desk. 'Glad to know I still serve some kind of useful function around here.'

Pam spoke without looking up from the papers arranged in neat piles on her desk. 'You do.'

All heads turned to her.

She looked self-conscious when she found everyone staring at her. 'Entertainment value?'

A hush befell the room. This was all wrong. She'd passed comment on Malkie without venom or animosity. If anything, an almost playful dig. She seemed to realise what she'd done.

Old Pam returned. 'What?' All heads turned away again.

Malkie and Steph shared a look, Steph's expression questioning, presumably thinking of his and Pam's earlier meeting. Malkie shook his head and broke eye contact.

Malkie tried to concentrate on a typical log of calls to Crimestoppers, more red herrings than a Russian fishing trawler, but knew he was only killing time.

When Gucci spoke again, three heads turned to her.

'Well, bugger me.' She stared at her screen.

Malkie waited a second, no more, before breaking.

'Well?'

Gucci realised all eyes were on her. 'Davie Jessop's mate with the van, Angus Campbell. He's a painter and decorator.'

'Interesting.' He felt Steph's eyes on him. 'In an open-minded and not at all bias-confirming kind of way.' He heard Steph sigh.

'Get the—'

'Registration? Yes, boss.'

'Aye. Right. Then—'

'Do an ANPR search. Tell me ev—'

'Every camera that caught it within, say, a five-mile radius, to keep the search manageable?'

Malkie glared at her but couldn't hold it for long. 'Aye, all that. Just what I was about to say. Excellent. Carry on then.'

He heard Steph tut and she scowled at him. She slammed her chair under her desk and walked away.

Fuck's sake, Steph. What's eating you?

Malkie and Gucci shared a look. Rab glanced between them as if unsure what was happening.

Malkie started after her. Gucci stopped him.

'Leave her for now, boss. Leave it until she calms down.'

'Aye, but calms down about what, Lou?' He held his hands out, helpless and clueless.

Gucci held his gaze for a second, then sat back at her desk. 'DVLC then ANPR. Hour after glorious hour of trawling databases. Everything I dreamed of when I signed up for the exciting world of policing.'

Malkie wanted to head back to the Jessop home, even if just to annoy the SOCOs, but he found some mind-numbing but necessary paperwork to make him look busy until Steph reappeared.

After an hour, he could take the suspense no longer.

'Anything, Lou?'

'Not yet. I'll tell you as soon as I find anything useful, boss.'

'Point taken. Carry on.'

He watched her shoulders rise and fall and heard her sigh.

Idiot. Find some other way to make yourself useful.

As he trawled the case file for something to leap out and bite him on his investigative backside and give him some hope, his phone rang. He grabbed it, hoped for something to offer him some distraction.

'Malkie? Callum.'

Malkie almost recoiled from the phone. He stood and headed for the back of the office and the meeting rooms. He saw Gucci and Lundy watch him with frowns on their faces but cared only that they heard none of the conversation.

'We're not supposed to talk, Callum. Could endanger your perceived objectivity and that could wreck any grounds Pam might find to reopen the case. You know this, mate.'

He heard silence. Was Callum embarrassed by his own foolishness? Or did he have something to report that he dreaded giving voice to?

'I need you to meet me. Now. Alone.' A pause, then, 'I'm sorry, Malkie.'

Malkie felt a weight drop into his guts. What the hell had made Callum almost unable to speak?

'Where?'

More silence.

'Where, Callum?'

'Livi Village. Your dad's house.'

Malkie felt ready to throw up. He'd been back there just once, days after the fire to rake through the ashes and blackened debris of nearly twenty years of his life and decades more of his dad's. And his mum's.

'Why? Is it absolutely necessary, mate?'

Another empty pause. 'Aye. Aye, I think it is. Can you come now? Before it gets completely dark?'

Malkie peered through the meeting-room window, saw Gucci and Rab peering at their screens, looking exhausted. He was hardly adding anything useful to their efforts.

'Ten minutes.'

'OK.'

'Callum?'

'Aye?'

'Am I going to regret this?'

'Not as much as I am, Malkie. Not as much as I am.'

THIRTY-SEVEN

The cellar door opened.

Andrea's face peered around the door. 'Can I trust you, Elizabeth?'

Elizabeth could think of no reason Andrea would ask that question, but she felt a rush of hope anyway.

'Yes. You can.' She poured every scrap of sincerity she could muster into her answer.

Andrea plucked at her lower lip with two fingers, seemed to agonise over something.

'I want to let you out for a while, but...'

Elizabeth's heart leaped in her chest.

'But if you run...' Her face said the rest.

'Come with me, Andrea. Go to the police. You're a victim of domestic violence. The fact that they're your brothers doesn't change that. You need to stop them. They're the Jessops, for God's sake. Can you imagine what they'll do to me, Andrea?'

She ran out of words, could see them bouncing off of Andrea without effect. Her mind had gone elsewhere. 'I messed up, once before. They had a boy in here, couldn't have been more than thirteen.'

Elizabeth's stomach turned at the thought of whatever Andrea's rotten family had done to a child barely older than Sophie.

'I took pity on him. He couldn't stop crying and he'd wet himself. I untied him and he pushed me over. By the time I reached the top of the stairs he'd disappeared. There are thick trees all around this place, and he was much younger and faster than me.'

Andrea slid her back down the door frame to sit on her heels. Again, she looked broken.

'When they got home, Stevie lost his temper. He slapped me so hard I fell over. I started crying. He told me to stop snivelling, but I couldn't.'

She paused, seemed to need to summon strength to continue.

'He kicked me in my stomach and my ribs, twice. Cracked two of my ribs.' She cried now, quiet and desolate.

'When he left the room, still angry at me for being so useless...'

She swallowed, gulped, had to brace herself to continue.

'Davie told me he would be having a word with me too, as soon as Stevie went home. Davie...'

Elizabeth turned around on the bed, lowered her feet to the floor, sat on the edge of the mattress. She wanted to reach for the woman, could only begin to imagine her pain and her humiliation, but she feared how Andrea would react to a move towards her.

'Davie didn't actually lay a hand on me, at first, but he did a fine job of making me think he was going to. He lifted his fist to me several times, then laughed when I cowered and screamed. He really enjoyed himself.'

She went quiet. Elizabeth could find no words, at first, until her own troubles reimposed themselves on her mind. Regardless of this poor woman's awful situation, regardless of how Elizabeth's heart ached to persuade Andrea to go with her, now, to the police, Sophie mattered most. Always.

'I promise, Andrea.'

Andrea looked up at her, confused.

'Not to run away. If you think you can trust me, I'd really love to get some air. This cellar is awful.'

Andrea stood, wiped her cheeks with the back of her hand. She smoothed her skirt down and brushed some invisible fluff from her cardigan – both fresh, clean clothes, Elizabeth noticed – then opened the door wider.

Hope bloomed in Elizabeth. She stood. Much too quickly. Realisation dawned on Andrea, who retreated behind the door and closed it to within a few inches of the frame.

'I'm sorry, Elizabeth. I can't trust you, but I admire you for that. I would too, if...'

Elizabeth made a move for the door, even as she felt her world fall apart around her, but she had no chance of reaching it before Andrea pulled it closed and turned the lock.

Elizabeth screamed and banged her fists on the door. 'Andrea. Let me out, you fucking bitch. They'll kill me. You know they will. Andrea. My daughter needs me. Andrea?'

After a few seconds, her muffled voice came through the door.

'I was nearly a mum once, Elizabeth. I made it to the fourth month.'

A pause, and somehow Elizabeth knew the woman's heart was breaking.

'Stevie knew I was pregnant when he...'

Andrea sobbed. One part of Elizabeth would tear Andrea apart to get back to Sophie, but another part of her hated how much she'd be prepared to do just that.

She curled up on the mattress and sobbed until she had no tears left.

THIRTY-EIGHT

When he parked outside what used to be the garden he played in and read in as a child, Malkie stayed glued to the car seat for long minutes, until Callum appeared inside the battered old wooden gate. As he climbed from the car, he looked at Callum and dreaded what was coming.

What the hell have you found?

Callum stepped forward and extended his hand. 'Been a while.'

Malkie found himself in no mood for pleasantries, even less so than usual given Callum's entire demeanour, like a doctor about to deliver a terminal diagnosis. He shook Callum's hand, found it sweaty and trembling.

As they strolled together up the path to the remains of the front door, Malkie did his best to break the icy sense of dread that filled him but failed.

'How's retirement treating you, Callum?'

Callum didn't respond, kept his eyes on the house. Or rather, the remains of it.

Malkie didn't try again.

The fire and the months since had finished it off. It now

bore no resemblance to the home he remembered. Just about all of the ruined furniture and other trappings of domestic life had been gutted and taken away. Only the lowest few feet of the internal and external walls remained. He wondered why the site hadn't been levelled and cleared out, until he remembered the numerous letters he'd ignored from the council asking him with semi-sympathetic but increasing insistence to get people in to do just that. Why he couldn't bring himself to do that – he didn't even need to be present for it – was yet another question he'd become deft at ignoring.

He decided in that moment that his dad must never see this, if he hadn't already made the trip by himself.

Graffiti adorned one of the front-facing walls. Buckie bottles and takeaway food wrappers and empty syringes littered the ground around the outside of the front door.

Poor kids have no chance these days; nothing to do and parents they hate going home to.

Callum held a hand out, indicated Malkie should step to the left.

To where his mum's bedroom window used to open out onto the garden she'd always loved so much, that she'd always taken so much pride in until her illness – the illness he never spotted – robbed her of the energy to perform even the lightest of the faffing-about she lived for.

He stepped with care, as if afraid even eight months later he might destroy vital evidence. He spotted a sheet of what looked like a rain-rotted section of timber cladding, one of the yard-square sections of teak strips that used to adorn the outside of the building. He stood on it like it was a crime-scene stepping plate. The entire lawn around it looked like a swamp, only a few patches of weak and shrivelled grass hanging on to life in the saturated mud, but he felt firm ground underneath the wood.

He turned to Callum with a face that demanded no more

delays. He looked even more apologetic than before and pointed to the sheet of cladding Malkie stood on.

He stepped off, and Callum lifted it, his eyes downcast.

Malkie saw nothing at first except mud and stones and an old copy of the *Livingston Herald*, mashed into the ground, the top pages crumpled and peeled back from those beneath. Malkie glanced at Callum, his eyes asking what he was supposed to be seeing.

Callum's face drained to a grey cast, and he licked his lips before he could speak.

'Under the newspaper.' His tone filled Malkie with so much dread he wondered if he had the courage to look, but he did.

Callum lifted the muddy papers with a pen. Underneath, Malkie saw a battered and scratched old steel-cased lighter, the kind with a lid that opened to reveal a flint thumb wheel, pressed into the mud.

As much as he didn't want to assume it might be significant and all that might entail, Callum's eyes told Malkie it was the very thing he'd been meant to find.

'Don't touch it, Malkie. Just in case.'

Malkie's stomach churned; did Callum's terrified manner mean he'd realised he'd fucked up, way back on that terrible night when two men lost the centre of their lives?

Callum's face betrayed his guilt. 'I missed it. I should have seen it, but I missed it. It was buried under so much rubbish and pressed into the mud, under that sheet of timber when it fell from the wall as it collapsed. Whatever. I should have spotted it.'

'But that could have been dropped any time, couldn't it?'

'I wish I could say yes, but I can't. Look at the mud under and around the newspaper.'

Malkie did so, took a moment to notice what he thought Callum wanted him to see.

'Ash? Is that why the mud around it has black patches?'

'Aye. But the mud under the newspaper isn't black at all.'

Malkie stood. Callum remained crouched, held the wooden sheet up with his fingertips. Malkie knew what he needed to do: call Pam. If this was evidence, then he needed to be nowhere near it for the sake of getting the case reopened, and he wanted Callum nowhere near it for the sake of his retirement. Malkie knew better than most how badly a man can fuck up despite the best of intentions and the greatest diligence; Callum was *good people* and his fallibility – no matter how disastrous – didn't warrant a ruined life. And he harboured no doubt that it would do just that. Callum's manner already spoke of how badly he was flogging himself for this possible screw-up. If it turned out he had, indeed, been negligent and derailed any chance of Malkie and his dad seeking justice, he thought Callum might not survive that.

Callum crouched down onto his heels again. With a pen from his pocket, he lifted one corner of the topmost few pages of the newspaper. The sheets lower down had turned grimy and dank but had been protected to some extent by the pages above. Malkie took his phone from his pocket and took a photo. He took another with the flash enabled in case the greying of the sky rendered the first useless. Then, Callum lowered everything back into place with extreme care.

They peered at Malkie's phone screen as he faffed with the settings and worked out how to zoom in.

On the top edge of one page, they could read the faint print.

17th July 2024. The day the fire started. The day his mum died.

Callum stared at him, didn't need to say any more. The lighter had been in the mud, under the newspaper, before the fire started, and the date on the newspaper suggested it had been dropped there only shortly before.

Had someone stood here, outside her always-open window, and murdered her?

His world lurched. Callum caught him by one arm.

'Christ, I'm so sorry, Malkie. I'm so, so sorry.' He looked about to throw up.

Malkie dragged himself back from a waking nightmare of ashes and smoke and screams and collapsing timber walls.

'Fuck.'

Callum looked at him as if he expected Malkie to kill him, like he thought he deserved nothing else.

Malkie grabbed a hold of his better half, fought down the urge to shout and scream and condemn the miserable excuse for a man wringing his hands before him.

'No. Stop that, Callum. Fucking stop that.' He pulled him by the arm back towards the garden gate.

They stood. Silent. One lost in renewed grief and shocked fury, the other in abject self-loathing.

'I was so sure it looked like such an obvious case. How could I have been so complacent? How could I have been so bloody stupid?'

Malkie let the man flog himself, knew he probably needed to vent his guilt before Malkie would get any sense, any usefulness, out of him.

When Callum's muttering and tears dried up, Malkie took him by both arms and waited until the man looked at him.

'Callum. You fucked up. Maybe. We don't even know if that thing is relevant or not, might have been dropped there any time in the last eight months.'

Callum's look told Malkie neither of them believed that.

'No, Malkie. When I first arrived that night, I could see how pristine your mum kept this garden. There was no way any rubbish was left lying around it. And it's *under* that newspaper, stuck in the mud.'

Malkie knew what was coming but let the man finish his *mea culpa*.

'It had to have been on the ground before that section of

cladding fell on it, before the fire gutted the house. And it fell there around the same time as the fire.'

A penny dropped in Malkie's mind. 'You knew already, didn't you? You knew the date already?'

Callum's eyes confirmed it. It explained why the man had seemed so sure of his own shame before he even got Malkie to the scene. He hadn't been worried he *might* have missed something; he already knew he'd fucked up.

Malkie crossed the pavement to his car, turned and rested his backside on the bonnet. Callum joined him. They stood in silence. Malkie decided he had to deal with this without ruining a good man's life. He'd failed to save Walter Callahan. And others, his inner idiot reminded him. He refused to let Callum's uncharacteristic – he was willing to bet – error wreck the rest of his life.

'OK. Callum. You go home. You tell no one you found this, and you tell no one you showed me this. I'll tell DS—'

'No.'

'Sorry?'

'I said no, mate. If you admit you knew, and were here, and tampered with the evidence, anything your colleague finds that might confirm your mum was... Any new evidence she finds here will be hopelessly tainted. I doubt that lighter will be enough to reopen the case even if it's plastered with some bastard's DNA, but it might reach the evidentiary threshold for reopening if it's discovered by someone else. Someone who can be trusted to know how not to foul a possible crime scene.'

Malkie chewed on this, agreed it made sense, but who...?

'No. Not happening, Callum. We'll find another way.'

Callum turned to him. 'You can't stop me, Malkie. If... if this turns into something, if it goes any way to proving that fire was no accident...'

He swallowed. Closed his eyes for a second. 'Then I'll take the hit. I won't lose my pension, probably won't even be disciplined or charged with anything. Just like your bosses, our lot like people to fade away into retirement rather than bring bad publicity down on them. I'll be fine.'

Malkie felt tears demanding release. 'You won't. We both know that. You'll kick yourself for the rest of your life.'

'Aye. But that's the point. My life, my retirement, is probably safe, whatever they do to me. Yours isn't.'

Malkie found himself ashamed to realise he wanted Callum to take the hit for this, rather than see Pam's investigation collapse.

Callum straightened himself, smoothed his waterproof jacket down. 'I'll contact DS Ballantyne tomorrow and tell her I came back because I never quite got over that night either. I'll tell her I found the lighter. You just have to plead ignorance when she tells you about it.'

Malkie opened his mouth to protest again, but Callum cut him off.

'That's my decision, Malkie. Whatever you decide, I'm confessing my mistake to your colleague. If you don't want to drag yourself down with me and jeopardise any chance you have at getting justice for your mum, you'll hang me out to dry as if you can't bear to look at me.'

Malkie – as much as the thought appalled him – allowed himself to admit the man was right.

THIRTY-NINE

Malkie had driven to the LESOC without realising he meant to. It was becoming a habit; one he didn't want to break.

Dame Helen Reid sat on the top of the three granite steps that led into the main hallway of the Georgian pile converted with a modern, zinc-clad annexe into the refuge it had become for ex-service people, and the place Malkie had first met Deborah.

She flicked some ash from her cigarette and nodded at him as he approached.

'What happened, Malkie? Last night when you visited? How did Deborah end up hurting herself? She reopened a skin graft she only got done last week.'

Her tone carried a demand for an explanation but no indication of blame; she would simply need to know, and Deborah would have talked the incident down.

'She over-reached herself, Dame Helen. That's all. Thought she could reach all the way around to the other side of my ample girth. You know what she's like for acknowledging her limits.'

She considered Malkie for long seconds before replying.

'Just make sure she doesn't push herself too hard too fast, please. Don't let her own stubbornness derail her recovery.'

'I won't.' He turned to go inside but Dame Helen touched his arm, made him stop.

'Sit, Malkie.'

He sighed but knew better than to argue.

'What else is troubling you?'

How does she know?

'My dad and I fell out over something. I can't remember ever actually falling out with him before. It feels rotten.'

'Over what?'

Don't mince your words now, Helen.

He took a moment, debated how much to tell her, realised he wanted to tell her all.

'I found out I have a daughter. You know I told you I nearly died when I was a teenager? There was a girl involved. It went really bad and her brothers attacked me.'

He took a breath. 'I found out just a month ago that girl got pregnant. Yes, by me. She didn't tell me. For twenty-seven years.'

'Ah. I see. And now your father is unsure how he feels about you having such a strong personal link to someone he's spent his life hating for nearly getting you killed.'

'Exactly. I think he's worried he'll see Sandra in Jennifer's eyes and not be able to feel anything but loathing for the girl.'

'Sandra is your ex and Jennifer is her daughter? Your daughter?'

'Aye. I can't cut Jennifer out of my life, but I don't want to put my dad through any more pain than he's already suffered. Actually, that's another thing; we're re-examining my mum's death, too.'

He suddenly realised just much how he was dealing with and felt an urge to lie beside Deborah and watch crap TV swell inside him. He stood. 'Don't worry. I don't burden Deborah with all this nonsense.'

Dame Helen looked up at him. 'You're a good man, Malkie, you really are. I never had children, I was always too busy, too stupid, thought there would always be a next year.' She looked up at him and he saw a mix of cold flint and compassion. 'Don't hurt Deborah while you deal with all of this. Protect her from it, or rather, from what it's probably doing to you. Please. She'll try to hurry her rehabilitation so she can support you, even if that means harming her recovery. She's stubborn that way.'

Malkie nodded. She reached up and squeezed his hand then opened her cigarette case and turned away. Malkie climbed to the top step but stopped before passing through the doors that slid open before him with barely a sound.

'It's not stubbornness, Dame Helen. It's determination. She's scared that if she starts giving her recovery anything less than one hundred per cent, she'll stall, maybe even go backwards. She's an amazing woman, and if I can get her to listen to me any more than she listens to you, it'll be a miracle.'

Dame Helen turned and looked up at him. 'Yes. Fair point. But we keep at her, yes?'

'Always, Dame Helen. She's never getting her saddle back on Indie if we don't.'

She smiled and turned back to light her new cigarette. 'Call your father, Malkie. Don't worry about what you'll say, just call him then wing it, OK?'

As he climbed the stairs, he pulled his phone from his pocket. He couldn't bring himself to risk another conversation that might sour his mood just when he and Deborah needed to repair the damage done during his last visit. He texted an 'Are you OK, Dad?' and left it at that.

Outside Deborah's door, he steeled himself. He believed they'd left themselves still in a good place considering the distress she'd suffered. That he'd stayed on another half hour or more without any major embarrassment being apparent on her part led him to hope they'd suffer no lasting discomfort from the incident.

A second after opening her door, he knew otherwise.

She smiled at him but couldn't hold it. She looked back at the TV without saying anything. He closed the door behind him, crossed to her bed, leaned over her, took her chin in one hand.

'Hello, you.' He kissed her. Not passionately and not with any great energy, but he held his lips against hers, tasted her and let her feel the love he poured into her. Her eyes glistened in the light from the TV in the otherwise dark room. He smiled at her, kissed the tip of her nose, then laid himself out beside her. She lifted her head, and he snaked his arm around and held on to her shoulder.

'I don't suppose there's some shitey soap opera we can suffer through, is there?'

She laughed. 'Oh, shut up. I like them.'

'I know, but I still love you.' The words escaped his mouth before he knew he was going to say them.

He looked at her, shocked by his own comment. His admission?

She stared back at him, seemed surprised too.

As he wondered whether she might repeat the sentiment back to him, she leaned over, more carefully than the previous night, and rested her head on his chest, pushed him down onto the bed.

They lay, quiet, for minutes. She seemed as happy to enjoy the muted rubbish from the TV as he was. She played with his tie, curled it round the scarred fingers of her damaged hand. She reached up and tugged at the knot. It came away in her hand.

'Clip on. In case some scoundrel grabs it while I'm trying to administer justice.'

She turned it in her hand then dropped it on the mattress

on the far side of him from her. She slid her fingers between his shirt buttons to where his own burn scars lay.

He tensed, still not able to let go of his revulsion at the permanent reminder of the night he lost his mum.

Deborah pulled her fingers out again. 'I'm sorry.' She sounded distraught.

'No. Don't be. It's me. Sometimes I manage to forget it looks like it does, but sometimes it hits me again.'

He sighed, long and tired. 'And then I think about you, and—'

'No. Let's not, Malkie. Please? You have yours and I have mine, and we deal with them the best we can, right? Together?'

He pulled her closer, kissed her on the forehead. 'Aye.'

She snuggled into him. 'Good day?'

He surprised himself. 'Actually, maybe.'

'Tell me.'

'We got a wee result on the woman we're looking for. She's still in danger and I'm still scared shitless we won't find her in time, but we might have got a lead on one of the bastards we think might want to hurt her.'

'Will that help you find her?'

'No. We got him leaving the country. Now we need to catch him coming back in and try to follow the creep, see if he'll lead us to her.'

'She's lucky to have you looking for her. You'll find her.'

Deborah's unconditional faith in him both warmed and scared him. Would he disappoint her if he later had to report that Elizabeth Dunn's body had been found dumped in a wood somewhere?

'Stop that.' She slapped his chest.

'What?'

'Catastrophising. I can hear your idiot brain dragging you down.'

'I can't help it.'

'But you had a good day today, no?'

He couldn't answer her. Couldn't lie to her by omission.

She looked up at him. 'What? And don't lie.'

The woman was merciless. In fact, every woman in his life was merciless. Was it just natural mothering that they seemed to think all men needed?

'You remember Callum Gourlay?'

'The fire investigator?'

'Aye. He found something. Might have found something. Outside my parents' home in Livi Village.'

'What?'

'A lighter.'

She raised herself up on one elbow, winced in pain but ignored it. She needed no words to communicate her realisation of the importance.

'Aye. Exactly. Neither Mum nor Dad smoked, and she kept that garden spotless. It might have been dropped there weeks or months after the fire, but...'

'You don't think so.'

'There were other things that point towards it having been there for a long time.'

'Like eight months?'

'Like eight months.'

'Oh, Malkie.' She pulled herself up to get her face closer to his. Malkie recalled Dame Helen Reid's gentle warning and moved to push her down again. She ignored him.

Eye to eye, she gazed into him. Even her right eye, blind and scarred with milky-grey striations, drilled into him, into his soul, demanded he hear her.

'I love you too, and I'll get you through this. I promise you.'

Love flooded him. Was that the first time any woman had ever professed love for him other than platonic affection? Did Sandra Morton ever say it to him? Almost certainly not. Theirs was not a romance, more a teenage rite of passage that went as wrong as any could.

He stroked the ruined side of her face, felt the texture of her scars, soft and warm despite how they looked.

'You and me against the world, Flight Lieuy Mad Bitch Deborah?'

'Damned right, Dirty Old Man.'

They watched some drivel on TV for an hour. Deborah fell asleep on him, as usual. She stirred when his phone buzzed and chimed.

A message from his dad.

> I'll be fine. Invite her. I'll behave.

He sighed; no unqualified enthusiasm for the idea, but a sign that he wanted to try. For his son's sake, if nothing else.

Deborah murmured against his chest. 'Everything OK, Dirty Old Man?'

'Getting better, Debs. Getting better.'

FORTY

Morning briefing saw Malkie nearly fail to persuade Thompson to ask the Fiscal for twelve more hours to question Davie Jessop, Steph caught Malkie's eye then nodded towards the reception area. He grabbed his coat and followed her.

As they passed the area behind the front desk, Sergeant Bernie Stevens glanced at them. Malkie offered her a weak smile; couldn't be sure just how shoogly a peg he was still on as far as she was concerned. She nodded back at him but with none of the obvious disdain she usually showed him.

Maybe I can be a proper adult one day, after all.

After a stop at the coffee cart in the public area of the Civic Centre, which housed the *polis* and the courts and the PF's office, they wandered the grounds outside to find an empty bench. Steph chose the one next to where he and Sandra Morton had sat when she had dropped her bombshells, first about having been pregnant and miscarried, then about him being a father after all. He wanted to ask Steph to move further along, choose a different bench, but he told himself he had his big-boy pants on today.

She took a while to speak. Malkie occupied himself trying

to hold his coat lapels closed over his chest with one hand to keep out the biting February temperatures. Steph's nose and cheeks had flushed and her breath came out in visible puffs, but she showed no sign of feeling the cold through her thin jacket other than the way she held her coffee cup.

'I saw Dean again.'

Malkie's heart sank. He waited for her to continue rather than barge in with well-intentioned but ever-clumsy questions.

'I met him for a coffee. Can you believe that? He called me, insisted we meet, so I insisted right back that we do it somewhere public and busy. Hence, coffee.'

She sighed. 'I should have known better, shouldn't I?'

'Depends.'

'On what?'

'On what happened. Did you...?'

'No, not this time. Didn't lay a finger on him. Not in a public place. I chose somewhere with lots of people not because I was afraid of him. Because I was afraid of what I might do to him in the absence of any witnesses. Bastard.'

Malkie noted another instance of Steph using Language, against type, but said nothing.

'He's threatening me, again. Says he has a video of me attacking Barry Boswell. Says he'll report that he saw me – not someone like me – running away from the attack on Boswell a few days ago. I told him I was curled up with a bottle of gin and a George Clooney film, but he asked me how well that would stand up as an alibi if someone happened to report seeing me at the scene of Boswell's assault.'

She leaned forward, rested her elbows on her knees, stared at the ground.

'It's never going to stop, is it, Malkie?'

Malkie fished for something encouraging to say but came up with something so far up the inappropriate scale he would have been proud of it in other circumstances.

'Chicken wire the bastard.'

She laughed. 'Shut up. I'm being serious.'

He said nothing. She had to look at him to check just how serious he was being, and he didn't give her anything. Part of him *wanted* to chicken wire the bastard.

She shook her head, and her smile disappeared. 'No. We can't. I can't. I wouldn't. Never.'

'Never ever?' he asked in a sing-song voice.

She smiled but only just. 'No. Stop it. Next suggestion.'

He let his mind drift. His ears heard traffic on the Almondvale Boulevard. Where Martin Jessop got smacked into by a boy racer in a souped-up Volkswagen. He opened his mouth.

'No.'

'No what?'

'No, we're not pushing him in front of a passing car. Or bus. Or truck. Not happening.'

He deflated. They ruminated in silence for a while until Malkie could bear it no longer.

'You know what Rab told me once? He was going to creative-writing classes but stopped on the advice of the tutor. He said one of the techniques they taught about creativity was to let your imagination run riot, go wild, really reach, you know? You'll come up with a lot of utter pish but somewhere in the pish might lurk a wee nugget that might actually work.'

She frowned at him. 'So?'

'So, let's do that. Let's start with something so awful even I wouldn't wish it on the bastard then work back to something maybe we can use? Even if just for the therapeutic value in it?'

She looked sceptical, but Malkie forged on.

'Let's bury him up to his neck in manure in a pigsty and run a hose on him until he drowns in shitey water.'

She shook her head at him, cast him a stern and disapproving look, but he saw a gleam in her eyes.

'OK. Too good for him. I agree.'

She slapped him on the arm.

'Ouch. How about we loosen the bolts on his balcony and get him so pissed he falls against it and drops to a nasty and sticky and very flattened death? No, SOCOs would see through that in a second.'

He felt himself getting into the swing of the exercise.

'How about you let me beat the shit out of you – Aye I know, but go with me on this one – then we blame it on him, somehow?'

She looked at him, and he was shocked to see interest there.

Really, Steph? I'm still joking. Just how mad are you at him?

She shook her head. 'No. I love you to bits for offering, but I'd have to fess up and resign and never sleep well again. Plus, I'd reduce you to a nasty wet stain on the ground.'

He shrugged, decided to give up his new therapy technique as a bad idea.

'What then? I can't bear to see you like this, all tense and angry and potty-mouthed. It's not like you. Well, not the potty-mouthed bit, anyway.'

'Shut up, old man.' She punched his arm.

He sensed that in other, more private circumstances she'd have allowed herself to lean her head on his shoulder, just for a while. In full view of the Civic Centre and the windows of their side of the open-plan police-station offices, she'd rather have her fingernails pulled out.

Malkie gave her a few minutes before deciding enough was enough.

'Do you feel like telling me, now, what you've already decided you want to do about him?'

She screwed her face up at him; he knew she always hated the rare occasions when he saw right through her.

'I think I'm going to have to give him more rope, let him think he's got me, make him stick his neck out. Maybe I can get him to double-up on his accusation about Boswell, but I'll find some way to verify my evening with George Clooney.

'Discredit the scumbag. Dean, I mean, not George Clooney. Obviously.'

'Aye. Future-proof myself against all and any future allegations from him.'

Malkie mulled this over, decided he liked it. 'I like it, but you need to iron-clad your alibi first, aye? Get it lined up and in your back pocket before you stick your neck out and goad him into making an even bigger arse of himself than he is already.'

'Aye. But it would work. Get him off my back without me crossing any lines. Well maybe a wee toe or so, but nothing I'd feel a need to resign over.'

'Then we just remind him periodically how much shite will fall on him if he even suggests you were involved in anything nefarious.'

'Nefarious?'

'Aye. Nefarious. Good word. Got it from one of Rab's short stories.'

'Any good?'

'Awful.'

They heard a shrill and demanding whistle from the direction of the Civic Centre and spotted Gucci outside the reception doors, waving at them to come back inside with some urgency.

As they walked back to the office, Malkie turned to Steph, grabbed her arm with excessive and fake excitement.

'And if that doesn't work, we wrap him in chicken wire *and* bury him up to his neck in a pigsty full of manure, aye?'

Steph tutted and shook her head but smiled.

When they reached the end of the lawns, Gucci could wait no longer and crossed the access road towards them.

Malkie felt a small spark of hope; Gucci looked excited.

'North Lanarkshire found nothing at Andrea Jessop's registered address in Glasgow, all dark and empty.'

'And you rushed out here to tell us that?' He regretted his tone as soon as he heard himself.

'No. Stevie Jessop owns two vehicles: an old Capri as well as his white Transit.'

Malkie could see there was more, but Gucci made him ask. 'And?'

She grinned. 'ANPR caught his van on the access road into Newcastle ferry terminal just after sixteen thirty last Thursday.'

Malkie and Steph shared a look. Too good to be true?

'Newcastle ferry goes to Amsterdam, doesn't it?'

Gucci was ready for him. 'Town called IJmuiden, but aye, as good as Amsterdam.'

Malkie strode inside the reception area. Preoccupied, he didn't think to make an effort to schmooze Desk Sergeant Bernie Stevens and only realised as he reached the door that she had already pressed the release button. He glanced at her, surprised, used to her making him wait several seconds. He nodded to her, and she nodded back. He yanked the door open and strode through towards the CID desks like a man on a mission.

When he reached his desk and Steph and Gucci had caught up with him, he clapped his hands.

'Right, troops. Gucci has, again – he nodded his recognition to her and Rab rolled his eyes – come through for us. Stevie Jessop's Transit van was spotted on ANPR entering Newcastle ferry terminal last Thursday. That means Amsterdam, which could mean wacky baccy; I'm not aware of the Jessops having graduated to Class A yet. I want ANPR searches fanning out north up the A1 from Newcastle, and west along the A69 in case they come up via South and North Lanarkshire.

'Lou, Rab, take one each and get markers put on that van. Lou has the registration. I want to know the instant it comes back into the country because I'm bloody certain Stevie Jessop will be in it, and if we don't find Elizabeth Dunn before he gets to her...'

He ran out of words; couldn't bear to voice what they'd all be thinking.

'He'll make her suffer. We know what those lowlifes are like, right?'

All three nodded their agreement. All three knew how much he'd understated the cruelty Stevie Jessop was capable of.

'I need to talk to Pam.'

Steph flashed him a look. Was she worried he wasn't sharing his troubles with her?

Even in her present circumstances, she wouldn't forgive him for that.

FORTY-ONE

Elizabeth heard footsteps on the stairs outside, and braced herself. They sounded light, not clumsy and heavy like Davie or Stan, but she had it in her head that every time that door opened might be the last.

The key turned in the lock, then nothing happened for several seconds. When Andrea's face appeared, she looked around as if ready to duck back and slam the door shut again as if expecting an ambush. When she saw Elizabeth sitting on the bed, she relaxed, but a look of dread remained.

She stepped inside and stood, feet together, hands clasped behind her, and took a few moments to summon the courage to say whatever she'd come to say.

'I want to let you out for a while. I can't bear the thought of you sitting in here all this time. It's not right.'

She looked at her feet. 'I want to trust you, Elizabeth, I really do, but how can I? If I were in your position, if I had...' She swallowed, took a breath. 'If I had a child worried sick about me, I'd do anything to get back to her. Anything.'

She raised her eyes, made herself look at Elizabeth, but she flinched and nearly looked away again. With a visible effort, she removed her hands from behind her back, and Elizabeth wondered just how terrified this poor woman had to be of her own brothers.

Andrea held a pair of handcuffs.

'No. Please. For the love of God, Andrea.'

Something broke in the woman. She threw her hands out to her sides as if pleading for an alternative. 'What, Elizabeth? What can I do? If I take a chance on trusting you and you do what I or any other mother would do, if you run, they'll kill me. And if I leave you rotting down here in the dark and sleeping in clothes you haven't changed for days, how can I live with myself?'

Tears broke through, poured from her, but she kept a watch on Elizabeth. Her sobs lasted only a few seconds, then left her looking broken and deflated, the handcuffs hanging at her side from a limp hand.

'What can I do?' Her voice small and ashamed and miserable.

'Nothing.'

Andrea looked up at her, her eyes hopeful.

'You're right. You can't let me out on trust, because you can trust me as little as I would trust you, if…' She couldn't finish her sentence.

Andrea fidgeted with the cuffs as if they were a gun that might go off in her hand. 'Stevie took these from a policeman he left unconscious in a gutter one night. He's always bragging about them, like they're some kind of trophy. The officer he assaulted had to retire on medical grounds. Stevie doesn't know when to stop. Actually, he does know, he just never wants to.'

Some small measure of steel returned to her. She stood straight, wiped her eyes with the back of one sleeve of her cardigan, fixed her eyes on Elizabeth as a decision obvious to both of them had been made.

Elizabeth saw no other choice. She remembered the way

Andrea had been dressed when they first met, as if just back from a run. And she did look fit. No lightweight, either; she saw little spare fat in her face, but her thighs were thick and her shoulders and arms carried some bulk. Had to be toned muscle. No, even if she could break free and run, she doubted she'd get far.

As perverse as the situation was, as much as Elizabeth feared being handcuffed, and as much as she believed Andrea loathed herself for her actions, she could see the sun and sit outside for a while in handcuffs, or stay here and rot.

She turned her back on Andrea and crossed her wrists behind her.

'No. Front, please.'

Elizabeth turned back again and held her hands out. Andrea threw the cuffs on the floor. Elizabeth picked them up and slapped them on her wrists. They felt cold and brutal.

After stepping forward and checking at arm's length that they were secure, Andrea surprised Elizabeth by hugging her. She heard Andrea's tears return, and her small voice say, 'I'm sorry. This isn't me.'

When Andrea stepped back again, Elizabeth gave her arm a squeeze. 'I believe that.'

They shared a moment and a small smile, then Andrea turned and led Elizabeth up the stairs.

'They're not here, I take it?'

'No, and stuck out here they can only arrive by car, so we'll hear them in plenty of time to get you back downstairs. You'll be safe. We'll be safe.'

Elizabeth got her first real look at Andrea's home.

Thick stone walls, ancient-looking cross-sparred window frames well-maintained and painted and adorned with white curtains with a faint floral print. Outside, trees and a gravel path and a flower bed that Elizabeth needed no horticultural experience to know was a labour of love. The sun and the colours flooded her eyes like a balm, and she suddenly dreaded the inevitable moment she would need to walk herself back down to the cellar, because she'd resigned herself: even if she managed to escape, what would the price be? Crack Andrea over the head with something and if that didn't kill her, her brothers would? Could she do that for Sophie? The answer came in an instant: yes, she bloody could, but she loathed herself for it anyway.

The flower motif continued through the hallway and into the kitchen; everything soft and gentle but nowhere near crossing a line into twee.

The kitchen held a massive, solid wooden table and similarly heavy-looking chairs. A huge Aga range filled all of one wall, and she felt heat radiate from it. She sat on a chair and held her hands out, felt warmth caress her fingers and chase away a chill that hadn't left her since she'd arrived. Andrea looked appalled to see just how cold her guest had been.

Andrea fussed about, made tea and sandwiches, kept one eye on Elizabeth at all times. She had seemed to regain some scrap of confidence, as if Elizabeth seeing the outside world and not making an immediate break for it reassured her.

Andrea sat opposite Elizabeth and slid a steaming mug and plate of sandwiches across. The tea, the same as she'd been given in the cellar, tasted a world apart in brighter and less claustrophobic surroundings.

She drank and ate, and felt, if not good, then less desperate and miserable than she had since she became nothing better than a cheap criminal.

When she replaced her mug on the table, she noticed how filthy her fingernails had become. This seemed one too many insults to her dignity. She glanced at the door to the outside world. Could she make it? Could her fierce determination to return to her family dig reserves of strength out of her she didn't even know she possessed?

Andrea noticed and scowled. She stood.

'Come.'

FORTY-TWO

'No.'

Malkie stared at his hands clasped but fidgety on the table in the meeting room. 'You have to, Pam. Callum's adamant, so I want to see it.'

She sat forward; was that a subtle psychological sign that her interest had been piqued? That she wanted to hear more?

'No.'

Fuck.

'I won't be doing anything wrong by visiting the scene of my mum's death, not if I'm accompanying you and you can confirm I stayed in the car the whole time.'

'Damn it, Malkie. I'll check it out, but you don't go near it.'

Malkie waited.

'I'll go look at it, but that's all I can promise, OK? I may not even be able to declare a new crime scene based on one bit of metal, even if it's still forensically viable after all this time. But I'll look at it. If it's there, I'll bag it and show it to Thompson, ask if she'll authorise some SOCO budget on it. Best I can offer you, mate.'

Pam stood.

Malkie stood. 'No. I'm coming with you.'

Her eyes flared and she opened her mouth to tear him a new arsehole, but he raised his hands, cut her off.

'I'll stay in the car. I promise. If you think it worth bringing in, I'd appreciate a look after you've bagged it, but that's all I'll ask. I swear.'

He held three fingers up. 'Scout's honour.' He grinned.

She didn't. 'You were a Cub Scout? Really?'

'Aye, still got my woggle somewhere.'

She sighed at him. 'Only you can make the word *woggle* sound rude.'

'I know. It's a talent. Anyway, I'm coming with you. I said I'll be good.'

She seemed to sag. 'How can I refuse. I'm not a complete ice queen, you know.'

Malkie bit his tongue as he stood and followed her. She collected her coat from her chair and advised her DCs she would be back in an hour, then walked off towards the rear exit and the pool-car garage without bothering to check Malkie followed her.

When Pam parked outside the garden gate, Malkie's memory flashed on Callum Gourlay standing before him, broken and ashamed of himself, of what may well have been his sole major screw-up in decades of service to the Scottish Fire and Rescue Service's Fire Investigation team.

Did Pam believe his story about Callum calling him and Malkie refusing to go with him to the house?

She pointed at him. 'You. Do not. Move. Understood?'

He started to lift his hand to give her another Boy Scout promise, but settled for a 'Yes, Pam,' instead.

She shook her head. 'Oh, grow up.' She sounded just like Steph; was it him after all?

Pam closed the door behind her then turned back to the window. Malkie lowered it.

'Left-hand window, nearest the front door, yes?'

'That's what Callum told me, aye. Right beneath it, right where some fucker could have been standing when he—'

She silenced him with a raised finger and a look that promised an early return to the station if he pushed his luck. He clamped his lips shut again and heard her remove something, a responder evidence kit he assumed.

When she returned, an agonising ten minutes later, she looked troubled and held two evidence bags, a small plastic one and a larger paper one. Malkie's heart leaped; she shared his interest in the find. The small one had to contain the lighter and the larger, the newspaper.

When she'd sat back in the car, she held the plastic one up for Malkie to see. He lifted a hand to it, a reflex action, and she pulled it away from him.

'Look. Don't touch.'

He lowered his hand but held both out palms up to show compliance.

The lighter looked different somehow, out of the ground. Less suspicious. He felt a rush of doubt. Was he setting hares running that would just come back and bite him on the arse?

Didn't matter. The truth mattered. Justice mattered. Closure mattered. He hated that word, closure, but finding himself in need of it in so many ways these days, he allowed it to take a temporary place in his acceptable terminology list.

Pam sent a text, then waited until a chime from her phone announced a reply. 'The boss says she wants to see it first before she'll commit to reopening and spending on forensics. Well, prints to begin with.'

'What's in the other bag?'

'A newspaper. It was covering the lighter.'

He pretended to chew on this for a moment. 'What date?'

Pam sighed; she'd have expected the question because it's what she would have asked. 'The seventeenth of July last year.'

Malkie held his hands out. 'There you go. And it was *under* the lighter? Which means it was there around the time my mum died.'

'Slow down, Malkie.' Her tone softened, and he doubted many in the station had ever heard that happen. 'I agree it looks...' – she thought for a second – 'interesting. That's as far as I'm prepared to go, for now.'

'I'll take that. Thanks.'

Pam started the engine and Malkie settled in for the short journey back to the station.

He couldn't settle his mind on whether he and his dad really were ready for where this might lead.

Doesn't matter. We're going there.

FORTY-THREE

Elizabeth followed Andrea to a door in the hallway, nausea washing through her in waves. She couldn't believe Andrea would hurt her, but just how afraid was she?

Andrea opened the door and ushered Elizabeth inside.

A tiny bathroom with a shower and one window too small for anyone to squeeze through. The door, like every other door she'd seen, even the internal ones, looked to be heavy, solid wood, and on the way in she noticed a lock on it too. Did every door in a property of this age have a lock and key, or did the bathroom just not have an inbuilt lock?

Andrea gestured for Elizabeth to go in, then twirled her fingers to turn her around. She removed one wrist from the handcuffs then backed out quickly. Elizabeth heard the lock turn.

The decor was as gentle as the living room she'd glimpsed on her way to the bathroom. She wondered if Andrea had always been the feminine type, or if she'd decorated the place as a refuge from the ugliness of her family. She hoped the poor woman found the peace she craved here. Until the next time her bastard brothers appeared.

Andrea's jogging gear hung over the glass shower partition. Elizabeth lifted them down, folded them and laid them on the toilet seat. She stripped, turned the shower on and held her fingers under the flow. It took a while for hot water to come through, probably not unusual in a building of this age. When it did, she stepped under and moaned in pleasure. Her hair felt gritty and sticky as she wet it and the silky flow of shampoo over it lifted her spirits while she lost herself in the luxury of what would, any other day, be a normal part of her routine. She needed two washes and a healthy dose of conditioner to feel human again. Then she washed herself, and even that restored her like she'd never take for granted again.

When she stepped out, she saw Andrea had left her fresh clothes: joggers and a sweatshirt, even some new underwear still in the wrapper. Elizabeth had been blessed with a modest cup size, so she could survive a few days without a bra. She remembered telling Andrew how she once thought she'd grow up big and bosomy, like her mother. When Andrew had asked her what happened, with a fake disappointed look at her breasts, she'd replied that she'd obviously got lucky.

She stood, dried her pixie-cut hair and finger-styled it, then dressed.

When she knocked on the door, the key turned, and it opened only a few inches. Had Andrea been waiting outside the door all this time? Of course she had; she was so terrified of her brothers her head would be filled with fear that Elizabeth, unwatched, would manage to escape, somehow, even from that bathroom. As Elizabeth had learned herself, clear-thinking and logic would always be an early victim of this kind of experience.

'Can you hold your hands out please, Elizabeth. Sorry.' Andrea's tone revealed just how sorry she was.

Elizabeth manoeuvred both hands between the door and the wall and Andrea refastened the opened cuff. When she pushed the door fully open, she looked no less ashamed of herself as before.

'Thank you, Andrea. Really. Thank you.' She reached out to give Andrea's hand a squeeze, but she snatched her arm back and stuffed the handcuff key back into her jogger pocket.

After a moment when neither found words, Andrea nodded to the kitchen. 'Let's at least get some sun on you, shall we?'

At the back door, Andrea draped a puffer jacket over Elizabeth's shoulders, then opened the door.

Blinding sunlight blasted in, made Elizabeth screw her eyes shut. She stepped outside, felt an icy blast of air that seemed to pour over her face and neck and left her feeling more awake than for days. Even if she got away, even if she could outrun Andrea with cuffs on and one side of her face swollen and agonised, she had no idea far she might have to run before the cold took her.

Andrea led her to a patio set and sat her down. A jug, two glasses, an ice bucket and two bottles sat on the table along with a bowl of fresh cherries. As Andrea poured measures of gin into Elizabeth's glass, she looked at her, appalled.

'You do like gin, don't you?'

Elizabeth could drink it but wasn't a huge fan. 'I love it, Andrea. Thanks.'

Andrea's relief was palpable. She finished pouring them both healthy measures topped up with tonic and ice and then dropped a handful of cherries into each with a flourish.

Each lifted their glass, Elizabeth feeling clumsy with her hands so close together. Andrea seemed to trawl her mind for something to toast to and came up blank, as their shared situation dictated.

Elizabeth saved her. 'To doing what we need to do?'

Andrea's smile was weak and guilty. 'To doing what we need to do.' Elizabeth had to wonder if she saw a gleam of something in Andrea's eyes, something cold and dangerous. Could she dare to hope it was more than just empty sentiment for her?

They drank, then shared the silence for long minutes. Birds sang in the dense forest that ringed the property. She heard a car drive past, its engine muffled by what sounded like quite some distance. Too far to stumble to in her condition and in these temperatures.

No wonder the Jessop brothers had brought her here. She shivered and nausea forced her to replace her glass on the table.

Andrea couldn't help but notice. 'I'm sorry.'

Elizabeth leaned over, reached for Andrea's hand. Andrea started to reach back but recoiled when she saw the steel of the handcuffs glint in the sunlight.

Each returned to their individual thoughts.

Elizabeth cast her eyes around. 'Your garden is lovely.'

Andrea smiled, but barely, as if she felt undeserving of the compliment. 'I only work part-time now, so I get to spend a lot of time on it. Too cold now, of course, but you should see it in the spring and summer. The colours... I landscaped a lot of it myself, but I haven't had the strength for quite some years.'

Elizabeth noticed she rubbed her wrists. 'Arthritis?'

Andrea realised what she was doing and laced her fingers together. 'No. It's, er...' She seemed to make a decision. 'It's osteoporosis.'

'Really? You can't be much older than your forties, can you?'

Andrea took a moment to continue. 'I developed osteoporosis as a side-effect of some problems I had with my weight.' Her eyes remained downcast throughout this admission.

Elizabeth's mind filled in the gaps, and her heart ached for the poor woman. She risked asking, as gently as she could, 'Stress-related weight problems?'

Andrea nodded but kept her eyes down. 'Stevie and Davie made my life difficult for many years. I... I handled their bullying badly. When they found out how badly they could hurt me, even our father made them stop. They always despised me for being so weak.' The shame in her voice made Elizabeth angry beyond words.

They lapsed into an embarrassed silence, and Elizabeth wondered just how many people Andrea had ever shared this with. She felt a need to reciprocate, to share back. But she could barely bring herself to recall her previous, troubled life even in the privacy of her own mind, let alone articulate it and hear it spoken out loud.

'I don't have any brothers or sisters.'

She saw Andrea look up, her eyes eager. Did this woman have any friends at all?

'I always wished I had. I thought it would be good to have a big brother to look after me.' She wondered if even the word 'brother' now did nothing more for Andrea than trigger memories of past trauma, but she made herself continue.

'My parents tried their best for me, but I could never really share the secret stuff with them, you know?'

Andrea managed a weak smile.

'When I left home and went through uni – economics degree – and landed a job on a whacking great salary, I was full of myself. Only-child syndrome, maybe. Thought I could take on the world because that was all I'd ever been told, that I could do anything I wanted.'

Memories of just how sour that had gone flooded her, and she felt dirty.

'I learned the hard way how the patriarchy is alive and well in the finance industry, even these days.'

Andrea's voice surprised her. 'Did someone hurt you?'

'No. Well, not physically. I was young and fit and – I was told – attractive, and it never occurred to me to avoid any kind of behaviour that wasn't strictly professional. I was friendly and loved to party, you know?'

Andrea's eyes said loud and clear that no, she had no idea what a life like that was like.

'Anyway, a man decided I was fair game. A man far more senior than I was and far more powerful than I realised. He tried it on with me. Wouldn't take no for an answer. I had to get physical with him.'

She stalled, realised she'd never shared this much detail about her awful experience with anyone except Andrew.

'I complained, raised a case with HR.'

Again, Andrea's eyes spoke for her. 'And that ended badly for you, didn't it?'

Elizabeth felt shame sluice through her. Shame and fury. She'd been vilified and character-assassinated and made out to be nothing more than a cheap slut trying to extort cash from a pillar of the Scottish establishment. Her mind flashed as highlights reel past her: a tribunal; press stories; friends who forgot and friends who remembered whatever suited their careers best.

She roused herself, found Andrea watching her with empathy so raw it burned in her eyes.

Elizabeth scanned the garden again, desperate to direct the conversation to more positive ground. She noticed what looked like the side of a hot tub, poking out from behind one corner of the building. Ten feet from it, a bench, massive and heavy-looking, a marble seat supported by a black-painted wrought-iron back and sides. It looked older than the cottage.

Andrea's eyes followed Elizabeth's and she seemed every bit as keen to move on to more banal and less painful things. 'That damned hot tub isn't mine. Well, I bought it, but...'

Elizabeth frowned at her, questioning.

'Stevie uses it, he and Davie and that awful man Stan. They use it when they come here. First thing I have to do every time they appear is clean it, fill it and heat it, even if that means I'm still filling it when they go upstairs to trash my bedrooms.'

She drifted for a minute, and Elizabeth saw specific thoughts chewed over.

'They come and get drunk in it for a night or two, trash my home, then leave again. Costs me a fortune and I can't bring myself to get into it anymore, but better they're getting drunk and shooting up in it than bothering me, I suppose.'

'Shooting up? They do drugs in your home?' Elizabeth's loathing flared in her.

Andrea nodded. 'I was tempted – just once – to...' For a moment she looked not ashamed, but regretful, as if she'd missed some opportunity.

To do what? To call the police and hope the amount of coke was big enough to see them put away for life? Or worse, had she been tempted to take some herself to numb the worst of her repeated ordeals? Worse still, had she considered overdosing on the stuff? Let them find her dead, and prints and DNA from her brothers all over the bag?

Andrea seemed to return from somewhere and remember Elizabeth was there. 'Oh no. My stupid bloody big mouth. Please forget I said that.'

For some reason she couldn't explain for now, Elizabeth needed to ask more. 'What do they take?' Her memory flashed on drunken arseholes at financial-services parties pumping all sorts of rubbish into themselves. Because they could afford to, at first. Conspicuous consumption. Wasn't that the expression? Later, she'd taken some small but guilty pleasure in hearing a few of them had been arrested and sent to prison.

When she returned to the moment, Andrea's face had taken on a whole new fearful pallor. 'They've only ever brought tiny little bags with them, but...'

'Andrea?'

'I saw a big bag a while ago. Like the size of a bag of sugar. I saw Davie pulling it out of the engine of Stevie's van. He's so thick he stood there with it in his hand, turning it over, sniffing, hefting it, you know? Like he thought no one could be watching him here.'

Elizabeth felt ice flood her veins and her stomach turned over. The Jessops. Drug dealers. She was a dead woman.

Andrea reacted to Elizabeth's sudden realisation. She stood.

'I'm sorry. You need to go back downstairs now. They could come back any time.' She stood but couldn't meet Elizabeth's eyes.

Was this the time? Would she get another opportunity to get back to Sophie? Justify the risk of Andrea hurting her, of losing Andrea's trust? Would she tell her brothers and that would be the last she'd see of the woman, her only lifeline in these dire circumstances?

While Elizabeth agonised over what to do, Andrea appeared behind her and took one arm. Her grip was firm now.

She'd blown it. Andrea would never trust her now.

Paralysed by indecision and fear, she allowed herself to be guided back into the house and down the stairs to the cellar.

She couldn't even find the energy to thank Andrea for the short and merciful period of respite.

As she lay on her back on the bed, she couldn't stop thinking about the fact that the man she'd killed was the nephew of a drug dealer.

And a Jessop, of all people.

FORTY-FOUR

As they drove back to the station, Malkie's phone chimed at him. A text from Gucci.

> When will you be back, boss?

> Minutes. Why?

> Stevie Jessop, Newcastle ferry terminal, twenty minutes ago.

Stevie would take at least two and a half hours to drive back to central Scotland, so he had time to plan his approach.

Only then did he realise he had no idea what his approach would be. He thought fast; the troops would expect him to lead them. The best direct action he could take would be to confront Stevie as soon as he arrived home, see if the appearance of him and Steph and a couple of Uniforms seemed to rattle him, which might confirm possession of a package of weed. That alone, if they managed to catch him unawares, might give them reasonable cause for an immediate vehicle search, although he doubted a man like Stevie Jessop would allow himself to let that happen.

Aye, wait at his home address, nab him as he stepped from his van, try to rattle him a bit. If nothing else, put some awkward questions to him about his brother.

He'd barely stepped into the CID area of the office when Gucci beckoned him over to her desk, an eager look on her face.

'10:03. Jessop's van.' She pointed to a black and white CCTV photo. He could see a figure behind the wheel but no real detail.

'And the registration is definitely his?'

'Aye. It's his.'

She turned her seat to face him. Rab turned too.

Malkie scanned the office. 'Where's Steph?'

Gucci looked to Rab; neither looked happy. Gucci went for it.

'Thompson asked her for a word in private. They only talked for a few minutes, then Steph charged out with a face like thunder, grabbed her things and stormed out the back way.'

'Did she say anything?'

Rab frowned. 'Steph or Thompson?'

'Steph, of course.' Rab flinched at Malkie's loud snap at him. 'Sorry, Rab. Did Steph say anything?'

Rab shook his head. 'Nothing, boss. Just grabbed her stuff and left like she was worried she might punch something. Thompson's still in there.' He nodded towards the meeting rooms.

Malkie saw Thompson hunched over some papers on the table, her head in her hands. He knocked on the door and entered without waiting for an invitation. He said nothing, just sat opposite her and waited.

Thompson shuffled the papers together and returned them to a manila folder. She sighed, squeezed her fingers in her eyes.

'Steph's stepfather, Dean Lang—'

'I know who that fucker is.'

She frowned at him but didn't make a thing of it. 'He's bloody called Crimestoppers, again. I had a marker put on his name and he was only too happy to waive his anonymity this time.' She took a breath. 'Claims some copper threatened him, tried to strangle him. In public. Says he has video of it, and a witness.'

'*Some copper?*'

'That's all he said. For now.'

She threw her pen across the room, a feeble way to vent her fury, but the only alternative was a mug that looked full of cold coffee.

'I thought she was better than that, Malkie. Didn't you?' Thompson looked appalled, as if Steph had been some kind of standard for professionalism in a police officer. Until now.

'She is. Lang is a sneaky wee fucker. Sorry, Susan.'

'No, you're fine with *fucker* in this case.'

'He's been pushing Steph's buttons ever since she found out about... Well, you know. I knew it had rattled her, but I had no idea it went so deep into her. Although, I'm not sure I'd handle it any better if I found out someone had raped my mother, and I was the result.'

Memories of his own mother, weak and pale in bed, exhausted; how could he not have seen she was dying?

'Malkie. Stop that. Focus.'

'Sorry. Anyway, I thought she was handling it. You know what she's like, like some bloody motor that just keeps going no matter what hits it.'

They sat in silence for a moment, Malkie asking himself how he could have underestimated the strain she was under to have been acting so out of character. He guessed Thompson would be asking herself similar questions; had she failed in her duty of care as Steph's senior officer and – Malkie didn't doubt – her friend, too?

'She dragged me out to the grounds earlier today. Admitted

she was struggling. Would you believe we joked about how we could bump him off without getting caught.'

Thompson managed a small smile. 'Chicken wire?'

Malkie smiled back. 'She's mentioned it to you too, has she?'

'On more than one occasion. If I ever find out she's been shopping in B&Q I'm putting a tail on her.'

Their fondness for Steph couldn't fight off their worry for long.

'Should I desk her for a while, Malkie?'

'Christ, no. That would kill her.'

He worked the problem through in his mind. Thompson sipped her coffee, grimaced, and put it down again.

'She needs to stay active. Until – if – Dean makes a formal complaint, you do what the manual says you have to do, but for now, I'll keep her close, keep an eye on her. I honestly don't know what else we can do.'

'And Dean?'

'I could have another word with him.'

'*Another* word?'

Damn it. I should not have said that.

'I gave him a warning after he ambushed Steph in his flat with... Barry Boswell.' He couldn't bear to name Boswell's relationship to Steph; there were plenty of other words he could choose to describe him, but not that.

Thompson's eyes turned severe. 'You didn't touch him, right?'

'Of course not.'

Well, unless you count pushing him against the balcony of his seventh-storey flat and threatening to launch him towards the ground.

'Well, not much.'

Thompson heaved a sigh. 'Oh, Malkie. Seriously?'

He couldn't answer and disappointment joined the irritation on Thompson's face.

'He won't report me, I don't think. I think I put the shits up him pretty well.'

'You?'

He stared back at her. 'Aye, me. Contrary to expectations, I can be quite scary when I get my temper up. Anyway, I can remind him.'

'No. Don't you bloody dare. Does it not occur to you how he could spin that? Coppers closing ranks, physically intimidating an innocent man to protect one of their own?'

'Innocent?' Malkie's temper over-topped.

'Yes.' She shouted now; had to take a breath but held a finger out to warn Malkie not to speak until she'd finished. 'That's the way his brief would spin it, and you should have thought of that. Oh, you bloody idiot. Does Steph know?'

He nodded, couldn't speak.

Thompson shook her head, her disappointment plain. 'There's no helping you sometimes, mate. And enough people want to.'

He leaned forward on the table, folded his arms, stared down at the pen-marked lacquer on the wood.

'I was angry. What those fuckers did to her. It was too much, Susan.'

She sagged back into her chair. 'I know. It was. But you going after him like that is never going to help, Malkie. You see that, don't you?'

Malkie felt his anger rise. 'I do, but some people don't respond to anything other than direct and in-your-face danger. You know the type.'

'Aye. I do. And I also know that type can be sneaky as hell.'

She stood. The bollocking was over.

'Do not go anywhere near Lang or Boswell again without a damned good and verifiable reason. Understand?'

Malkie sulked. How was he supposed to look after Steph when he couldn't take direct action?

'I said, do you understand, Detective Sergeant McCulloch?'

Shit. Full title. She's seriously pissed off this time.

'Yes, ma'am. I understand.'

He opened his mouth to complain some more but the shake of her head and the threat in her eyes shut his mouth again. She left and he returned to his desk.

Steph reappeared, leaned in, rested her fists on his desk, leaned into his ear.

'What the hell have you done now?'

'I told her I had a word with Dean, the last time. She didn't take it well.'

Steph groaned. 'And did you tell her I know you did that?'

He trawled his short-term memory of the conversation. 'I don't think so, no.'

'Great. So, she'll guess I do, and now she knows I didn't mention it to her. Thanks for that, mate.' She stomped away back to her desk, dropped into her chair, and squeezed her fingers into her eyes.

Nice one. Even by your standards, mate.

Rab, of all people, gave him a way out.

'Stevie Jessop got ANPR'd coming into Edinburgh on the Old Craighall roundabout, ten minutes ago.'

Steph and Gucci turned in their chairs. Malkie expected a glare from Steph, but she blanked him.

'Damn it, he could be less than a half hour from home by now. Steph, with me, please. Rab, Gucci, stay here but be ready to grab a couple of Uniforms and get there pronto. I don't want us arriving mob-handed or he'll squeal about victimisation and just cause, etc. We're only going to have a word with him about the sad death of his nephew Martin, but if he gives us the smallest reason to think he's brought something exotic back from Amsterdam, I want you there ASAP.'

FORTY-FIVE

Malkie parked up at one end of the street on which the Jessop home sat, close enough to see clearly and no closer.

The journey had been less painful than he might have feared, Steph too focused on their high-speed drive to take more bites out of him.

The wait when they arrived, though, was excruciating. As hard as he trawled his mind for something to say that wouldn't set her off, he came up blank. He'd screwed up trying to threaten Lang, he saw that now. At the time, he'd been blinkered by rage, furious beyond measure at what Lang and Boswell were putting her through. The best person Malkie could ever remember knowing being menaced by two of the worst, and legally, he had no recourse until one of them actually did something that got witnessed. His helplessness stuck in his throat. How many times had he bemoaned the difference between justice and the law? Was a modern-day Police Scotland officer even allowed to voice criticism of the vast gulf between the two? And now, a woman who devoted herself to upholding the law for all without prejudice was in danger of having her career wrecked by two animals and he could do nothing about it. Not without pushing his luck and risking his career along with hers.

He wanted to rant about it to her, to reassure her that he understood the perversity of the situation and that he burned to do something more effective than give Dean an official, recorded warning. Although a warning was unlikely to be followed up by an ever-dwindling number of officers with too many more urgent cases to worry about than a troublesome wee weasel like him.

'He's here.' Steph didn't snap at him, but her tone told him she'd moved into professional mode, one that may or may not include forgiving him yet.

Malkie removed his seatbelt and straightened in his seat, as if that would improve his sight line.

'Get down, you idiot.'

Not yet forgiven, then.

Stevie Jessop parked outside his home. He took a few seconds to leave the van. Malkie could only hope he wasn't looking forward to a discussion with his genius brother Davie.

When he did climb out, he stared straight at them.

'Fuck.' Malkie opened his door. Steph did the same.

As they walked towards him, he planted his feet apart and crossed his arms over his massive chest. He wore a body-builder's style of vest, to allow appreciation of as much of his hard gym work as possible. His forearms looked thicker than Malkie's thighs.

'What's the fuckin' idea? Arrestin' ma brother? For what?'

'Can we talk inside, Mr Jessop?'

'Don't suppose I can refuse, can I? Paula told me you've put a fuckin' copper *inside* my house? Are you takin' the fuckin' piss or what? I have kids.'

Malkie's temper broke early. He stood nose-to-nose with Stevie, his natural fear of anyone with a thicker neck than his temporarily washed away by a wave of rage.

Stevie's arms unfolded and he held them at his side, veins bulging and his hands in tight fists. His chest became even more massive as he puffed himself up to his most intimidating, but Malkie was seeing nothing but red mist.

'Yes. We have a fucking copper inside your house because your fucking idiot brother invited us in, and my colleague here discovered feasible fucking evidence that Elizabeth Dunn has been here. So yes, I think we should fucking talk inside your fucking house, don't you? Fucker?'

He felt Steph's hand on his arm. He maintained his glare into Stevie's eyes but clamped his lips shut.

Stevie looked surprised; he wouldn't be used to people standing up to him. And while the man could break Malkie like a sodden twig, even he knew better than to assault a CID detective with a Uniform standing nearby. He backed up a step.

He glanced at Steph, who Malkie knew would be staring at him like a punchbag she was considering beating the shite out of, then turned and walked towards the house.

As Malkie threw the front door open and it slammed against the hallway wall, heavy and hurried footsteps on the stair preceded the Uniform's face appearing over the banister, looking ready for trouble. Eager, even. He had to be bored to distraction.

Stevie spotted him. 'What? You might be allowed to hang around in my house, but you stay out of my way, copper. You hear me?'

The Uniform took another step down, his face dark and promising violence, but Malkie held a hand up.

'Thanks, mate. Just stay on that door, make sure no one goes in there until the SOCOs get here, aye?'

He gave Malkie a look that promised instant aid given the smallest excuse, then nodded and disappeared again.

Stevie had gone through to the living room where Malkie had interviewed his brother. He threw himself into a chair and glared at him. Malkie stood in the doorway and returned his look.

'When will you release my brother. He's done fuck-all wrong.'

Malkie pretended to be taken aback by this information. 'Oh. Sorry. In that case... Detective Constable Lang, can you call the station and have Davie Jessop released, please, with an apology for our terrible mistake, aye?'

Steph didn't move an inch.

'I think my colleague has a problem with one wee fact, Mr Jessop.'

Stevie waited. He was known to be smarter than his brother. Still no Einstein but a scabby dug would be smarter than Davie.

'How can you be so sure your brother has done nothing wrong? You've been out of the country since Thursday, haven't you? Somewhere nice?'

Stevie said nothing for a moment. He would correctly assume that Malkie knew exactly where he'd been.

'Amsterdam.'

Malkie grinned. 'Lovely. Bit of sightseeing, coffee and cake, aye?'

A feral gleam appeared in Stevie's eyes. 'Never touch the stuff, mate. I treat my body better than that.' He folded his arms across his chest as if to accentuate the thick ropes of muscle that ran the length of his forearms.

'Yes. Very impressive, Mr Jessop.' Malkie sat on the sofa, propped his elbows on his knees and clasped his hands, leaned forward as if he were there to talk about home insurance.

'We found Elizabeth Dunn's bracelet hanging in the hedge outside here.'

'Who's she?' Stevie feigned innocence but it looked all wrong on him.

Malkie sighed; this kind of game never stopped boring him.

'Elizabeth Dunn is a shoplifter, who your nephew, Martin, was chasing when he was run over. Oh, and sincere condolences for your loss, by the way. Anyway, she's gone missing.'

Malkie was pleased to see some reaction from Stevie. A flaring of his nostrils. Even more tightening of his arm muscles. A warning in his eyes.

'Mr Jessop?'

'No idea. Never heard of her. All I know is all this happened while I was out of the country, so if you don't mind, I'm knackered after a bad night's sleep on the ferry and a long drive home. I'd like you both to fuck off, please.'

Malkie held his gaze but knew he had nothing to compel Stevie to talk. As the man had said, he had about the best alibi possible. Which didn't mean he had nothing to do with Elizabeth's abduction; he doubted Davie would have done something so stupid without Stevie's instructions. But however much he could prove Stevie and Davie had called each other several times in two days, no clever technology could confirm what they said to each other.

He had nothing on Stevie. He knew it and Stevie knew it. Time for a change of tack.

'So, did you bring anything nice home with you? From Amsterdam?'

He watched the man, his eyes scanning him for any of the minuscule non-verbal clues he'd learned about at Tulliallan, anything that might betray nervousness.

He saw nothing.

'Nothin'. I did have lots of coffee and cake, took in a couple of sex shows, you know, the ones where they do it on stage right in front of you? Brilliant. But mostly I just walked along the canals and contemplated my life and all its blessings, you know?' He grinned, looked pleased with the quality of his *fuck you* shite.

Malkie grinned, chummy and conspiratorial. 'And I

suppose you couldn't visit the sex capital of Europe and not get your own wick a bit wet, right?'

Stevie made an obvious act of checking the hallway. 'I would never dream of indulging in that kind of thing, Detective. I love my wife, and she meets my needs nicely. You look like you could do with some, though.' He grinned back at Malkie, seeming more pleased with himself with every exchange.

'Well, I'm glad to see your brother being arrested hasn't ruined your sense of humour. You're not worried about him, no?'

Stevie's grin vanished. 'Like I said, I don't know fuck-all about what you seem to think he's been up to, so I can't really comment, can I?'

Malkie felt it happen: the admission to himself that he had nothing. Not on Stevie, anyway; Davie was fucked.

Malkie stood. 'Thanks for your time, Mr Jessop. I'm sure your brother will let you know if we ever release him so you can collect him from the station.'

Stevie's expression turned dangerous. 'He'll be home sooner than you think, Pig.'

'Hmm. We'll see.' Malkie left, Steph preceding him. He glanced up the stairs towards the bored Uniform. 'I'll try to hurry the SOCOs up, mate.'

'That'd be great. Thanks.' Malkie doubted he'd heard anyone sound more pissed off in weeks.

In the car, both Malkie and Steph sat in silence until Malkie saw fit to pass comment.

'Fucker.'

Steph said nothing. Still mad at him or too pissed off at Stevie to risk opening her mouth?

'All we can do is watch him, hope he's impatient to get to Elizabeth Dunn.'

Steph spoke now.

'But if we miss him and he gets to her before we do...'

He started the car, slammed it into gear and took off before either of them felt compelled to complete that sentence.

FORTY-SIX

The tedious admin stuff over with again, Malkie leaned forward and clasped his hands on the table.

'So, Davie—'

'No comment.'

Although Malkie had expected nothing else, he ached to reach over, grab Davie Jessop by the scruff of his police-issue sweatshirt and slam his smug face into the tabletop.

He took a breath and smiled; how many times had he watched some scrote sit in that same chair and pull the same legal armour on? Or so they thought. His brief, Paul Drayford – a plain-looking man in a grey suit that Malkie thought looked like the same supermarket ones he bought – should have warned him that '*No comment*' wasn't the magic bullet most thought it to be. Interview under caution was the first, and sometimes the only, opportunity most people got to secure themselves a sympathetic hearing and – in worst-case scenarios – leniency once in a witness box in front of a Beak.

'I'm sure you'll have already been advised how unhelpful that response is if relied on too heavily.' He glanced at Drayford, who shrugged as if to say *I can tell them, but I can't make them.*

'So. Mr Jessop. May I call you Davie?'

'No comment.'

Drayford rolled his eyes. Malkie assumed he'd sat back from the table so his client wouldn't see such reactions; he must have known from his pre-interview conversation with Davie that the moron would behave this way.

'Did you abduct—'

'No comment.'

'It's in your interests to—'

'No comment.'

Malkie almost chuckled, a genuine release of his amusement at the idiocy of the man in front of him who thought himself invincible and unchargeable as long as he gave them nothing.

Drayford managed a full sentence. 'My client has the right not to say anything at all if he so desires.'

Davie turned to him and grinned. 'No comment.'

Malkie shared a look with Renfield. He thought for a second, settled on a change of tack.

'Mr Jessop—'

'No comment.'

'Noted. A man who we believe resembles you was seen to abduct a woman called Elizabeth Dunn from her home. Was that you, Davie?'

'No comment.'

'Fair enough. When you willingly allowed my colleague, Detective Constable Lang, to use your bathroom, she happened to spot something which drew her attention.'

Nothing.

'Do you know what that was, Davie? What she found?'

'No comment.'

'Aye, you said. We found Elizabeth Dunn's bracelet hanging in your hedge. Can you explain that?'

Malkie saw it and didn't doubt Steph did too. That momentary tightening of the musculature, the flick of the eyes to anywhere but the *polis* but then right back again in case they gave something away by not keeping eye contact. Davie had to swallow before answering.

'No—'

'Comment. Yes, we know. You know we have SOCOs there right now?' He glanced at Steph, who nodded. 'Aye, some very good SOCOs are there now, dusting that room for fingerprints, and if they find Elizabeth's, we'll get them to check for her DNA too. Will we find her prints there, Davie?'

Davie took a few seconds to get his next 'No comment' out.

'Would you like some water, Davie?' Malkie reached for the non-breakable plastic jug on the table and poured some into an equally non-breakable plastic tumbler and slid it across to Davie. He looked at it for a moment, then grabbed it and downed it in one.

'Thirsty work, all those *No comments*, isn't it?' Malkie smiled at him as if chatting about how pleasant the weather had been for the time of year.

Davie wiped his mouth with his sweatshirt sleeve.

'Thing is, Davie. I think we *will* find Elizabeth Dunn's prints there. And your brother, Stevie, was out of the country at the time, so it seems to me that only you and Stevie's wife would have been home during the time frame within which Elizabeth Dunn was abducted. But the person who Elizabeth Dunn's husband described looked nothing like Paula. Oh, and by the way, we found your van.'

Davie took a second. Drayford scowled; was this news to him?

'What van?'

Malkie feigned surprise. 'He talks. Excellent. Now we can

make some progress.' He clapped his hands together. 'The van we think she was bundled into. We found it – well, I'm sure you can tell us where we found it, can't you?'

Drayford found himself something to object to, something useful to do. 'DS McCulloch...'

Malkie held his hands up. 'Fair enough. Point taken. Anyway, that van is now in a garage being examined by some other forensics people. Someone tried to burn it, but they were obviously not too bright because they left it only half-burned. Large stretches of the dashboard and one of the handles on the back doors were left relatively undamaged, so we're hopeful of a result there.

'So. Mr Jessop. If there's anything you'd like to share with us, now would be the time.'

Davie's jaw clenched and unclenched several times. He stared at Malkie like a trapped animal weighing its chances up. Malkie waited, glanced at his watch.

Drayford leaned forward. 'I think my client would like to take a break, DS McCulloch.'

Davie took a second to tear his eyes from Malkie to look at his brief, then looked back at Malkie and nodded. 'Aye, I need a break. I don't feel well.'

Malkie held his gaze for a moment before reaching towards the buttons on the recording device. 'Interview suspended at two-fourteen p.m. at the request of Mr Jessop's legal representation.' He stabbed the button, then stood. Steph stood too and opened the door to the corridor.

Malkie leaned over the table. Davie shrank back.

'This is looking bad for you, Davie.'

On his way out the door, he remembered. 'Oh, by the way, did I mention that your brother's home?'

Davie's face told Malkie this wasn't necessarily good news for him.

. . .

In the small, dark and airless cupboard that was used as a remote monitoring room, Malkie and Steph reviewed the video.

Malkie paused it at the moment he'd got Davie to stumble. 'You think he'll buckle?'

She considered. 'I don't know. Did you see the look on his face when you told him Stevie's back? I think he's a hell of a lot more scared of his brother than he is of us.'

'Not surprising. Stevie has a reputation. He's said to have a serious problem controlling his temper.'

'Aye, so I've heard. He crippled a woman for giving him the finger from their car. Dragged her out into the road and kicked her so many times he fractured her spine.'

Steph opened her mouth to speak, but Malkie had a good idea what she was about to say. 'Aye, if we get to arrest him, I'll let you hurt him. Just a wee bit, though. OK?'

She scowled at him but didn't deny he'd guessed right.

Malkie checked his watch. 'We need to make him let something slip. How hard can that be? He's about as sharp as a brick.'

A knock on the door stopped Steph from responding. Gucci's head appeared. 'They're back.'

She stood back to let them leave the room. Before they opened the door to the interview room, he stopped beside her.

'Anything from the SOCOs at the Jessop house?'

'They lifted some prints. They're running them now.'

'Do we have both Jessops on file?'

'Oh yes. Nasty pieces of work, those boys.'

'Aye, the worst. Anything from the van?'

'Same. Prints have been lifted, should have the results soon. You're going to have enough to hold Jessop for twenty-four hours, aren't you?'

'Aye, but it's his brother I'm worried about. Anything from the Uniform at their house?'

'Nothing. Stevie hasn't come out. But...'

Gucci's expression had Malkie dreading what was coming next.

'Our man's on his own so he can only watch the front of the house. We were told to pull the other Uniforms off the Jessops. Resourcing restraints, you know?'

'Brilliant. Just bloody brilliant. How long has he been there on his own?'

'Couple of hours.'

'I'll relieve him as soon as I'm finished with Davie.'

'Go get 'im, boss. You got this.'

Malkie didn't know whether to thank her for her encouragement or tell her to stop patronising him. That told him the Jessops and his failure to find Elizabeth Dunn were starting to get to him.

Steph started the recording and did the boring admin stuff while Malkie sat and arranged himself. Malkie noticed that Davie's brief looked even more pissed off than before. He wouldn't have thought that possible.

'So, Mr Jessop. Have you—'

'No comment.'

It was surly this time, sulky.

Not so cocky now. Has he realised how much shite he's in?

'We'll get the results, soon, of some prints our SOCOs lifted from your spare bedroom. Still got nothing to say, Davie?'

'No comment.'

Drayford looked bored now, probably wondering what he'd done to deserve this one.

'Davie. I'm trying to help you here, mate. If you did this for your brother...'

Davie's reaction was subtle, but Malkie caught it. A scowl from Drayford suggested even he had caught it.

'Is that it, Davie? Did Stevie tell you to kidnap her? Did he want her ready and waiting for him when he got back from his holiday? Were you only following orders, Davie? We all know what Stevie can be like. I'm not sure I'd have the guts to disobey him if I was in your place. Mind you, if he did put you up to it you can maybe ask for some consideration for dobbing him in. Ah, but then he'd go down with you and he wouldn't like that, would he?'

Davie's eyes took on a fearful look. The man would never win any awards for his acting ability.

Malkie stared back at him.

What was it, Davie? Stevie wouldn't be stupid enough to kidnap Elizabeth the same day your nephew was run over. He's smarter than that.

When it hit him, it made perfect sense.

'Stevie had no clue what you were doing, did he? You wanted to show some initiative for a change. Why, Davie? Did you want to impress your big brother? Show him you're not the useless idiot he thinks you are? Is that it?'

Malkie leaned forward, ramped up the intensity of his gaze and his posture.

Davie didn't move and yet he seemed to shrink, too.

'What will he do to her, Davie? How much will he hurt her for causing Martin's death? That's how Stevie will see it, isn't it? He's going to go apeshit, isn't he? He'll kill her.'

'No comment.' Davie's voice small now, and miserable.

'He will. You know he will. I believe he's fond of Martin. Or rather, he was. He'll flip, won't he?'

Misery flooded Davie's eyes. Malkie hoped even Davie had the brains to see, now, how this might pan out.

'If Stevie kills her, Davie, you become an accessory to murder. That's a hell of a lot more years than you'll get for just abduction and assault. Actually, I'm not sure. How much for kidnapping and assault, Detective Constable Lang?'

Steph leaned forward, grinned at Davie. 'Oh, lots, boss.'

'You might get out before your fifties. Maybe. If you behave yourself, keep your nose clean and your head down, that is.

Apparently, you meet some really bad people in prisons these days. Isn't that right, Detective Constable Lang?'

'Yes, boss. Lots of very bad people in prisons these days.'

Davie turned in his seat, looked to his brief.

Drayford sat forward. 'Detectives, rather than repeatedly stating the obvious, are there any other questions you want to ask my client at this time?' He still sounded bored, like he just wanted it all to stop. Malkie had to wonder what drew some lawyers to public service. Maybe the guy just wasn't good enough to cut it in private practice. That was the way of the world, and the reason why far more poor people ended up doing time than the filthy rich.

'Davie? One last chance? Tell us where she is before Stevie gets to her. Save him, and you, from going down for much, much longer than you already will. It's in your best interests, mate.'

He held his hands out as if to impress on Davie that he wouldn't get a better offer.

The fingers of one of Davie's hands drummed on the tabletop. He chewed the thumbnail on the other. Malkie could almost see his little ferret brain weighing up his options and finding none of them very attractive. Keep it shut and hope the Pigs wouldn't find her, or lead them to her, do his time, then face his brother down the line, years from now.

Davie glanced at his brief, who shook his head and shrugged as if to say, 'Too late for me to help you now, you idiot.'

'No comment.' He sounded fragile now. Breakable.

FORTY-SEVEN

Malkie left Davie to stew.

He headed for the house to relieve the Uniform who'd been left to watch Stevie without support. It happened too often these days. So often that he felt like punching journalists who carped on about the lack of Uniforms visible on the streets and Police Scotland's ever-lower arrest rate for volume crimes. Shoplifters like Elizabeth Dunn. No, not like her. He refused to condemn her. She'd done what she could, all she thought she could do, to give her daughter the best chance of escaping the viciousness that teenage kids loved to dish out without the slightest appreciation of the damage they caused.

He found the Uniform looking about as bored as any person could. He'd slumped down in his car seat, and had both windows wound all the way down, Malkie guessed to let the frigid February air in to keep him awake. Malkie parked up behind him, gave the poor sod time to see him arrive and get himself looking like he'd been awake and alert the whole time. He strolled to the passenger side of the patrol car and let himself in.

'You mind?' he indicated the window.

'Aye, of course, sir.' He closed the driver's side window too.

'Malkie.'

'Sorry, sir?'

'Call me Malkie, unless Senior Management are around, OK? I hate being called "sir".'

'Will do.'

Malkie reached over and offered his hand. 'And your name is?'

'Mark. Mark Renfield.'

'Are you new?'

'No, but I transferred in from A Division after my mum's husband died. Moved to Livi to be closer to her.'

'Look after her, mate. Mums are important.'

Renfield stared at him.

'My mum died last year.'

'Sorry, sir. Malkie.'

'Aye. Thanks. Anyway, seen anything?'

Renfield returned his attention to the Jessop home, a hundred yards away on the other side of the road.

'No. Mrs Jessop went out about half six, but no sign of Stevie Jessop all day.'

'I assume you've taken a walk past a few times; in case they forget you're here?'

Renfield chuckled. 'Oh, they know I'm here. Even if I wasn't sitting here in the patrol car, Mrs Jessop keeps hanging out of an upstairs window until I notice her, then giving me the finger.'

'Charming. But no sign of Stevie?'

'No.'

'At all? Not once?'

Renfield frowned at him. 'I'm here on my own, sir. All these properties have back gardens that back onto each other, but I can't watch both front and back at the same time. And if I took a wander around to the parallel street, he could see me missing and leg it out the front.'

Malkie held a hand up. 'Easy, mate. I didn't mean anything. I know you got left here on your own, and I'll have words to say with your inspector about it, later. Relax, OK?'

Renfield sagged in his seat. 'I've been dreading one of you lot making an appearance and giving me a hard time for not being able to divide in two and watch every side of the place. If I'm honest, sir, me sitting here has been a waste of time. He could have been out the back any time in the past two hours.' He looked as aggrieved as Malkie considered him entitled to be.

'Which is why you should have had support. And I'll have words with someone.'

Renfield nodded. 'Thanks. I've just been expecting a bollocking I didn't deserve.'

'Don't worry about it, mate. I've had more bollockings than you've had haircuts, most of which I did deserve, and I haven't been booted out the door yet.'

Renfield smiled.

'The SOCOs have been, aye?'

'Aye. Been and gone. Just one. He was only in there ten minutes, though. When they left I came out here to the car to get away from the smell.'

'That's fine. At this stage in the investigation, my DI would only sign off on a basic search and dusting for prints. That wouldn't have taken long.'

They sat in silence for a while, until another car drove past them and parked outside the Jessop home. A minicab. Paula Jessop climbed out with three ALDI carrier bags clutched in her hands. She looked their way, took all three bags in one hand, and extended one middle finger at them. Then she went inside.

'That's odd.' Renfield sat forward, his face troubled.

'What?' Unease crept into Malkie's gut.

'She left in a Capri, but comes back in a minicab?'

Malkie made the connection in an instant and was out of the car and sprinting for the Jessop house. He banged on the front door. Paula Jessop took an age to open it, then stood in the doorway with a cigarette in her mouth and one of the smuggest and most triumphant smiles Malkie could remember seeing plastered on anyone's face.

'Where's Stevie?'

Paula removed her cigarette and yelled back into the house. 'Stevie. *Polis* want to talk to you.' She made no effort to sound convincing. She pretended to listen for a few seconds. 'He must be asleep.' Then, again, the grin.

Malkie made a show of scanning the street. 'Where's his Capri?'

'Nae idea.'

'You left in it earlier but came back in a minicab.'

'Did I?' Still no sign of any attempt to be convincing.

Malkie backed off, held her eye contact. 'Thin ice, Paula. Thin ice.'

'Whatever.' She slammed the door closed.

Malkie returned to the patrol car. 'Can you hang on here another half hour, Mark?'

Renfield sighed. 'Aye, but I'm going to bloody soil myself if any longer than that, sir.'

'I'll get someone to relieve you. I need to go do detective stuff.'

He paused before leaving. 'Thanks, Mark, and don't worry about this, OK? Anyone gives you a hard time, tell them to talk to me, aye?'

Renfield's response was wry. 'Won't help as much as you seem to think, sir, but thanks.'

Back in his own car, Malkie pulled away from the kerb too fast as he quick-dialled Steph on the dashboard display. She answered in a second.

'I was about to call you. Davie Jessop has asked to talk to

you. I think he might be about to crumble.'

'Brilliant timing.'

'Why?'

'I'm pretty sure Stevie's out and about somewhere.'

'Wasn't there a patrol car watching him?'

'Aye but his partner was called away on some other job, left one poor sod to watch both sides of the house without getting close enough to give them an excuse to bleat about harassment. Wasn't his fault. Cutbacks.'

'Any idea where he's gone?'

'No. But his idiot brother will know. I'll be there in ten minutes. Get Gucci and Rab on background checks again. Concentrate on the sister. What was her name?'

'Andrea.'

'Aye, her. Get everything we have on her. And ask Glasgow Uniforms to do an urgent drive-past, try her door again.'

'Will do.'

'Steph? Are we OK?'

A pause, then, 'We will be. See you in ten.'

FORTY-EIGHT

Elizabeth hadn't seen Andrea for over eight hours or been brought any food or water, when she heard a car arrive outside.

She started trembling and couldn't stop it. Was this the monster they called Stevie, at last? Was her time up, one way or another? Would she see another dawn?

Tears spilled from her, and she felt the shame of dampness in her underwear. She couldn't remember ever feeling fear this cold and debilitating, the brutal realisation that at best she was about to experience pain and suffering like never before. At worst...

She sobbed. Prayed. Pleaded with the universe that she didn't deserve this. She did what she did for her daughter. How could that be wrong? She hadn't wanted that security guard to die, would never have wanted that. Why did he have to follow her so far? Why didn't he check the road before he ran across it? How could that be her fault? Why was this happening to her when she'd been nothing but kind to people?

She heard voices, loud and angry but muffled through the thick wood of the cellar door and the one at the top of the stairs.

He recognised one as a woman's. Andrea. The other was male. It could be that Davie creep; the accent didn't sound like Stan. Either might hurt her again but she suspected they wouldn't do too much damage until the one called Stevie arrived. Did she at least have more time until that happened?

Footsteps thundered down the stairs. She moaned, terror flooding her, her mind unable to process her situation, unwilling to accept the reality of it even as she knew this was no nightmare.

The lock turned and the door flew open to slam against the wall.

A huge man stood in the doorway wearing shorts and a T-shirt and – of all things – flip-flops. Tall and massive, his head nearly touched the top of the doorway. His arms hung by his side, but his fists pumped as if eager to hurt her.

Stevie Jessop. Ice ran in her veins. She remembered him now. Her old life at Gleann Darragh. A business investment application. He wanted one hundred per cent financing to buy out a crappy old gym already on the company's books. He wanted GD to fund him to refit the place and buy all-new equipment, with no contribution from him other than his self-claimed expertise in the industry and his assurance that he 'knew the place'. She'd failed to hide an amused smirk as she turned his idiotic plan down, and she remembered the fury and the hatred in his eyes, despite her best attempt at mollifying apologies.

She prayed he wouldn't remember her, but a spark of recognition appeared in his eyes. He frowned, took a second. When the penny dropped, he breathed hard and his eyes glowed with hatred the likes of which Elizabeth couldn't believe she'd survive.

'You. Little miss up her fuckin' self in the swanky office. Didn't know a good business right in front of her and pissed herself at my idea to make something of it. Oh, this is gonna be sweet.'

'Please. Don't. I'm sorry. I was stupid. I should have listened to you. And I didn't mean for your nephew to get hurt. I promise. Please don't hurt me.' Her last words broke into sob-choked fragments, stuck in her throat as her fear turned to frantic panic. She pulled her legs up, wrapped her arms around them, backed into the corner on the mattress.

He watched her and breathed. Just as she dared to hope the worst wasn't yet about to begin, he charged across the room and grabbed her by the hair.

She screamed, now. She clutched at his hands as she felt her hair tear at the roots. Words poured from her, an unintelligible stream of begging and pleading and demanding he stop.

He dragged her into the centre of the cellar and dumped her on the floor. She curled into a ball even as she recognised the futility of trying to protect herself from what had to be coming.

He reached down, gripped her chin in one hand and lifted. She smelled beer on his breath, so strong she wondered how he stood so steady.

She looked up at him. Hope flared in her for a second, before his other hand, balled into a fist, smashed into her face like a lump hammer. She was driven back down, slammed to the floor. Her face erupted in pain. She screamed again, curled up again.

He grabbed her hair again. She tried to hold her face down, away from him, but his strength appalled her. She had no chance if she didn't want her scalp ripped from her head.

'Finance this, you fuckin' whore.'

A second punch bludgeoned her, and she felt concrete smack into the back of her head.

She had time to see him reach for her again, his teeth bared, his eyes wild, before she felt herself spin away into blackness.

. . .

When she woke, agony exploded through her. She couldn't open one eye and felt pain slice through her lips and mouth when she moaned at the inconceivable degree of pain that burned through her.

She tried to sit up, but shards of glass sliced her insides. She lifted her blouse and saw bruises, a mass of yellow and purple. The sight of her own flesh so battered made her gasp, and fresh agony clamped around her ribs like razor-sharp talons.

She lay back, waited for her suffering to ease. She begged the pain to fade, promised she wouldn't move again. She raised her fingers to her face, to her closed eye, felt a swelling like she couldn't believe, massive and tight and hot.

She cried. This was wrong. She didn't deserve this. Sophie didn't deserve to be terrified. Or Andrew. And if Sophie had to grow up without a mother? Would she survive that? Her mental health and Elizabeth's determination to remove every source of pain and stress that threatened to rob her of happiness might all come to nothing now. She might end up causing more damage to her daughter than if she'd done nothing in the first place.

If Andrew's condition deteriorated beyond his ability to care for her, had she damned Sophie to a future defined by temporary foster homes and over-worked social workers? It occurred to her that an animal like Stevie Jessop was no different from Andrew's MS: merciless and pitiless and incapable of anything like sympathy for the suffering they caused. Then she hated herself for wasting time contemplating the nature of her captor. All that mattered was getting back to Sophie. Even any further suffering Elizabeth might be about to endure took second place to survival.

Survival for Sophie's sake. Nothing else mattered.

She forced herself to sit up. She thought she could ignore her agonies through sheer force of will, but she screamed. Then she feared the sound of footsteps on the stairs, drawn by the sounds of her having regained consciousness and being ripe for another beating.

When she did hear footsteps, she lost all capacity for coherent thought. Terror sluiced through her. She tried to stand, to cross to the door, to look for something to hit him with, even as she knew nothing she could do to him would leave so much as a mark on him.

She collapsed to her knees, her forehead on the floor, and prayed for it all to stop.

He grabbed her by the hair again and dragged her towards the door. Every nerve in her body burned. She couldn't believe the deluge of pain that engulfed her, but somehow, she held on to consciousness and held on to his hands to stop him from tearing the skin from her skull.

He dragged her up the stairs, through the kitchen to the outside. Icy air blasted into her; Stevie hadn't bothered to give her a coat despite the frigid night. Around the corner from where she and Andrea had sat and drank gin, she reeled to find Andrea handcuffed to the bench beside the hot tub, the chain secured around a bar of the massive iron frame that supported the marble slab of the seat. She'd been battered just as brutally as Elizabeth. She too had no coat, and she hugged herself as if already on her way to a cold and miserable death from hypothermia. Stevie threw her against Andrea who shrank back into the bench, her face as bloody and bruised and swollen as Elizabeth knew hers must be.

When Stevie stepped to one side, she saw the man called Stan lounging in the tub, his eyes dead and uncaring.

Andrea didn't lift her head, didn't look at Elizabeth, but she reached out one hand and took hold of her fingers. Elizabeth squeezed back.

'Aw. Fuckin' sweet, that. Eh, Stan? Haudin' each other's

hands, stupid wee lassies. She always was the runt of the family, weren't you, sis?'

Stan didn't react, looked asleep. Stevie unlocked the cuff that secured Andrea to the frame of the bench and slammed it, tight and hard, around Elizabeth's wrist. Both women winced as he yanked on the chain to test it.

Stevie removed his T-shirt and climbed back into the steaming tub. Stan handed him a beer. They clinked their bottles together, downed long gulps each, then laid their heads back on the hot-tub head rests and sighed.

Both closed their eyes, which told Elizabeth they had no fear her and Andrea might escape. The sun had gone and dark had descended. She gazed up, saw stars twinkle in a clear black sky. That explained why the ice in the air made her shiver despite the pain it inflicted on her ribs. A universe that allowed school bullying and MS and men like the Jessops was one hell of a lonely and uncaring place. She expected to die tonight. Andrea too, by the looks of what Stevie had already done to her. To his own sister. She couldn't comprehend the man's complete absence of conscience or empathy. And it terrified her.

The stars that gazed back at her gave not one solitary damn. They would continue their impossibly old journeys across the heavens long after she had been dispatched, long after the damage her death and Sophie's inevitable orphaning would do. She trusted Sophie possessed the steel to survive, that she'd live on for her mother, once she knew all that Elizabeth had done for her, however misguided and disastrous.

When she lowered her eyes again, she found Stevie watching her. What had she expected to see in the man? More rage? Disgust? A hunger for revenge for the death of Martin?

She saw only cold hatred, which seemed somehow the worst outcome possible. How much hurt could he cause her and how long could he drag it out for without the fury to push him too far too fast and end her quickly. Did he mean to make her suffering last an age?

As if he heard her thoughts, he nudged Stan, nodded at her and laughed. Stan smiled, but the man seemed incapable of any emotion more expressive, such as actual laughter. They clinked their bottles again.

'Welcome back, bitch. You took your time. We waited but we got bored. I'd invite you in, but you'll just bleed in the water. Probably piss yersel' too. Eh, Stan?'

Stan's lips curled in disgust. 'Aye.'

Stevie sat up, leaned forward, and moved to the side of the tub closest to her and Andrea. He rested his massive arms on the edge of the tub and propped his chin on his hands.

'You wondering what I'm going to do to you, aye?'

She said nothing, terrified that anything she came out with would be just another trigger, another excuse for him to inflict his cruelty on her. She felt Andrea stiffen beside her, felt her grip on her fingers tighten. A warning? To keep her mouth shut? After all, who knew the depths of Stevie's cruelty better than his own brutalised sister? She squeezed Andrea's fingers back and hoped Stevie wouldn't see the minuscule shift of their fingers.

'I'm going to finish this beer. Then I'm going to have another beer. Then I'm going to do some coke to really get me in the mood. Then I'm going to break some of your fingers. What do you think, Stan? Sound good to you?'

Stan had laid his head back again and only held a thumb up.

'See? I liked Martin. He's not really a nephew; we just called him that. He was the son of a mate of mine who's doing life in Barlinnie. I promised him I'd look after his son. The lad knew me since he was a wean and called me his Uncle Stevie so I adopted him. Davie played along with it, called him his nephew as well. It was only this fuckin' bitch that didnae.' He lobbed his beer bottle at Andrea. Her eyes were still downcast, and Elizabeth didn't dare reach to stop it for fear of more agony through her core. The bottle hit Andrea on the forehead. She flinched and clutched her head but made no sound and kept her eyes down, mute evidence of how terrified she was and how much more cruelty her brother was capable of. Elizabeth started to wonder if even now she had no idea of the depth of this man's sickness.

She saw no chance of either of them surviving this.

FORTY-NINE

When Malkie charged into the CID area of the office, he saw nobody cast any excited looks his way and swore under his breath.

'Nothing?'

Steph and Gucci looked up and shook their heads, miserable and frustrated. Rab glanced over and looked like he had something to report but needed to finish his call first.

Malkie sat at his desk. 'Andrea Jessop?'

Gucci lifted her notebook and turned to him. 'Fifty-three years old. Retired teacher. I called her last place of work; said we were concerned for her safety—'

'You didn't lie there, Lou.'

'I spoke to a friend of Andrea's called Elaine Michaels who said Andrea owns a wee cottage somewhere. Not too far from Glasgow apparently, because they drove there for a party after a night out in the city. Elaine was already half-cut before Andrea drove them there, and fully hungover when Andrea drove her home the next morning. She slept the whole journey back home. Sorry, point is she remembers nothing about how they got there except that they drove over the Kingston Bridge then onto a motorway. That's it. That's all she remembers.'

'So, M8 west or M74 south?'

'That'd be my guess.'

'OK, so...'

'I was checking the ANPR database for her registration – petrol blue 2022 Audi – when you arrived.'

'Brilliant. Cheers, Gucci. Steph, has Davie Jessop said anything else?'

'Nothing. He's called for the doctor twice, though. Said he felt light-headed and claustrophobic, again. Given the all-clear both times, though.'

'What a surprise. Rab?'

Rab asked the person on the phone to wait for a second. 'SOCOs ran the prints from the Jessops' boarded-up bedroom, a clear match for the samples we took from Dunn's home. And it was a single, full, thumb and five fingers print, not a casual touch, she meant it to be clear and unambiguous. She was leaving us a message. Nothing conclusive from the van, though.'

'We don't need to place him in the van. We've got Elizabeth Dunn telling us she was there. Steph, shall we have another crack at him?'

'Oh, yes. Let's.'

Thirty minutes later, Malkie listened to Steph record the preamble for a further interview with Davie Jessop and his brief. Paul Drayford looked hugely pissed off to have been on call again when Davie needed a lawyer.

When Steph nodded to Malkie, he started on Davie.

'Your brother's gone AWOL, Davie. If he hurts Elizabeth Dunn and he goes too far, you remember what I said, aye? Accessory to murder carries a hell of a lot heavier tariff than kidnapping and assault. So, Davie. Still got nothing to say?'

Davie glared at him. He chewed his lower lip so hard it turned white, and Malkie expected blood at any time.

'Why am I still here? This bloke' – he indicated Renfield with his thumb – 'says you have to let me go after twenty-four hours.'

Drayford squeezed his fingers in his eyes and sighed.

Malkie felt for the man. 'Unless we have sufficient reason to believe we might be in a position to charge you, Davie. At the moment, we have more than enough to charge you with Elizabeth Dunn's abduction. If her bracelet hanging in your hedge wasn't enough, our forensic people found Dunn's prints in your boarded-up bedroom. If we find her dead and we can't tie Stevie to it, you'll be next in line.'

Drayford roused himself. 'Please.'

Malkie held his hands up. 'Fair point. I just meant if all of that happens, Davie, well... You'll be our prime suspect. Is that better?' He looked to Renfield, who nodded, but with a face that defied Malkie to push his luck any further.

'So. Davie. Mate. Where's Stevie?'

Davie opened his mouth, then seemed to agonise over what to say and clamped his mouth shut again. He looked about to scream.

'Davie? Come on, mate. You know what Stevie's capable of, don't you? And he was really quite fond of Martin, I believe?' He looked to Steph again, who performed her part of the double-act without flaw.

'I believe he was, boss.'

'So, he's going to be bloody pissed off with the woman he considers to have caused Martin's death, isn't he?'

Davie's eyes darted from person to person. He sat forward, leaned on the table, clasped his hands. His breathing became short and fast.

'Feeling claustrophobic again, Davie? We can put you back in the custody suite for a while if you like. Although it just occurred to me: I believe a standard cell in Saughton or Addiewell is about sixty per cent of the size of one of ours. And, of course, you'll have a roomie.' He pronounced this with enthusiasm, as if selling a luxury holiday room.

Davie dropped his head until his chin almost touched his chest. He clasped his hands on the table and opened and closed his fingers, flexing them then squeezing so tight Malkie heard his knuckles crack.

Bastard's going to fold.

Malkie waited, allowed silence and tension to work their magic.

Davie leaned to his left, whispered to Drayford, who shook his head and whispered back. Davie looked less than happy at what he'd been told.

When he turned back, Malkie knew the man was about to buckle. He worked hard not to let his eagerness show on his face.

Davie licked his lips. Closed them again. Dropped his head then lifted it again, looked to the ceiling, whispered 'Fuck' to himself.

'If I tell you, Stevie will kill me.' Whining now, all trace of his previous arrogance gone.

'He'll kill you? His own brother?'

Davie sneered at him like he was talking to an idiot.

'Sounds bad, Davie. So, if he does kill Elizabeth Dunn and we nick him for it – and we will, Davie – Stevie will want a word with you whenever you both get out. Unless he gets some pals of his to have a word with you on the inside, of course.'

Drayford cast Malkie a look, but he put no real conviction into it.

Davie licked his lips again, looked ready to burst.

'Davie. Last chance, mate.'

Davie looked at him. His eyes seemed to plead with Malkie for a way out.

If Malkie could think of one, he'd still hang the fucker out to dry.

Davie seemed to realise no help was coming, and he almost fell forward onto the table as he moaned his misery.

'Carstairs.' He barely whispered the word.

Malkie suppressed a thrill. 'Can you repeat that a bit louder for the recording, please, Mr Jessop?'

Davie lifted his head, all fight gone from him. 'Andrea's cottage near Carstairs.'

Kingston Bridge then a motorway. Carstairs fitted that.

'Your sister, Andrea?'

'Aye. Andrea.'

'Where, exactly?'

Davie's words sounded like they were being ripped physically from him. 'Last stretch of the A721 before Carstairs. Turn-off to the right after a roundabout, heads south.'

He sagged even further down towards the table. He rested his forehead on the wooden surface. 'Stevie will kill me. He'll fucking kill me.'

Malkie heard him sniff. He pulled a couple of paper handkerchiefs from a box beside the recording equipment and pushed them into Davie's fingers. Davie swiped them away.

'Are you happy, you fucking Pig? You happy I grassed on my own brother? You happy he'll fucking kill me for this?'

Despite years of experience littered with examples of exactly the worst times for Malkie to push his luck, he did just that.

'Fuckin' ecstatic, you piece of shit.'

Davie erupted, threw himself across the table. He and Malkie tumbled to the floor.

Steph slammed her fist at the alarm strip that ran around the perimeter, halfway up the walls, and an alarm sounded outside the door. Davie piled into Malkie, landed on top of him, hammered fist after fist into his face. Malkie had rarely felt pain like it, even in this job, Davie's fury explosive. By the time he saw Steph appear over Davie's shoulder and drag him off, his head had already started to spin. He sat up, with difficulty, saw Drayford banging on the door to the corridor, his face frantic.

Steph slammed Davie face down onto the floor, twisted one arm behind his back so hard that he screamed. The door flew open, and two Uniforms charged through. They cuffed Davie, lifted him by his arms which made him scream again, and dragged him away, back to his cell.

Steph knelt beside Malkie. She held up one hand in front of his face. 'Malkie. Malkie. How many fingers, Malkie?'

Malkie forced himself to focus. He felt nausea turn his stomach, feared he might throw up all over her.

'Twelve.'

Steph released a breath. 'He's fine.'

When the station nurse came through the door, she tutted and bent to study his face. 'Christ, you're going to swell up like a rotten melon, Malkie.'

'Thanks, Doreen. Lovely bedside manner, as always.'

He sat up and everything swam around him. He knew it would pass but it couldn't stop soon enough. He leaned over, got one leg under him and a hand on the floor, braced himself to stand. Steph and Doreen took a shoulder each and pushed him back down.

Steph grabbed his face in one hand and leaned over him. 'Stay down, you idiot. You've taken a hell of a blow to the head.'

He bit down on the pain, forced his mind to form words. 'Carstairs. Andrea Jessop. Tell Gucci...'

'I will, boss. Now, please. Lie back and try not to be such a rotten patient?'

He gave up, let his head settle back to the floor. He thought he might pass out, but from somewhere deep in his mind, a voice refused to let him.

Find her. Save her. Nothing else matters.

He sat up too quickly for Steph to stop him. He batted her hand away then held a warning finger up. He felt his left eye already tightening. His face hurt like a bastard, and he felt blood trickle down his neck.

Doreen wiped him clean then applied some gel from a tube and began to dress his cuts. 'Malkie. For God's sake, please. Just sit there for a while, OK? If you pass out and do yourself any more damage, I'll get my arse kicked, so do me a favour, OK?'

He held a hand up in surrender, then leaned himself forward to rest his elbows on his thighs. The pain in his face hammered at him, demanded he lie back down and sleep it off, but he feared what news he might wake up to.

No, the bitter end was the only thing he cared about. He wasn't losing another one.

He drifted...

His dad plonked his Police Scotland cap on his head and beamed at him. 'Those bad guys have no chance, Malcolm. Not with you on their tails. I'm proud of you, son.'

Seventeen-year-old Sandra Morton lay under him, pulling him down by his neck as she unbuttoned her blouse.

A fresh-faced girl stood before him, looked eager and impatient at the same time. 'Constable Lang, sir. Your new DC. Looking forward to working with you, but should your face be all purple and swollen like that?'

His mum booped him on the nose. 'Silly sausage. You can't do your paper round today. You've got the measles.'

Mum?

He allowed huge, empty blackness to swallow him.

FIFTY

Stan's face lit up as he reached for a metal biscuit tin on a tray fixed to the side of the tub. Stevie opened it and frowned.

Elizabeth felt Andrea tense again.

Stevie pulled a ziplock plastic bag full of brown powder from the tin, held it up for Stan to see.

'Has Davie given up for Lent or something? I thought there'd be less than half this much left. Thought I was going to have to cut some of the load of ninety per cent I just brought in.'

Stan peered at it. 'Looks darker than the last lot, boss. You sure that been cut?'

Stevie frowned at the bag, then at Stan. 'Fuck's sake, man. Aye. Well, a wee bit spicier than what we sell on. Fifteen per cent, no more than that. Do you no' trust me?' He grinned and slapped Stan's forehead with the bag. Then he opened it and pulled two fat joints from the tin.

Elizabeth heard Andrea whimper, too faint for either of the animals in the hot tub to hear. Did she already know how much more of an animal her brother could become on hard drugs? Had she seen him high? Did she know just how much worse their ordeal was about to get?

Elizabeth felt tears spill from the one eye she could still open. She considered running, figured Stevie might be forced to bring her down if she made it anywhere close to the nearby road, maybe finish her without meaning to, at least cut his amusement short? She placed weight on her feet. Andrea squeezed her fingers again, tight, but Elizabeth refused to sit and wait for more humiliation, more degradation, more torture.

As she leaned forward to stand, pain lanced through her, from her ribs up through her neck to her head. She felt consciousness slip from her in a black wave of crushing pain, but she managed to hold on, to fight it off.

She had no chance. Even if she could bear the agony enough to run, Stevie would catch her at a casual stroll.

She leaned on Andrea and wept.

Andrea lifted her head to watch her brother.

Stevie unrolled both joints on the tray and sprinkled brown powder from the bag into both. He rerolled them into new papers and sealed them, stuck one between his lips and handed the other to Stan. Stan eyed it and scowled but put it in his mouth.

Stevie's face broke into a grin. 'You up for another twenty?'

Stan shook his head. 'No. You always win. I can't afford.'

'Fuck that. You work for me, you do what I say, you Serbian tosser.'

'Lithuanian.'

'Whatever.'

Stevie lit both joints then held his beer bottle up. Stan did the same. Stevie leaned in and peered at both bottles. 'Close enough. More in mine in fact, so you have an advantage, you fucking pussy.'

Stevie counted to three, and both downed their beer in one and took huge drags from their joints. Elizabeth thought they'd never stop inhaling and she'd never seen one man's chest grow so massive before.

Stan coughed first. Stevie exhaled, long and controlled, then grinned at Stan.

'That's another twenty you owe me, mate. Lightweight.'

Stan shook his head. He opened his mouth to protest but stopped.

'That's bit rough, boss. You sure it's cut?'

'Aye. You know I always do it myself. I never let Davie cut my supply; he's too stupid. And that stupid old cow' – he pointed at Andrea – 'doesnae even know where I stash it. Her own house and she's got no clue. Probly too scared to look, fuckin' shites hersel' at her own shadow. What about it, Andrea? Did you ever find it? Where I stash my highly illegal hard drugs in your wee fairy-tale cottage? Did you?'

Andrea stared back but said nothing. Elizabeth couldn't imagine the humiliation of having had her perfect little retreat, her secluded and private escape from her disgrace of a family, invaded and ruined by these animals.

Stevie laughed, but it turned into another cough. He cast a defiant eye at Stan and kept smoking, rested his head back again.

'Boss...'

'Aw, shut the fuck up, Stan. I'm trying to party here. Fuck's sake. And finish that joint, or you're sacked.'

Stan shut his mouth and leaned back, but his eyes betrayed his unease. He took another drag, but Elizabeth, even in the state she was in, saw that he barely inhaled.

They opened more beers. They smoked and drank, and steam rose, slow and graceful, from the hot water to the black sky above them.

Andrea squeezed Elizabeth's fingers and watched them.

FIFTY-ONE

He felt a slap. Hard. Had to be Steph.

'Malkie. Wake up. You need to stay awake, mate.'

He felt a thick blanket of fatigue wrap itself around his brain and demand he sleep.

He fought it.

His mum knew he always did his level best not to let people down.

His dad knew he'd never rest, never stop chasing.

Steph once had no idea of the shambles of a police officer he was.

Used to be.

He had a daughter now, didn't he? What was her name? He should know her name, shouldn't he?

Another slap. Harder.

'Malkie. Wake up. Fuck's sake, mate. Wake up.'

Faces. Staring at him. Staring down at him. One concerned, one distraught. Hands lifted him. He sat up. The world span around him but slower than he remembered from before. Noises were muffled and echoed in his ears. He heard his own blood pounding at the sides of his head. That was a good sign, wasn't it?

He remembered.

Davie Jessop. Crumbled, at last. His sister, Andrea. Carstairs. Cottage.

He surged to his feet. Steph and Doreen grabbed his arms, but he shook them off. He swayed, defied the room to keep turning around him, refused to close his eyes, glared at the walls as they slid past and yet remained right in front of him.

After long seconds, the spinning slowed and his urge to puke faded to only faint nausea. He shook his head, regretted it.

'Aspirin. Give me some aspirin or I'll kill someone.'

Steph stepped in front of him. She planted one hand on his shoulder and the other on his chest. 'You idiot. You stupid, stubborn, idiot.' Her eyes glistened.

When he felt as much clarity had returned to him as was going to, he barged out of the room, along the corridor through to the CID desks and dropped into his seat. His head pounded.

He yelled to no one specific, 'Aspirin. Please. And charge that fucker Jessop with assaulting a police officer. And find Andrea Jessop's address. And wake me when you do. Christ, I wish I was a drinker.'

Doreen appeared beside him with two pills in one hand and a glass of water in the other. She handed him the pills then held the glass out to him.

'These are stronger than aspirin. Much stronger.' She put her hands on his shoulders and peered into his eyes. After a second, she turned to Steph. 'He's going nowhere but A&E then home and he doesn't drive for twenty-four hours, OK?'

Malkie opened his mouth to protest but shut it again when he saw the look on Steph's face. She indicated towards the back door to the station car park. He headed that way in as straight a line as he could manage.

'Steph?' Thompson's tone made them both turn to her. Her

expression told them she'd rather have her fingernails pulled out than have whatever conversation with Steph that was coming.

Steph took Malkie's chin in her hands. 'You. Do not move from here. Understand? I'm taking you home. Or to A&E.'

He saluted her. 'Yes, boss.' He pointed to the floor at his feet. 'Right here.'

Steph flashed him one more warning look then followed Thompson into her office. As Thompson closed the door behind Steph, she gave Malkie a look that carried some ominous warning, but he was damned if he could guess what it was.

He headed for the back door; he had a woman to find. He couldn't remember her name right now, but he would find her.

As he staggered across the car park towards his car, Steph appeared in front of him. The look on her face promised violence.

'What part of *don't move* did you not understand, Malkie? What does it take to get through to you? You think you're the only one who wants to find her? You don't think maybe I could do with a good result? The shite I've been having to deal with the past few days?'

She wandered away a few paces, took a breath, then turned on him again.

'No. I've had enough. Ruin your own life as much as you want. Get in your car with concussion, see what other poor bastard you mow down before you crash into a tree or a lamp post and kill yourself. Just stop thinking you know better and that you have to save the entire fucking world and stop ignoring those of us who do and have only been guilty of bloody caring about you, you stupid, stupid man.'

She deflated, held her hand to her forehead as if she felt a massive headache coming on. When she spoke again, her voice was small and quiet.

'Please, Malkie. If you won't go to St John's, then let me take you home to your dad. Just know when to stop, to let others take over. Please.'

Malkie hung his head. She was right. She was usually right. Bloody annoying.

'I can't, Steph. Not won't. Can't. I can't let myself fall asleep tonight wondering if I'll wake up to hear she's been found dead while I was tucked up in my bed, doing nothing.'

He leaned back on his car, felt like sliding sideways to the ground and sleeping on the cold, hard concrete.

'I can't. If I could and just wouldn't, I'd agree with your assessment of my utter idiocy. But I can't.'

She leaned on the car beside him. 'I can't let you drive, mate. You must see that, no?'

He took an age to get his next words out, figured he had a fifty-fifty chance of getting the bollocking of his life.

'You drive then. But let me—'

Steph folded her arms and defiance returned to her. 'No chance, mate. You heard what Doreen said.'

'Who's Doreen?'

She gave him one of her looks, in no mood for his shite.

He braced his hands on his hips, stood straight, looked to the black sky, heaved in a huge lungful of icy February air, then faced her again.

'Either you drive me, or I drive me. No, wait, that doesn't sound right. You drive. If you don't, I'll get a cab back here after you drop me off and I'll drive myself.'

He pointed somewhere to the west. 'I am *not* giving up on Elizabeth...' He frowned.

'Dunn, for God's sake. Elizabeth Dunn. You're making my point for me, Malkie. You're in no fit state.' Steph's expression broke his heart: she was frightened for him. With all she had on her plate at the moment, with a stepfather trying to ruin her career and a rapist father in the background intending who knew what atrocity for her, she was terrified for him.

Never, ever deserve you, Steph.

He folded his arms; put on his best *I'm not arguing* face.

Steph slumped, then lifted her head to the same black sky as if looking for divine assistance. 'God help me, Malkie. You're a walking car crash and the most stupid and stubborn officer I've ever had the misfortune to be partnered with.'

He swayed and swallowed and waited.

'Why I still love you will always be a bloody mystery to me. Get in.' She took his arm and led him back towards her car.

She strapped him in because he couldn't find the bit to click the seatbelt into. 'Carstairs?'

He took a second to clear his thoughts. 'Aye. And get Rab and Gucci on to finding out where in Carstairs. Tell them if they don't find anything, I'll come back and bleed all over them.'

'Idiot.'

'I know.'

As she pulled out of the car park, she quick-dialled her phone on the dashboard screen. 'Lou, guess what?'

'He won't go home?'

'Good guess.'

Malkie flapped a hand at her. 'Less backchat to your senior officer and more action, please.' He paused as his head swam. 'Lou, do whatever Steph says.' He leaned back on the headrest and waited for his brain to stop pounding.

Steph tutted. 'Lou, send me the registration of Stevie Jessop's Mercedes Sprinter, then get on Google Maps and find me all small properties south of the A721 between a roundabout where it crosses the A706 and the town boundary, OK?'

'On it, boss. Look after our Fearless Leader, aye?'

Malkie couldn't miss the fond but sarcastic smile in her voice, even over the phone.

They drove. West then south through the suburbs until they

hit the A71, and Steph stamped on the throttle. Malkie tried to close his eyes, to settle his mind for what might come. He shook his head to dislodge a creeping sense of dread, then regretted it as blood pounded in his ears and an ache swelled in his head again. A pained groan escaped him.

'That's it. I'm taking you to A&E. No arguments.'

'No.' His temper broke. He forced himself to calm down and lower his voice.

She looked at him, not with a warning as he expected but with worry so raw, so vulnerable, it almost made him give in to her. To let it go. Try again tomorrow. Hope that Elizabeth Dunn stayed alive until—

'No. You take me anywhere but Carstairs and I'll find my way there myself after you leave me, Steph. You agreed you'd help me as long as I didn't drive.'

'I didn't agree to that, actually, and you're in no fit state to quote me, and you need medical attention, Malkie. You might be concussed, and that can kill you.'

Malkie took her left hand where she always rested it on the automatic gear lever. 'Lou is going to find Andrea Jessop's cottage, then we're going to find it, then we're going to find Elizabeth Dunn and get her home safely to her family.'

He laid his head back and closed his eyes, fought off a wave of exhaustion and desperation.

'If we don't... If she...' He couldn't finish. Tears dropped from his eyes. 'We're all she has, Steph.'

Steph pulled over and turned to him. She rested a hand on his shoulder, then moved it to his cheek.

'And if it kills you? If you *are* concussed and it kills you? What then, mate? What about your dad? Me? Lou? Thompson? Maybe even Rab?'

He chuckled at that, but then she dropped the big one on him.

'What about Deborah?'

His breath caught in his throat and debilitating grief swamped him. If he left Deborah alone now, after giving her – after they had given each other – something to look forward to? Did he have the right to do that to her? To Steph? To his dad?

He punched the front side of a fist against his forehead. 'Aw, Steph. Is this what my mum meant when she talked about hard adult decisions when I grew up?'

She waited a second. 'You're growing up?'

He laughed despite himself but succeeded only in snorting. He wiped his nose on the back of his coat sleeve, was relieved to see nothing.

'How about this? Open your window so you don't fall asleep because that'll finish you if you do have concussion. I'll get us down to Carstairs, will only take twenty minutes or so, then we get some fresh air and walk around a bit, let me see you're OK, before we act on anything Lou finds. Deal?'

'Deal.'

She lowered the passenger-side window and pulled away.

'Thanks, Steph.' His words now slurred and sleepy. 'You do have a heart, don't you? A very warm and loving one, I think.'

'Shut up, and don't go dying on me or I'll kick your arse.'

FIFTY-TWO

Ten minutes in, Stevie Jessop tried to stand.

He slipped, fell back into the water. Stan had to grab an arm to stop his boss from going under. He pushed him back into his seat.

Stevie shook his head. Stan frowned at him.

'Oh, fuck off, Stan. Stop being such an old woman. Fuckin' miserable prick. No wonder yer wife topped hersel'. Poor wee cow.' His words had started to slur.

Stan glared at Stevie, who seemed oblivious. Stan reached to his side and pushed his barely reduced joint off the edge of the tub to the ground.

Stevie tried to stand again, but fell back again coughing, his breath seeming to struggle in and out of him, shallow and laboured.

'Something's wrong, Stan. I don't feel good.'

Stan surged forward, sent water pouring over the side of the tub. He took Stevie's head in his massive hands and peered into his boss's eyes.

'Fuck.' He settled Stevie back into his seat. Stevie's arms

and legs moved in feeble desperation to keep his head above water.

Stan stood and stumbled from the tub. He held Stevie's head out of the water as he felt for a pulse in his neck, then shook his head. 'Too late, boss. I warned you.' He walked away towards the front of the cottage, still shaking his head and muttering something in Lithuanian.

Stevie lifted his head, reached for the side of the tub nearest the women and with a supreme pull on his meagre remaining strength, he pulled himself over to rest one arm and his chin on the edge.

'You?'

Andrea stared back at him, silent for a moment; then, 'Behind the wood pile. You stashed it behind the wood pile in the living room.'

'You...'

'I did, Stevie, and I'm glad I did. Whatever happens to me now, I'm happy I've killed you. I'll hate myself for it later but right now I'm going to watch you drown and try to tell myself I had no choice. Not for myself, and not for Elizabeth.'

Stevie seemed to reach deep inside himself for one last surge of strength, but he found nothing. His breath barely visible in the frigid night air, he clutched his chest as if his heart had iced over, then slipped slowly down out of view. Before his eyes slid out of sight, they widened in terror as water surged down his throat and into his lungs. He couldn't cough and he couldn't splutter. He'd have felt himself drown but been able to do nothing about it.

When the sounds of the water slapping on the insides of the tub stopped. Andrea's grief broke through. She cried quiet, miserable tears, and Elizabeth tried to lift her arms to embrace the woman.

And realised they both remained handcuffed to a marble

and cast-iron bench that looked heavier than they could lift together even when fully fit. With broken ribs and so many other injuries she'd lost count of, she had no chance.

They had no chance.

FIFTY-THREE

'Are you up to this?'

'Aye.'

'You promise?'

'Aye. I only threw up once. I've been fine since.'

Steph studied the passenger side of her car. 'If that burns my paintwork, you're paying for a full respray, mate.'

Malkie spluttered. 'How? I only threw up because you were driving like a nutter. You must have done eighty all the way. No wonder I got ill.'

She grabbed the lapels of his coat, held them under his chin. 'I did forty all the way for just this reason. You threw up because you're concussed. Or were.' She held up one hand. 'How many fingers now?'

'Same as last time. Nine.'

'Idiot. Anyway, while you were cleaning your vomit off the outside of my car, I got a message from Gucci.'

'What? Why the hell didn't you say so?'

She fixed him with one of her looks. 'Like I said, it arrived while you were de-puking my car, less than three minutes ago.'

He relented, held his hands up. 'Sorry. What has she got?'

Steph showed him the screen on her phone. A map of the area both sides of the A721 to the north-west of Carstairs. Three tiny red circles marked locations, all far off the main road and surrounded by trees.

'So, let's start on them, then. That one first.' He pointed at the northernmost mark.

Steph tutted and wiped her screen with her sleeve, then headed for the driver's door.

Inside, she took a while to start the car. Malkie waited. She had something to say; he'd known her too long to miss the signs.

'Dean Lang is in intensive care. On life support.'

Malkie's heart stopped. As hard as he tried to stop the thought forming in his mind, he failed.

You didn't, did you, Steph? Please God, tell me you didn't.

She seemed to read his mind. 'Don't you dare ask if I had anything to do with it. Don't you dare.'

'Never crossed my mind, Steph.'

She gave him a withering look; she'd known him too long too.

'I never touched him. Not after that day outside the coffee shop.'

'What day? What coffee shop?'

Her face darkened. With guilt or shame or both. 'What coffee shop, Steph?' His head pounded but he ignored it.

'He asked to meet me. I did.'

'Oh, Steph...'

'I know, OK? I know. Stupid.'

'What happened?'

'He said things.'

Malkie waited; wasn't sure he wanted to know but at the same time had to.

'He talked about Boswell. Called him my—'

'I get it. What did you do to him?'

She hung her head. 'I attacked him. I didn't hit him, but I

had him backed up against a shop window with my hand around his throat.'

Malkie groaned.

'And...'

His stomach turned over. He amazed himself by shutting his persistent nausea away and focusing his confused and wandering thoughts on her.

'And?'

'And someone got it on video. Or so he told Crimestoppers.'

'Aw, fuck.'

'Indeed.'

'And now he's near-dead? How?'

'Fell from his balcony, seven floors onto a car roof. Miracle he survived, they're saying, but he might end up vegetative for life.'

'We can hope so.'

She reached over and squeezed his hand. 'You can't say that, mate.'

'Bastard doesn't deserve any better.'

She started the car but hesitated before pulling away.

'I agree, but I refuse to hope for that. I can't be that person.'

'Let's go and find Elizabeth Dunn, partner. Let's save a life that absolutely is worth saving.'

FIFTY-FOUR

Stan reappeared, fully clothed and clutching a holdall, as Elizabeth and Andrea struggled to pull the bench by the chain towards the hot tub. Each tug on the chain set both of them off screaming in pain. They managed to move the thing an inch, but Elizabeth feared one or both of them would pass out from pain or blood loss and if that happened, they were both dead. Every tug on the thing sent shards of agony lancing through her ribs so agonising they eclipsed all else so she was capable of nothing more than clutching them and praying for the excruciating pain to fade again.

The damned thing might as well have been bolted to the patio slabs for all the chance they had of moving it ten feet without blacking out from their injuries.

'Help us, Stan. Have a heart. Please.' Andrea sobbed and reached out to him. 'Free us and we'll tell the police it was all Stevie and Davie. I promise. They'll believe that.'

Stan seemed to consider for a moment. Then he shook his head, and Elizabeth felt all hope leave her. As he walked back to the van she'd been brought here in, she held on to Andrea to stop her from collapsing to the icy gravel.

The van's wheels span, spraying gravel all over them, and Stan drove away, left them to die.

Elizabeth lifted Andrea back to her feet.

'Andrea. Andrea, listen to me. Where does Stevie keep the key to this thing?' She indicated the chain that joined them.

Andrea took a moment to return to reality, then she pointed. 'He put them in the pocket of his shorts.'

Elizabeth studied the ten feet between where they sat and the nearest edge of the tub. It might as well have been a mile away.

They sat again, huddled close as adrenaline drained from their veins and cold seeped into them. She'd read an article once about how it felt to freeze to death. Funny thing was that it said you actually feel warm. She glanced at the tub. Hundreds of gallons of hot water that would stay hot all night and would save them from the cold if they could only get into it.

She cast her eyes around the garden behind them, looked for anything that might let her saw at the chain. But Andrea's pristine garden lay devoid of clutter of any kind. Anything she might have been able to use would be in the shed, thirty feet away on the other side of a perfect, putting-green-grade lawn.

Elizabeth yanked on the chain in sudden fury and Andrea screamed in pain. Elizabeth clung to her, held her close, let the woman sob into her chest, even as blood seeped over both of them from fresh wounds to her wrists.

She didn't deserve this. Andrea deserved it even less. Stan could have unlocked them, but she figured he'd be on his way to a ferry port or an airport by now.

They held on to each other.

Five minutes. Then she'd persuade Andrea to try again. If she had to strip the skin from her wrists to free her hand, she would. Whatever agony and whatever permanent disfigurement that might cause her would be worth it because her family needed her. Sophie needed her.

She *would* see her daughter again.

FIFTY-FIVE

The first property on Gucci's map turned out to be more dilapidated than Malkie's cabin had been when he moved him and his dad back into it. It looked like no one had lived there for decades, let alone years.

They scoured the trees around it for certainty but neither expected to find anything.

As they drove to the second location, Malkie felt his grip on his remaining reserve of stubborn hope leak from him. No capacity for self-talk remained, no furious determination that if he only wanted badly enough to find Elizabeth alive then some kind of karmic justice might kick in and they would.

When they approached the second site and he saw lights in windows, he roused himself from his creeping despair and decided this was the one. No white van but a Volvo estate parked outside.

It was enough. He wasn't beaten yet.

The young couple who opened the door of the holiday cabin were so nervous at a knock on their door in such a remote location that they barely looked at their warrant cards before letting them look inside.

When they returned to the car, Malkie nearly collapsed.

Weariness and despair dragged at him. He couldn't lose another one, couldn't live with himself if one more person died and he didn't stop it, if he failed again to save them.

He thought he heard Walter Callahan's voice tickle at the back of his mind. 'We do what we can, Mr McCulloch.' No, that was his mum. His mum said that. He and Walter Callahan never got a chance to become friends. Not before the poor bastard had died choking on his own blood because Malkie—'

Steph slapped him. Hard. Reality crashed back in on him.

'Stop that, right now. And stay awake, damn it. We have one more to check and if that's a bust, then we tell Gucci to keep looking. That's all we can do, Malkie, and I'm not going to watch you flog yourself for not doing what you can't bloody do anyway.'

She stopped. Her chest heaved as she hauled huge, furious breaths in and out. Her face was pale, but her eyes burned.

'Mate. What was it your mum used to say?'

He nearly broke. His heart ached and tears demanded to be released. 'She said we do what we can.'

'Aye, that was it. She was a smart woman, your mum. She must have passed some of her intelligence on to you, no? Get real, man. Do what you can, always, but don't go wasting a good copper because you realise that – shock, horror, hold the front page – you have limitations like the rest of us.'

Steph held a breath then went for it. 'I'm not having it.'

Malkie leaned back against her car, stuffed his hands into his trouser pockets, stared at his feet. Not in embarrassment or shame, as he usually felt at times like this, but with a dawning, long-resisted sense of acceptance, recognition of Steph's bare, basic, unarguable fact: we can't do what we can't do. The flip side of what his mum had told him so many times.

He stood now in the middle of rural South Lanarkshire,

possibly suffering from concussion, from something that could yet kill him, refusing to give up. And that was fine, to never give up, until there was nothing more you could do *but* give up.

They had one last location to check. That wasn't nothing.

That was a chance.

FIFTY-SIX

Both women agreed: one more try. All or nothing. Do or die.

Both had started shivering. Both admitted that their multiple injuries had started to blunt the brutal edge of their physical pains. And both agreed that had to be the worst possible indication of whatever little time they had left.

They stood, clutched the front iron bar of the of the bench frame in their free hands and wrapped the fingers of their captive hands the best they could around the chain.

After an aborted count of three, when both women broke and feared they couldn't do it, only to talk each other into trying again, they pulled.

Both screamed. Both cried out their agonies. Both swore and yelled and sobbed and hauled with strength born of outrage at their shared suffering and the prospect of their own miserable, cold deaths.

The bench moved another inch but Elizabeth's hand came nowhere near slipping out of the cuff no matter how much damage she hoped she could endure. The tub and Stevie's body, the key in his pocket, remained a vast gulf away. Any thoughts Elizabeth had nurtured that fear of their own deaths might send pain-denying adrenaline coursing through them died. Each effort to move the bench hammered her with pain so massive and profound and debilitating that even her furious determination was blasted away.

They collapsed again and sat, heavy and defeated, and held on to each other.

Both women's wrists bled, fat drops of blood, black in the moonlight, falling to the ground.

Would they bleed to death before they froze? Which would be better, or at least less awful?

Andrea slumped sideways. Elizabeth felt for a pulse, found one but barely. She held her free hand to Andrea's cheek and hoped the poor, tormented woman felt it and knew that in her last moments, she was loved.

Elizabeth surprised herself with that realisation. Regardless of any stupid theories about captives sharing a common experience drawing closer and becoming lifelong friends, she knew only that she and this woman, whom she hardly knew, would die together. They would be the last people to hold each other, the last to comfort each other. No one else in the world or in the entire, cruel uncaring universe would share their deaths.

And for that reason alone, Elizabeth loved Andrea. For being there as she died.

At least she wouldn't die alone.

As she felt exhaustion and blackness and – yes, it seemed it was true – impossible warmth spread within her, she prayed to the empty void above her that Sophie would know she'd done all she could, and always for her.

Could any loss of life ever be a good thing? She'd done what she'd done out of love, out of a need to protect her daughter the best she could against the unfairness and cruelty of her teen years at the hands of other girls blind to the damage they did until they, too, grew up to regret their ignorance.

The price she was about to pay would never be worth it, though.

No. No matter how vast the love, how brave the heart that sacrificed itself, there could never be such a thing as a worthwhile death.

FIFTY-SEVEN

As they approached the last location, a white Transit van thundered out of the side road they were aiming for and hurtled away to the south.

'That's it. That's Stevie Jessop's bloody van. This is it, Malkie.' She clutched his arm, and he realised she needed to win this one every bit as much as he did. She dialled Gucci and yelled the van's route and direction to her as she flung the car down the narrow and winding lane, flanked either side by thick stands of trees, until they saw lights in windows.

Malkie threw the passenger door open before the car came to a stop. He fell over in his rush to get to the house, felt sharp gravel punish the palms of his hands. Steph dragged him to his feet and together they entered the open door of a small, white, ancient-looking cottage.

Steph pulled her baton from her belt holster and flicked it out to its full, lethal length. Malkie had left his at the station, as usual.

Inside, they found a kitchen straight out of *Farmhouses Monthly*. A huge iron Aga range and a thick oak table. Glasses and beer bottles littered the top. They moved into a narrow and claustrophobic hallway with a door on each side. One opened into a bathroom, the other onto a set of stairs that descended into gloom. Ahead, a living room, also crammed full of rustic junk, nothing looking newer than a hundred years old. A stair at the back of the room led upwards. Steph headed for the stairs and Malkie returned to the steps leading – he assumed – to a cellar.

When he saw the heavy padlock on the outside of an open door at the end of a short hallway, his heart leaped and then crashed.

The room, dark and gloomy and close, held a bed and a chemical toilet and a table on which sat bottles of water, packs of sandwiches and toiletries.

But no Elizabeth.

Had he missed her? Was she in the back of Stevie's van being thrown about against the inside as he took her somewhere else to finish her? Was Malkie too late? Again? A crushing sense of déjà vu swamped him. Another one.

No. He had no idea what Steph might find upstairs or what they might yet find outside.

It was nothing but it was something.

He charged up the stairs, his mind furious and fixed on nothing less than complete success. His career – and his soul – might not survive otherwise.

'Steph? Anything?'

When she reappeared at the foot of the stairs, she didn't need to say anything; her expression betrayed a misery just as profound as his.

They headed outside, but he already felt broken.

FIFTY-EIGHT

She'd thought she'd heard tyres on gravel. Thought she'd seen a flash of light sweep across the garden from the front of the cottage.

She tried to lift her head but found she didn't want to. Sleep beckoned to her, promised a warm and comforting release from her suffering. She checked Andrea, found her white and still, barely a whisper of breath misting out from between her greying lips.

Elizabeth closed her eyes. She welcomed the slow, silent, gentle pull of the darkness, imagined herself tucked up under the duvet at home before Andrew's illness and before Sophie became the target of so much mindless cruelty from her peers. Her daughter happy and snuggled into her side, her husband leaning on one elbow and smiling at them both like the big, gormless, perfect idiot she'd first fallen in love with. Before their lives started to fall apart.

She thought she heard voices from somewhere far away.

No, she couldn't. Could she?

FIFTY-NINE

Malkie almost cried when he spotted the two women slumped sideways against each other on a huge bench.

Despite bruised and swollen faces, he recognised one as Elizabeth Dunn, so the other had to be Andrea Jessop. It looked like he was too late. Again. He lifted them both into sitting positions to check for pulses and noticed they'd been handcuffed to the iron frame. Surely even animals like the Jessops wouldn't treat their own sister like this, would they? But then, who else could she be? He found no pulse in Elizabeth's ice-cold wrist so he held a hand to her chest, pressed at her sternum. He found the gentle but determined beat of a heart even Jessop's cold cruelty had failed to kill.

Steph stood facing the hot tub, her phone in her hand. She barked a sequence of instructions, brief and efficient, to Gucci. 'Southernmost location you identified, Lou. Ambulance and...' – she reached into the water for a moment – 'and the coroner, SOCOs, the works. One fatality, possibly three. Aye, I know. Quick as you can, aye?'

She sighed as she replaced her phone in her jacket pocket before she disappeared back round to the front of the property.

She reappeared seconds later, her arms laden with blankets and towels. Together, they swaddled the two women like newborn babies.

While Steph carried on monitoring both women's pulses and their breathing, Malkie looked into the hot tub.

A huge slab of a man lay face down and unmoving, and Malkie knew it had to be Stevie Jessop. He turned the body over to confirm the identification. He felt no joy in the man's death, despite him having apparently left two women, one his own sister, chained together to freeze to death, but only after nearly beating both of them to death. He wished he thought artificial respiration might bring the fucker back so he could answer for all he'd done, but Malkie saw the remains of a joint floating on the surface of the water and a bag of white powder on a tray fastened to the side of the tub; he then knew nothing would bring Stevie Jessop back to suffer as he deserved to.

Malkie checked his pulse as a formality and was not surprised to find none.

While Steph stayed with the women to present a reassuring female presence if they should regain consciousness, Malkie headed to the kitchen. He couldn't make tea for fear of contamination of the scene, but he risked filling two coffee mugs with warm water.

He dabbed moisture onto Elizabeth Dunn's lips while Steph did the same for Andrea Jessop. Malkie found himself trying to rub heat back into Andrea's hands. Steph stopped him but didn't explain why.

When both women took a breath and licked their lips, Malkie and Steph glanced at each other with exhausted relief. No high-fives. No self-congratulation. Only a simple and desperate gratitude that they might yet end this day without more memories of deaths they'd failed to prevent.

They helped the women drink, only sips at first, but more as they regained consciousness.

When Elizabeth tried to lift her left hand, she stared at the handcuff as if seeing it for the first time. She looked to Malkie and frowned, took a moment then recoiled from him. He held his hands up then pulled his warrant card from his inside jacket pocket.

'We're police officers. You're safe now, Elizabeth. Safe.'

She took another few moments to calm down again, but then she forced words from her lips.

'Thank you. Thank you so much. I...' She broke down.

Malkie took her hand. 'Elizabeth, did Stevie Jessop put these on you?' He indicated the handcuffs.

She stared at them for a few seconds then looked towards the tub. 'In his pocket. The key.'

Malkie retrieved the key and removed the handcuffs. He winced at the depth of the wounds they'd sliced into the skin of both women's wrists and wished again that Stevie had survived to face a good kicking before his arrest.

With both of her arms free, Elizabeth reached for Andrea. She pulled one of the blankets around both of them and clung to her.

They sat in silence. Time for questions would come later.

Malkie rested himself against the back of the bench and – finally – allowed himself to believe this night would end well.

When he heard sirens and saw strobes flashing on the other side of the trees between the cottage and the road, he felt exhaustion flood him.

He let go, gave into it, slid sideways, and passed out.

SIXTY

Elizabeth heard voices, distant and muffled. Nearby. Male voices. Her heart pounded and ice filled her.

Had Stevie survived?

'Andrea.' She screamed, sat up, squinted into brilliant white lights that stabbed into her eyes that she felt like she hadn't opened in days.

'Elizabeth. Lie back. You're safe.'

'No. Jessop's still alive. Andrea...'

Hands pushed her back down. She fought back, writhed under them, clutched for air as if to drag herself up again. She felt a cold rush in her arm, then a wave of vertigo. Then darkness and a heavy, oppressive silence.

She woke. Lights stabbed at her vision, even through her eyelids. She reached up to shield her eyes. The back of her hand touched cloth on her forehead. A bandage?

'Elizabeth?' A different voice, one she thought she should recognise.

She turned her head, felt the world spin around her. She

saw white walls, curtains, devices hanging from metal poles covered in lights, flashing at her. A black display showed a dot crossing from left to right, trailing a fading line behind it.

A shape intruded on her field of view. A person. She screwed her eyes up, shut off enough of the blinding light to allow her to see.

Andrea's worried face came into focus. Elizabeth felt relief flood her. She clutched at Andrea's hand and Andrea squeezed hers back. They said nothing more for a while. Elizabeth felt tears burn in her eyes and she let them pour. This set Andrea off, and they laughed as they each wiped moisture from their cheeks.

'What are we like, eh?' Elizabeth's smile faded. She lowered her gaze to their hands, still intertwined.

'I don't know, Elizabeth. What was I like? To you, I mean?'

Elizabeth realised where Andrea's mind had gone. She tried to sit up, to hug her, but pain slashed through her ribs and she fell back into her pillows. Andrea leaned forward.

'I'm sorry, Elizabeth. For everything.'

Elizabeth felt anger flare in her. 'No, you stop that. You're not your brothers; you're nothing like them. You did what you needed to do to survive them. Good grief, having to survive your own brothers? No wonder you were conflicted, Andrea.'

'Conflicted? I locked you in the cellar.' Tears sprang anew and her voice turned strident. 'I put handcuffs on you. What kind of person puts handcuffs on another person? What kind of a person have I turned into?' She trembled, shook her head as if losing a battle with her own self-control.

Elizabeth took a monumental breath, steeled herself, and leaned over to take Andrea's other hand. She held on to both and made Andrea look at her.

'If I'd got the chance, I would have run and not cared a jot about what Stevie would do to you. What kind of a person does that make me?'

Andrea focused, pulled herself together with a visible effort. 'It would have made you a mother. Doing anything less would have been beneath you. I wouldn't have behaved any differently in your situation.' She went quiet, and Elizabeth remembered this poor, brutalised woman's story of having her own child murdered in her womb before it was even allowed to draw breath.

Elizabeth trawled her mind for her next words. This poor woman needed the perfect response, words that she would never forget, words that might help her forgive herself.

'We both did what we had to do. It wasn't our fault that meant hurting each other. We had to do what we had to do, didn't we?'

Her words, as clumsy and trite as they sounded to her own ears, seemed to pull something from Andrea, some small scrap of understanding. She smiled, weak and hesitant but a smile.

'I only wanted to save myself. You wanted to save your daughter. Very different. But thank you, Elizabeth. For saving my life, if nothing else.'

Elizabeth's mind flashed back to the two of them, freezing and dying, too injured and agonised to drag the bench they couldn't have hoped to move even if Stevie Jessop hadn't broken them both so badly.

'Stupid, stupid mistake he made, wasn't it? Mixing up his drugs like that?'

'Neither of them was ever very bright. And accidents do happen, don't they?'

Elizabeth searched Andrea's eyes for some tiny glimmer of admission of culpability, some small secret recognition they could trust each other to share, but she saw nothing.

Andrea stood. 'If you ever feel like dropping by for tea or perhaps a wee gin, I'd like that. I'll get rid of that damned hot tub, of course.'

They both tried to smile, but neither quite managed it.

Andrea's gaze became intense, as if she wanted to forge some kind of connection, if only the recognition of a shared experience both might struggle to forget. 'Thank you for giving me my life back.' She stood. 'Could I maybe meet your daughter, some day? Do you think that might be OK?' She frowned. 'I'm sorry. I have no right to—'

'I'd like that, Andrea. Very much. You have good heart, despite what you've lived through.'

She smiled, but Elizabeth saw yet more tears form. Andrea walked away before Elizabeth could think of anything more to say.

She lay her head back and hoped she could sleep. She preferred not to ask for more painkillers despite the shards of pain still lancing through her ribs.

'Elizabeth?' A man's voice this time. Hesitant. Hopeful but frightened.

Andrew.

She reached for him as he crossed the room, threw both arms around his neck, pulled him to her. He fell forward onto her, fell across her. Pain erupted through her rib cage, and she gasped. Andrew pushed himself up, weak and wobbly, to remove his weight, looked at her appalled, worry twisting his features.

'Elizabeth, I'm sorry. You pulled me. I couldn't—'

'I know. I know, Andrew. *I'm* sorry.'

A nurse appeared, stared down at her, concentrated for a few seconds, then nodded. Somehow, even in the absence of a smile, that nod comforted Elizabeth, made her feel safe.

She tried to speak again, found her throat dry and painful. The nurse held a glass and a straw to her lips. She sipped, then drank, then started to guzzle the water, but the nurse withdrew it.

'Steady, Elizabeth. Take it easy, love.' She patted Elizabeth's arm then wandered out of the room.

Elizabeth turned to watch Andrew lower himself with extreme care into a visitor's chair beside her bed. He paired his crutches together in one hand and laid them against the edge of the mattress, then picked up a remote control on a curly wire and pushed a button.

She rose. When her ribs started to complain she held a hand up and Andrew stopped.

She breathed, long and slow, for a few seconds, savoured the silence and the warmth and the safety she dared to believe she could now enjoy. Safety from brutality. Safety from losing everything.

'Who was that I saw leaving your room? Was that Andrea, the sister?'

'Yes, that was Andrea.'

'How is she?'

'Alive. Yes. She'll make a full recovery.'

'Aye. Thanks to you.'

She frowned at him. 'Me? What did I do?'

Andrew smiled, as if unsurprised. 'You left a trail. Your bracelet. You saved yourself and Andrea.'

She laid her head back into the pillows and closed her eyes, braced herself for what she needed to ask next.

'Does Sophie hate me, Andrew?'

'What? No. Of course not.'

'Is she embarrassed by me? Her own mother, a shoplifter?'

She heard Andrew sigh. 'Ask her yourself, you numpty.'

She opened her eyes. Sophie stood in the doorway, looking like she needed permission to enter.

Elizabeth sobbed as she held her arms out to her daughter. Sophie ran to her and threw herself into her.

'Mum. I thought I wouldn't see you again. I was so scared, Mum.' Her last words drowned in uncontrollable sobs.

They held on to each other for what felt like an age before pain from Elizabeth's ribs intruded on her joy. She pushed

Sophie off her but held on to her arms. Sophie turned sideways and lay down beside her, pushed into her, pulled an arm over her, and held her as if determined never to let her mother go anywhere without her, ever again.

Elizabeth took Andrew's hand. Tears sat on his eyelids too, but she knew the anti-depressants he took because of his MS had prevented him from being able to cry for months. One tear spilled. He caught it on a finger as it ran down his cheek. He looked at it and smiled as if wonders never did cease.

Elizabeth closed her eyes, held on to the only two things that mattered to her. She wondered if, given the same circumstances all over again, she would repeat her actions, despite knowing the damage she would do.

It troubled her that even after all she'd gone through, after all the pain and fear and misery she'd put herself and her family and even Andrea through, she couldn't tell herself with any conviction what she'd do.

SIXTY-ONE

'They got him, then?'

Malkie put his coffee mug down on the desk and read – slowly and carefully – from a sheet of paper with just two words on it. 'Aye. Stanislovas Petrauskas, Lithuanian, was a long-distance truck driver until he got a job as Stevie Jessop's main muscle. Moved to the UK eight years ago, applied for indefinite right to remain and got it but he probably wishes he never did, now. He made it as far as the south coast before being picked up. Given Stevie Jessop's dead body floating in Andrea's hot tub, we experienced no difficulty in issuing alerts on all airports and ferry ports. By the time he pulled into the terminal at Dover, we'd had a marker on Stevie's van for hours already. He pleaded ignorance of Stevie's death or either woman's imprisonment, but SOCOs found his DNA all over the cottage, including the cellar, and on the end of a barely smoked joint. Somehow, Stevie had sprinkled a healthy serving of ninety per cent pure cocaine onto the cannabis, and the autopsy confirmed that he simply overdosed. The Fiscal's office took no time to agree that more than sufficient evidence pointed straight at Stevie having used the wrong bag of his own Class A drugs and killing himself; a prime candidate for this year's Darwin Awards.'

Steph nodded to herself. 'Idiot.'

'Aye.'

'And Davie?'

'Singing like his life depended on it. Plenty to comment on now, oddly enough.'

'Idiot.'

'Aye.'

'And what about Andrea Jessop?'

Malkie smiled to himself in admiration. 'If she swapped Stevie's wee brown bags or topped one up with enough of the near-pure stuff to kill him and Stan, she was really bloody careful. SOCOs found Stevie's stash under some piles of wood in the living room but not a single print or hair or fibre to suggest she touched any of it. She's an environmental nut, had her gas supply disconnected years ago and never burns wood or coal. She left it there for rustic charm but apart from dusting it, it looked like it hadn't been disturbed in years. Well, not by her, anyway. Except – theoretically, possibly – to tamper with some wee plastic baggies of pre-cut skag in a tin and the aforementioned big, fuck-off slab of nearly pure brown.'

'From Amsterdam.'

'We have to assume so, aye. Anyway, SOCOs found ample DNA from Stevie and Davie Jessop and Stanislavski Wossis-name-ski, but not a trace of hers.'

'Interesting.'

'Aye. Andrea will be interviewed, but unless she told Elizabeth her nefarious plan like some corny spy-movie supervillain, I can't see how anyone can dispute whatever story she tells. Ex-schoolteacher, heart of gold according to her ex-colleagues. Never so much as a speeding ticket, never ran an overdraft or owed on her credit cards, serially abused by her own psychotic and violent drug-dealer brothers – if she ever sees a courtroom for this, no jury on earth would believe her capable.'

'What do you think. Could she have...?' Steph looked sideways at him, conspiratorial and sly.

He took a few seconds to be sure of his answer. 'I think she could of, aye.'

She tutted. 'Could *have*.'

'Aye, that too.'

They shared a companionable silence for a few moments.

'Any news about—' He caught himself just in time. 'The Scumbag?'

She smiled, again. A good sign. 'Still in a coma, still got a machine doing his breathing for him. Barry Boswell was interviewed but with them being old mates, if you can call them that, and so Boswell's DNA being all over Dean's flat already, there's little chance of forensically nailing Boswell for it. If it wasn't Boswell, we can hope whoever tossed Dean off his balcony left some kind of transfer of their own.'

'Whomever.'

'That sounds wrong. You sure about that one, old man?'

'Actually, no.' He grinned.

'Idiot.'

'Yes, Steph.'

Malkie mulled over his earlier word choice. 'It's an overused word, isn't it? Scumbag. But it's overused because it's just so bloody bang on. Like clichés.'

'Yep. Someone should invent a whole new word for people like him, but Scumbag will do for now.'

'And what's Boswell saying?'

'Claims he was nowhere near, hadn't seen The Scumbag for weeks.'

'You believe him?'

'Not for a second. Just a mention of Dean to Boswell had him shitting himself visibly in front of me. Dean admitted

Boswell had a go at him for that stunt he pulled on me and him in his flat, so he's probably worried Dean told me that and I'll finger him for Dean's sky-dive onto the roof of a 2011 Ford Fiesta. Anyway, doesn't matter what I believe.'

She took a moment, looked reluctant to go where her mind was taking her.

'What worries me is what SOCOs will get from the flat. I already know they'll find plenty of Boswell there, and some of me.'

He waited for it.

'And you, mate.'

And there it was. Because of one temper tantrum and a misguided attempt to put the shits up Dean Lang, he'd end up on a PoI list for a case of attempted murder. Or worse.

'Aye. Serves me right, I suppose.'

'Idiot.'

'Aye.'

Neither could follow that for a while. Steph managed first. 'Where were you? The night he fell from his balcony?'

He glanced at her, harsher than he meant to. She dropped her gaze, and he had a word with himself. He'd asked her much the same thing only a few days ago, and she'd reacted much the same way he'd been about to.

'I was at the cabin with Dad. Depends what time frame it gets narrowed down to. If it happened any time after about ten, I might be in trouble. For a while.'

Her eyes demanded an explanation.

'Dad went to bed at about nine. After he falls asleep half of Harperrig Reservoir could empty into his bed and he'd sleep through it.'

'So, any time after ten provides a window.'

'Aye, I'd have had plenty of time.'

She reached for his hand. 'I know you had nothing to do with it, mate. I just hoped you had a better alibi than that.'

Both looked to the door to the charging desk and custody suite, then separated their fingers as Pam Ballantyne stepped through, briefcase in hand, gloves and coat on. She stopped when she saw them both watching her. When she moved again, she approached Malkie but glanced sideways at Steph, no love lost.

'Malkie, can we talk?' She glanced again at Steph, who folded her arms and sat back in her chair. She managed not to grin but Malkie suspected one lurked in there somewhere.

'It's OK, Pam. Steph knows and I don't mind her listening in.'

Pam looked unconvinced but relented. She clasped her hands in front of her immaculately pressed grey suit trousers, as if preparing to deliver a speech.

'The item is with forensics now. DI Thompson has authorised budget for prints to begin with. But I'm afraid because we're only looking at the feasibility of reopening a closed case, it'll not be picked up as a priority. I can imagine that will be difficult for you but I can't really justify requesting the lab to expedite.'

Malkie wanted to applaud her fine and articulate monologue but he found himself less inclined to bait her than he had been for years.

'Thanks, Pam. I appreciate the update. Yes, it's frustrating but what can I do, right?'

'Yes. I do sympathise. I will of course update you immediately after DI Thompson if we receive any actionable information back.'

She seemed to stall, as if uncertain whether further words were necessary. Malkie put her out of everyone's misery.

'I appreciate that too, Pam. DC Lang and I were just about to head home. It's been a long few days.'

Pam found her feet again. 'Yes, I heard. Good result, that.

Well done, Malkie. I'll be off then.' She turned to go but hesitated. 'That was a great thing you did for that family.'

She glanced at Steph, and her manner stiffened again. 'Goodnight, Malkie. DC Lang.' She walked away, her pace brisk and severe.

Steph sniffed and arched her eyebrows, but kept her opinion to herself for a change. 'What item?'

He sighed. In the rush of the past day, he'd managed to ignore it even as it whispered in his mind.

'Callum Gourlay found an old-style flip lighter under some rubbish beside the remains of the house. He showed me. Both Callum and I think it feasible it was dropped there before the fire, possibly immediately before. As Pam said, it's only a preliminary fact-finding investigation for now. I'm just glad she's taking it seriously. She's not too bad, actually. I'm not sure anymore which of us rubbed the other up the wrong way first.'

Steph stared at him.

'Ach, give her a chance. Anyway, the lighter is way down on the forensics workstack, might take them days to get to it, but whatever is coming down the line, we'll weather it. Right, partner?' He stood, grabbed his jacket from the back of his chair. 'I have to go. Jennifer is meeting my dad tonight, so I absolutely cannot be late.'

She smiled. 'When can I meet her?'

'Hah. No chance. You and her, together? I'd be like a lion in a den of Daniels. Or Daniellas.'

'Do you even know what that story is about?'

'Not a clue, but it sounds good. You going to be OK?'

'No, but I'm going home to a bottle of gin and a couple of hours with Gerard Butler. You?'

'Terrified. Dad's dead set against the entire Morton clan, but I'm hopeful she might charm him. You've got my number, aye? In case, you know...'

'That's... frustrating. You OK?'

'I'll have to be. I've got a dad and a daughter to look after now. I'll manage. I'm getting better at fighting off The Wobbles, you know? Keeping my eyes up and looking forward.'

'The wobbles?'

'Aye, I don't use the "D" word anymore, don't want to give it credibility. I just have Wobbles these days, and I want to stay that way. I feel like I'm getting better, less of a pain in the arse, I hope.'

She punched him on the arm, a Steph hug, gentle and lingering and affectionate. 'We've noticed, old man. Keep it up. But right now, bugger off. Me and Gerard Butler have a hot date.'

He opened his mouth to correct her, but she talked over him.

'Oh, good grief. Gerard Butler and *I*, OK? Now piss off. Please.'

SIXTY-TWO

'This is either going to go really horribly wrong or just catastrophically. I can feel it in my bones.'

Deborah sighed down the phone at him. 'Oh, shut up. It'll be fine. You said she's adorable and your dad's a reasonable man. In fact, he's lovely.'

'Aye, alright, steady.'

'Make allowances for him. Poor old sod must be struggling. Can't be easy finding out you have a twenty-six-year-old granddaughter you've never met.'

'You think so?' He regretted the tone of disbelief that laced his last words. 'Sorry. Bit tense.'

'No problem, Dirty Old Man. When do I get to meet her?'

'Eh? What?'

'Kidding, you eejit. Time enough for that. Good grief, Malkie, you're so gullible.' She laughed, and it grounded him. Three months ago, he could never have dreamed he'd even consider another romantic relationship, let alone feel the depth of love for Deborah that still scared him when it caught him unawares. If he could navigate an actual adult relationship with Deborah, he could handle the far less intimate and challenging role of being a father to a fine young woman who didn't need fathering in the slightest. If anything, he expected to learn more from her than she would from him.

'Malkie. You there?'

'Aye. I'm here. Wish you were too, although at the same time I'm glad you're not.'

'Nice. Not hurtful at all.'

'Oh, shut up. I just meant I can deal with Dad better without you distracting me.'

'Is that what I do? Distract you?'

'In a manner of speaking, aye. Oh, shit. I hear a car. Damn it, I'm not ready for this.'

'Malkie. Malkie. Calm down. Take a breath. You've got this. I want a full report in the morning, OK?'

'Fine. Will do. Fuck's sake, this is terrifying.'

'Malkie?'

'Yes, Deborah?'

Click.

Dad loved doing that to him, thought it never got old, and he'd obviously told Deborah how hilarious it was.

Jennifer's car headlights danced down the single-track road from the A70 and Malkie forced himself to breathe. He checked the ice bucket was full and that the lanterns were lit all around the deck. His dad appeared, looking more dapper than Malkie could remember seeing him since... Maybe they could both do with another woman in their lives, in their different ways. Malkie's daughter, his dad's granddaughter. As long as his dad didn't dwell too long on Jennifer's mother, they might just come through this to everyone's benefit.

The old man came out onto the deck.

'Will you be OK, Dad?'

He took a moment. 'Yes. She's not her mother and she's not her brothers. I can hang on to that. I can't promise I'll be completely fine, but I'll do my best. For you, son.' He nudged Malkie's arm with his. A Dad hug.

When she pulled up outside the cabin, he took the torch from the hook by the door, opened her door, and lit her path to the deck.

His heart stopped when he saw his dad step forward to greet her; the old man's face had taken on a fearful cast. Had he only now thought through the implications, that this woman shared genes with the stupid wee girl who had nearly got his son killed?

We can't choose our genes. Can we, Steph?

She held her hand out. 'Hello, Mr McCulloch. Perfectly understandable reservations aside, I'm delighted to meet you.' She smiled at him, and Malkie watched his dad's heart melt from just those nine, perfect words. He'd always been a softie under his craggy and dour Scots exterior, and Jennifer – for all the right reasons – had played him like a fiddle.

He nodded, gracious. 'And it's a delight to meet you too, Jennifer. Please, sit.' He reached for the wine as he mouthed '*She's lovely*' at Malkie behind her back. Malkie rolled his eyes and Tommy grinned at him.

Malkie grinned. *Heart. Stolen. And it took only seconds.*

They ate and they drank. Conversation started slow and stilted and careful, but Jennifer refused to let the atmosphere turn bad. She asked Malkie about his day on the job and his dad about their plans for touring the east coast on the *Droopy Goose*. When Tommy asked if she could sail, she said she could learn, and they both believed her.

After dinner, she and Malkie strolled down to the water's edge.

'So, this is the famous Harperrig Reservoir.'

Something in her voice caught on Malkie's bullshit detector, and he narrowed his eyes at her.

She grinned. He suspected she blushed too, but it was too dark to see.

'I drove here a couple of times after Mum mentioned you lived here. There weren't too many cabins it could have been.'

'Did you watch me through a pair of binoculars from a lay-by or what?'

She laughed. 'No. I'm not a weirdo. I just parked up for a wee while and watched you from here. Shut up: I was curious.'

He laughed too.

They stood in comfortable silence and sipped their drinks. Malkie marvelled at the stark but magical reality of the situation; beside him stood an amazing woman, half of whose genes were his.

She pointed to his glass with hers. 'Mineral water? Don't you like wine? Actually, you're the *polis*, you shouldn't be giving me wine when you know I have to drive home.'

'You've only had one glass, daftie. And no, I hate wine. And beer and spirits and liqueurs. Hate them all.'

'But how can you be a tortured, middle-aged, burned-out, alcoholic detective if you hate booze?'

'I tick four of those boxes, and one day I hope to start on the fifth. Just never found something I can stomach yet.'

She considered this for a moment. 'We'll find something.'

She squeezed his arm then turned to walk back to the cabin. She stopped herself, leaned into him, and kissed him on the cheek.

'Take your time. I think your dad and I will be just fine together.'

He believed it. As she walked away, he stared out over the water.

'What do you think of your granddaughter, Mum? Wee cracker, isn't she?'

He pondered for a minute, thought through how the ordeal Elizabeth and Sophie and Andrew had been put through had only seemed to strengthen them, to bond them more deeply than he'd seen in most other families. Would he go as far for Jennifer as Elizabeth had done for Sophie? Would he risk everything for her safety or even just for her happiness? Would he learn to put aside his loathing of Sandra Morton – reduced but still bitter and painful– for the sake of his daughter?

He imagined his mum adoring the stupid, gushing, proud dad smile he couldn't keep from his face. Could he thaw the part of his heart that couldn't forget Sandra's past sins against him, so he could be as fine a parent to Jennifer as his own mum and dad had always been to him?

Yes, I bloody well can.

A LETTER FROM THE AUTHOR

I hope you enjoyed this, my fourth book. It started in my mind as a tale of a good person making a bad decision for the best of reasons. Malkie's non-negotiable promise to himself and others to become a better man reflects my own hope that the best of us still try to look out for the rest of us, where we can.

If you'd like to join other readers in hearing all about my latest releases, you can sign up here:

www.stormpublishing.co/doug-sinclair

Please check out my web site at www.dougsinclair.co.uk for information on coming books and some free short stories.

Can I ask you to be kind enough to leave a review of this book online? Let me know what you liked and what you didn't like, what resonated with you and what really didn't.

Some people will see much of me in Malkie. He's actually very different to me in many ways, but his journey absolutely is rooted in my own experiences. The word *neurodivergence* bothers me because I've yet to see any definition of exactly what fictional normality it is that *neurodivergent* people are thought to, er, diverge from. I suspect that the percentage of people going about their lives without any measure of neurovariety at all is minimal. Some, like me, are blessed with fantastic and patient and loving support frameworks and some of us really are not. I hope my stories bring hope to anyone struggling to ask for help. You are never alone.

And yes, I'm aware that I dangled a participle in that last paragraph.

You can connect with me on Facebook, or X, and I'd love to hear your comments – the good, the bad, and the ridiculous.

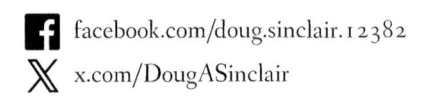

facebook.com/doug.sinclair.12382
x.com/DougASinclair

ACKNOWLEDGEMENTS

'Book Four' – various tender parts of me are bruised from repeated pinching, such is my stubborn brain's inability to think those words without wondering when I'm going to wake up.

I found my tribe, the UK crime fiction community, late in life, and I cannot credit enough the amazing people I've come to call friends (or at least acquaintances). Particular thanks go to the annoyingly talented Gordon Brown (not that one, the tall good-looking one) who introduced me to my equally capable agent Kevin Pocklington of The North Literary Agency, who then found my books an excellent home with Storm Publishing. I'm grateful to Oliver Rhodes and Claire Bord for taking a punt on me, and to my Super Ed, Kate Smith, without whom my books just wouldn't be as brilliant as my mum says they are. Same goes to my editorial support crew – Laurence Cole, Shirley Khan, Alexandra Begley, and to the honeyed voice of Angus King who narrates Malkie about as perfectly as I could hope for.

Thanks, also, to all who showed me patience and support when I needed it the most. Craig Robertson, Caro Ramsay, Douglas Skelton, Mark Leggatt, Neil Broadfoot, Michael Malone, Carla Kovach, Zoe Sharp, Alex Gray, Graham Smith, Alison Belsham, Noelle Holten, Sharon Bairden, Jacky Collins, Kelly Lacey, Suze Bickerton, Gail Williams – thank you so much, all.

Mum, you need to make room for another book in your trinkets and doodahs cabinet.

Maaike, please never stop being you.

Donna en mijn schoon-familie, dank u well voor alles. Ik hou van jullie. Heel veel.

The Twisted Sisters of Dumfries – Irene, Fiona, Linda, Anne, Jackie – thank you for letting me become an honorary, er, sister.

Andy & Al, Rich, Dave T, Meesh, Wendy – thank you for your love and support so humorously disguised as constant verbal abuse.

Eleanor, Fergus, Rosie, Lorne, Kathy, Henbo, Colin – thank you for being there for me for so many years they've actually become decades. Love you more than I'll ever admit.

Printed in Dunstable, United Kingdom